The Children Under the Ice

R.A. Douthitt

Cover design by R. A. Douthitt
Interior images © R.A. Douthitt and Tom Becker
Author photo © 2017 Tom Becker

Printed in the U.S.A.

ISBN-13: 9781980469797

DEDICATION

To all my students of writing:
Keep working at it. Never stop dreaming because
dreams do come true.

Thank you to Scott and Nathan for listening to my silly stories.

ACKNOWLEDGMENTS

Anyone who has written a book knows it isn't an easy task. It takes time, work, dedication, and patience. I have written five books. I couldn't have completed any of them without my fine editors, Christopher Moore and Wayne Purdin. Their high standards have made me a better writer.

I also acknowledge my wonderful beta readers, Lexi Carter and Christian Peterson. Their excellent suggestions for *The Children Under the Ice* have helped form this story into the book I wanted to write and one I wanted to read.

Finally, I thank my husband and my son for putting up with all my writing at the dining room table and for all the mess I make when writing a book. You both are the best and I couldn't do it without you.

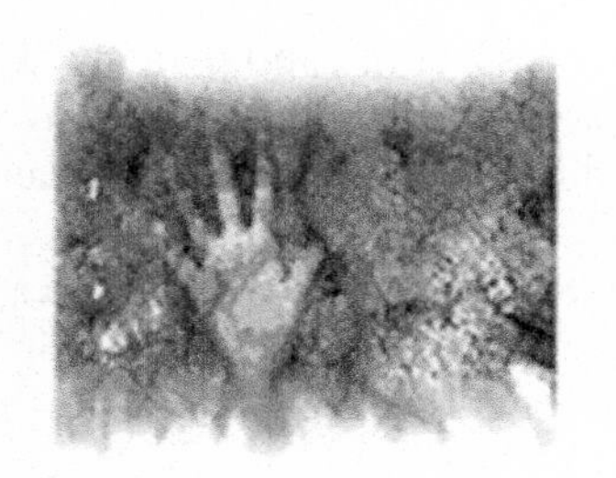

CHAPTER 1

1961

The body in his arms grew heavier as the sun set that fall evening. He could already see his breath in the crisp air. He listened for any noise. Mr. Davis stopped for a moment to look behind as though he had a suspicious feeling he was being followed. The nearby bushes showed no signs of disturbance. He shook his head.

"Don't look back, you fool," he mumbled to himself. "You know better than that."

Satisfied he was alone, Davis continued deeper into the woods. The arms of his victim dangled lifelessly while he walked. Finally, he came to the pond in the center of the woods; his favorite dumping ground. A few birds shot out of the bushes nearby. He turned again. The trees bent in the wind, but nothing walked among them. Still, he squinted his eyes as though an uneasiness had crept up his spine.

"Shh, this way," whispered Kevin. He motioned for the boys from school to follow him into the bushes. "He went this way."

"You'd better be right, Thompson," the taller boy named Gus wiped his nose with his hand. The boys left their bikes on the leaf covered dirt and tip toed after Kevin into the bushes toward the pond. They made their way through the thicket and came upon the clearing.

That's when they saw him.

Mr. Davis dropped the body into the small boat on the shore, adjusted his jacket, and then started to push the boat out into the water. He hopped in.

"Is that…is that a *dead* body he just put into that boat?" Gus asked. He covered his mouth. "I think I'm gonna be sick."

"Shhh," Kevin said when the other boys crept up.

"That's him," Shorty said as he nudged Kevin. "That's Mr.

Davis alright."

"See? I told you so." Kevin pointed. "He killed his wife."

Mr. Davis paddled the boat out to the middle of the pond and paused. Then, he took Mrs. Davis' body and dropped her into the murky water. Bubbles rose to the surface. She sunk quickly with the cinder block tied around her waist. He sat there watching her body, dressed in a floral print blouse and black slacks, disappear into the silent darkness below. A slow grin spread across his face as though he relished the fact that she was gone. *Finally gone.*

"Wow," Gus whispered as he watched the scene. "He really did it. We've got to tell someone."

"Who?" Shory asked. "No one will believe us."

Mr. Davis paddled back to the shore with a sheepish grin across his face, cherishing the moment. But it ended too soon. The boat bumped into the land and woke him from his trance. He stepped out of the boat and began to drag it onto the muddy shore of the pond.

Shorty nervously wringed his hands. "Okay, we've seen enough. Let's go."

Mr. Davis turned and jumped when he heard the voice. He nearly dropped the boat onto his foot.

"Oh no!" Kevin whispered, ducking. "He sees us!"

Mr. Davis looked up in time to see four wide-eyed boys from Sherman Oaks Elementary school staring at him through the bushes along the shoreline. Their eyes followed his every movement.

"What the heck are you kids doing here?" he shouted at them with such anger, the veins in his throat bulged and spit flew from his mouth.

Mr. Davis sprinted toward them.

"Run!" Kevin shouted to his friends.

They turned and headed into the woods, but before they could hide within the trees, Mr. Davis had grabbed Kevin by his jacket and spun him around. He pulled him close so his face was nose to nose with Kevin's.

"You're that Thompson kid, ain't ya" he hissed through nicotine-stained teeth.

Kevin nodded. His eyes bulged and his Adam's apple bobbled as he swallowed hard.

"Let him go!" Gus shouted.

Mr. Davis looked up at the other three staring at him with mouths gaping and he grinned. Then he rudely turned Kevin Thompson around to face the other boys. The boys looked at their friend, Kevin, shaking in the killer's arms. His large brown eyes watered.

"Leave him alone!" Gus shouted, "Let him go or else..."

"Or else what?" Mr. Davis asked.

Gus rubbed his forearms, trying to think of the words.

"We'll tell!" Shorty shouted.

"You'll tell who? The cops? Who d'ya think they're gonna believe, huh? Mr. Davis, the loyal bus driver? Or some good for nuthin' hooligans messin' around where they shouldn't be messin'? I know each of your parents and you should've been home a long time ago. All I have to do is tell 'em what I saw here in the woods."

"Oh yeah? What'd you see?" Shorty asked.

"Why, I'll just tell 'em I saw you kids messin' with a *dead body* here at the pond," Davis said.

"Hey, no way! You can't do that!" Shorty said. His round face turned pale.

"Yeah? I'll tell them my wife went missin' and I came here to look for her. And guess what I found? Some good-for-nothing kids. I'll tell the cops you killed her and dumped her body in the pond. Who do you think they're gonna believe?" he asked again. "Why, they'd never believe a bunch of losers like you." He cackled.

All four kids looked at each other, red-faced and sweating in the cold air. Kevin desperately tried to wriggle free.

"We know what you did. We saw you!" Shorty adjusted his glasses. "Why'd you kill your wife?" He immediately covered his mouth with his gloved hands, regretting the words as soon as he said them.

"That ain't none of your business, you little punk!" he spat on the ground. "She was a no-good tramp. No one will miss her."

"Please, mister. Let Kevin go and we won't tell anyone what we saw," Gus said, swallowing back tears.

"Yeah, we swear," the smaller kid named Brandon promised. He dutifully raised his hand as though swearing an oath. Brandon was a straight A student and belonged to the scouts.

Mr. Davis rubbed his chin stubble as though considering the deal. Then, he nodded his head.

Davis shoved Kevin toward his friends. They shivered in the cold evening air. He studied their frightened faces carefully. A few dead leaves tumbled by.

"You kids better not say one word 'bout this, got it?" he hissed. He looked deep into their eyes. "Or I'll come and get you."

He pointed to each one of them.

"And your *families* too," he smirked.

Their eyes grew wide.

"Yeah that's right. I'll come and get your families. You ever hear 'bout the boogeyman that lives in the woods?"

They looked at one another then nodded.

"Well, that's *me*," he said, pointing to his chest. "And I know where each one of you brats lives. Understand?"

They all understood.

"Don't make me come hurt you," Mr. Davis said. Then he pointed behind them. "C'mon, the bus is over there. Get in it. I'll take you all home. It's gettin' dark."

"But we rode our bikes here and—" Shorty said.

"I said get in the bus! Now shut up and walk," shouted Mr. Davis.

"Maybe we should make a run for it," Kevin whispered as they turned to head toward the bus.

Mr. Davis pulled a long knife from his jacket and grabbed Kevin from behind. He held the knife to his throat. "And don't get any bright ideas 'bout runnin' off, or your friend here gets it. You got that?"

"I think we better do as he says," Shorty rubbed his blonde hair.

"Ah man, Kev," Gus whispered. "This is bad. We're in big trouble now." Gus was the biggest of them all, but he was also a big baby. Kevin could see Gus shaking.

"Shhh," Kevin hushed him as they walked. "He can hear you."

Holding the knife, Davis followed behind the boys. They passed their bicycles lying on the ground. For a second, Kevin wondered if anyone would ever discover them. They walked until they were all on the school bus.

Once inside, they sat shivering in nervous silence as the bus began to move. Kevin looked out the window and noticed the long shadows along the road as the sun set behind the trees. Mr. Davis revved the engine and clutched the gear shift with such white knuckled intensity; Kevin thought he'd pull the clutch right off. It was as though Mr. Davis wanted to strangle each of the boys with those hands. Kevin had a feeling Mrs. Davis wasn't the first victim. He swallowed hard as he wondered just how many people those hands had killed.

Mr. Davis turned the bus around and started onto the bridge that went over the railroad tracks near the far side of the pond where they all played hockey in the wintertime. As the engine revved up, Kevin looked out over the trees. The woods looked so peaceful there set away from the main highway. *We'll get out of this*, he thought. *Somehow we'll get out of this*. Then, he wondered where his big brother, Doug was. *Where are you, Dougie*? Kevin thought. *Come help me*.

The bus made its way down the other side of the rickety old bridge, but instead of driving forward toward the neighborhood, the bus made a sharp turn left, so sharp that the kids fell out of their seats.

"Hey, what are you doing?" Kevin shouted.

"Sorry, kid," Davis said. "Can't take any chances."

Kevin yelled for him to stop and tried to rush to the front of the bus, but it was no use. The bus sped out of control. Kevin watched as they headed toward the pond. But before Kevin or the others could do anything, Mr. Davis drove the bus into the murky waters of the Sherman Oaks pond. It slammed into the water and immediately submerged almost up to the windows. The kids were thrown to the floor, forced to watch the bus driver escape through the window, leaving behind Kevin Thompson and his friends to haunt the pond, forever.

CHAPTER 2

1976

"All right, Mikey. Enough writing, time to come back to reality. We're late."

"Okay, Dad." Mikey angled his head and brushed aside his straight brown hair from his eyes. He shoveled one last spoonful of Cap'n Crunch into his mouth. He sat alone at the metal kitchen table his dad bought recently from the Salvation Army store outside of town. The night before, Mikey finished an article he'd been working on all week. He glanced over it with hopes it would be accepted into the school newspaper. "President Nixon and Watergate," he murmured the title under his breath. He erased some mistakes then used his hand to brush away the eraser scraps.

"Yes," he said to himself. "I like it. I hope my teacher does too." He gathered his pad and pencil together then looked at the clock on the wall.

He quickly grabbed the bowl and dropped it into the kitchen sink. It sunk into the acrid water alongside the pile of dirty dishes still soaking from the night before. Mikey pulled on his jacket just as his father opened the front door.

"Got all your stuff?" His dad removed his jacket from the hook on the wall and put it on.

"Yep," Mikey said as he picked up his textbooks. "Hey Dad! I just finished an article on—" He walked toward the door, and then froze.

His dad stood with a hockey stick in his hand. "Where's your hockey gear?"

"I'll get it afterschool," he said. "Uh, Dad, why are you holding my new hockey stick?"

"Don't you want to show it to your friends?" His dad had a sheepish grin on his face.

"Not at school, Dad."

"Why not? You know most kids your age would love to show off this new hockey stick." His dad turned it in his hands as though admiring it. "Don't you think so?"

"Yeah, well not me." Mikey walked past his dad and went into the garage.

As the garage door opened, Mikey could see that the snow storm the previous day had dumped several inches all over town. The snowfall was the earliest on record for Sherman Oaks. The storm meant the pond would be frozen solid. Perfect for hockey practice. Mikey knew his friends would be thrilled, but not him. To Mikey, snow only meant cold nights on the ice instead of researching at the library for his next article.

Mikey and his dad rode in silence on the way to school in the old Ford pickup truck. The houses slipped by the passenger side window. Some had snowmen decorated with hats and scarves out on the front lawn. Others had snow-covered Jack-O-Lanterns out by the front doors. It would be a cold Halloween this year.

"You just have to watch your shot, that's all," his dad said.

"Uh huh." Mikey tried to ignore him.

"You're getting better." His dad turned the corner. "Keep practicing and you'll be fine in the tournament. That Chad is one good player. You can learn a lot from him. And Stan, too."

I bet you wish they were your sons, Mikey sighed then leaned forward and fiddled with the radio dial. A country song by Conway Twitty came on.

A couple of his friends walked along the sidewalk on their way to school. He was glad he didn't have to walk to school in the cold air. Every morning his dad was able to drop him off on his way to work at the Sheriff's office.

Mikey noticed the truck slowing down.

"Do your friends want a ride?" his dad asked.

"Sure." Mikey rolled down the window and waved to his friends, Chad and Donnie. He smiled as they ran to the truck door. Chad wore his usual leather jacket over his black hoodie. His dark blonde hair covered his eyes. Donnie, towering over Chad, had his gloveless hands shoved into his pockets to keep them warm. His belly was so big, he couldn't zip up his coat. He had his homework folder under his arm.

"Wanna ride?" he asked. He scooted over as the two boys hopped in.

"Thanks, Mr. Thompson," Chad said.

"Yeah, thanks," Donnie said.

Mikey could smell the cold air on both boys. He cranked up the heater as the truck sped off down the street toward the school. Chad blew onto his cold fingers and Donnie rubbed his chubby hands together trying to warm them.

"Finish your science homework?" Donnie asked.

"Yep," Mikey said.

Donnie frowned. "I didn't."

"What else is new," Chad said with a smirk. He nudged Mikey.

"So," Chad whispered to Mikey. "Did you get it?"

Mikey nodded.

"Cool." Chad smiled. He snapped his fingers to the music as though he could hardly contain his excitement.

"And, I finished that article for the school newspaper," Mikey said. "You know the one about—"

"Crud," Chad interrupted. "I forgot that library book at home. It's overdue."

Mikey turned away.

The truck turned down the busy main street and drove passed the shops and restaurants with townsfolk bundled up in coats and scarves walking along the sidewalks. Finally, they entered the parking lot of Sherman Oaks School as dozens of elementary and high school kids walked across the campus.

Donnie swung open the truck door and hopped his large body out. His folder bounced off his belly and fell onto the snow spilling his math papers all over the ground. "Dang," he bent down to gather it up. He crammed it back into the folder.

"Let's go doofus." Chad shoved Donnie and waved to Mikey's dad. "Thanks again, Mr. Thompson."

"Thanks, Dad," Mikey said. He closed the door. He brushed his bangs aside and zipped up his jacket.

"Have a good day, son," his dad said without making eye contact. The truck took off leaving Mikey standing in the parking lot.

Thanks for asking about my article, Dad, Mikey thought. Then he turned to walk off.

"So? How is it?" Chad asked as they left the parking lot. "What's it look like?"

"It's a Northland hockey stick. Just like Maniago uses," Mikey said in a monotone.

"Far out!" Chad said. "That's the best birthday present ever. I can't wait to see it. Coming tonight?"

"Yeah. I just have to wait until after dinner. That's when my dad falls asleep on the couch," Mikey put his hands into his pockets, turned, and started to walk toward the lockers.

The first bell rang and all the kids entered the main building.

"Man, how come you didn't bring it to school?" Chad shouted. "I would have brought it and showed it off!"

Mikey chortled. "Yeah, my dad wanted to know the same thing."

"So why didn't you bring it?" Chad brushed Mikey's shoulder as they approached their lockers.

Mikey shrugged and dialed in his locker combination. Once it opened, he took out his textbooks.

"Hi, Chad." Some girls flirted as they walked by. Mikey knew all the girls liked Chad because of his blonde good looks and sports skills.

"Hey." Chad nodded toward the girls. He didn't seem to notice their flirtations. Mikey pulled out a notebook from his locker.

"Yeah, well, hopefully you can make it to practice tonight. This is gonna be the best tournament ever. I can feel it, Mikey," Chad said. He punched him on the shoulder. "I can feel it!"

"I wish I felt it." Mikey simply nodded, closed his locker, and headed toward his classroom.

§

Most winters in Sherman Oaks, Minnesota were wet with snow and ice. This year, the snow started in October making it tough for kids to concentrate on school and chores. Mikey noticed the students in their seats, staring out the windows as though hoping to see more clouds form in the sky. He knew the older folks complained, but the local kids cherished every moment of it. To them, snow and ice meant one thing: hockey. The early snowfall this year was a blessing for them. Now they had more time to practice for the big hockey tournament in January.

Outside of town was Sherman Oaks Pond where the kids

practiced. The kids with money went into town at the skating rink, but Mikey's friends preferred the pond.

The only problem was *the legend.*

Mikey knew most kids didn't care much for the legend. They just wanted to beat nearby Taylor Pines Elementary School that year in the hockey tournament. Chad and the others were willing to risk it all if it meant winning that trophy just once.

CHAPTER 3

Practice

"Come on Mike!" Chad clapped his gloved hands. "Give it all you've got!"

On the bleachers near the pond sat Lexie and Anya watching the boys practice.

"Go Mikey!" Lexie shouted. She and Anya sat huddled together, trying to stay warm in the early evening air. Mikey smiled and waved at Lexie. She swept aside her long blonde hair off her shoulder. She cupped her mittened hands over her mouth. "You can do it!"

He turned his body around then skated as fast as he could toward the goal. The new hockey stick in his grip felt awkward. He huffed and swung it hard hoping his aim was true. The clack of his stick hitting the puck echoed all around them. He skidded to a stop half way across the pond. Slicing across the ice, the puck slid past the goal and into the snow bank behind it.

Mikey sighed. He could see his breath in the cold evening air.

Stan, the team's goalie, ran into the snow and retrieved the puck. He threw it onto the ice and it stopped at Mikey's skate. He shrugged and used his stick to slide the puck over to his friend, Chad.

Mikey inhaled deeply. He could smell the pines mixed with the cold night air. He inspected the hockey stick then handed his stick over to Chad.

"Here, you give it a try. Maybe it'll work for you," he mumbled.

Chad took it and headed toward the goal with the hockey stick guiding the puck.

"Make it a good one, Chad!" Mikey shouted to his best friend who shot the hockey puck down the ice and toward the makeshift goal with ease. They all cheered when it went between Stan's legs and into the goal.

"Yes!" Mikey skated over to Chad.

"Man, this stick is the best!" Chad grinned and handed the

Northland hockey stick over to Mikey.

"Nah, you keep it for now," Mikey said.

"What? Whaddya mean?" Chad asked. His jerked his blonde hair out of his eyes. "It's yours!"

"Come on, we both know you're the better player. You keep it until after the tourney."

"Mikey, what about your dad?" Chad said. "If he sees you coming home without that new stick, he'll kill you."

"Yeah, well you let me worry about my dad, alright?" Mikey skated off the ice.

"Come on, guys, one more time!" Stan waited by the goal. He was the smallest of the group. He removed his mask. His cheeks were pink from the cold. "I have good feeling about this!"

"You gotta just keep practicing, Mike." Chad placed his hand on Mikey's shoulder and squeezed.

Stan skated over and tossed down his goalie mask.

"Practice your aim, Michael," he said through his Russian accent. "One more time, eh?"

Mikey waved him off.

"No, come on in, guys, it's getting dark out. We gotta get home now," he shouted to the others on the ice.

Donnie skated over to Stan. He towered over him. Stan craned his neck and looked up at Donnie. He winced as Donnie raised his big hand and pushed him over to the edge of the pond where Lexie and Anya still sat on the bleachers shivering.

"Ah come on, we were just getting started." Stan gestured toward Mikey. "You show great potential, Michael."

"Yeah, well, *you* let three pucks get by you," Donnie said as his big belly peek through his unbutton jacket. "I think it's time to pack up and head home. Besides, we've got homework tonight."

"Yes, Stanislav, we have homework in English tonight," Stan's sister Anya said.

"Stanislav." Donnie teased him as he took off his skates. "Time to go home, Stanislav!"

Stan tried to shove him hard, but Donnie, who was twice his size, didn't budge. He just laughed.

"You did great, Mikey," Lexie said. She watched Mikey take off his skates, his pads, and put his gear into his bag.

"Thanks, I guess. I could've done better," he murmured. He

quickly pulled on his snow boots. He usually liked it when Lexie came to watch, but tonight he wished she had stayed home.

"I dunno, Mikey, you'd better take the stick home." Chad handed the hockey stick back to Mikey.

Mikey reluctantly took it. He brushed his bangs aside then inspected the stick for a second or too. He squinted his eyes as though he didn't know what to think.

"For some reason, my dad thinks if I have the same hockey stick as the number one player, it'll make *me* a number one player, ya know?" He slid his hand across the handle then handed it back to Chad.

Chad nodded.

"As if my dad knows what it takes, huh?" Mikey frowned. "I don't think he was ever any good at sports in his entire life. Which would explain why he wants *me* to be good in sports, right?"

"Just take it home, Mikey," Chad said. "You're lucky to have it. I'd kill to have a hockey stick like this one."

Yeah, well, you're lucky to have a mom, Mikey thought, *and a dad who cares what you think.*

"You're the best player, Chad, you should have it."

"That's nuts." Chad shoved the stick at Mikey. "With more practice you could be the best too, okay?"

"I guess we'll see, huh?" Mikey leaned over and grabbed his bag.

"Come on guys, let's get outta here before something happens out here," Destrey said as he pulled his beanie tightly over his ears. His curly brown hair peaked out from under the beanie. He wasn't as tall as Mikey and Chad, but he made up for it in personality. He started the "joke of the week" at school and usually had the teacher in stitches.

They all slowly walked across the snow toward the neighborhood.

"Whaddya mean *before something happens out here*?" Donnie asked. He looked down at Destrey.

Destrey turned his head and looked back at the frozen pond.

"Ah come on," Donnie laughed. He his belly jiggled. "Don't tell me you believe in that ghost story crap, huh?" He took out a beanie from his pocket and put it on snug over his ears.

"You bet I do!" Destrey said. "And so do you."

"Ah, that story's for babies," Donnie said.

"Uh huh, then why don't you stay out here after dark and stand in the middle of the ice, huh?" Lexie challenged. She stopped walking and stood with her arms crossed. Her puffy winter coat made her look bigger than she was.

Donnie waved her off.

"Yeah, Destrey," Donnie challenged him also. "Why don't *you*?"

"Cuz I ain't crazy, that's why," Destrey said. "I know the story."

"What story?" Anya asked. "Tell me, what story?"

Mikey sighed as though frustrated. But deep down, he sort of enjoyed telling the story and the mystery that surrounded it. He'd always dreamt of being a newspaper journalist and found the facts about the legend fascinating.

"Well, most townspeople forbid their kids to play on the frozen pond in winter and swim in it in summer due to the mysterious disappearances. The legend has it that there's something sinister about the pond. Ever since the 1961 bus accident when several kids drowned in the school bus, people have been afraid to go in the water," he said.

Anya listened with eyes wide open. She turned her head and looked over at the frozen pond. A few wisps of snow scattered over its surface.

"And before that, several young women disappeared after having been spotted walking along the pond, never to be seen alive again," Destrey said. "Their dead bodies were pulled from the water. So you can see why people are...*afraid!*"

He gave Anya a sinister look and raised his hands as though about to strangle her.

"Local kids say it's the ghosts of the children under the ice," Mikey said.

Anya cocked her head as though confused. "Ghosts? Of children?"

"Spirits of the dead," her brother, Stan, answered in his thick Russian accent. She nodded.

"The angry ghosts look for those walking alone by the pond at night. If you're not careful, they'll grab you and pull you under the ice forever as revenge for what happened to them!" Destrey grabbed her arm.

She yelped and the group laughed.

"How do you know all this?" Anya asked Mikey.

"Mikey researched it all. He's great at research. He's going to be a newspaper reporter someday!" Lexie gushed.

"Really?" Anya smiled at Mikey.

"Well, I hope so…someday," Mikey said. He could feel his face turn red.

"Yeah, well, I think that's all nonsense," Donnie said as he walked over to Destrey.

"It's true!" Destrey said. Donnie just turned his big body away.

"All I know is that the killer of those children got away," Mikey said.

"Is this true?" Anya asked.

"Yep," Mikey said. "He was never caught."

The group walked on, talking about the legend and ghost stories as the sun made its way down behind the tall pines that surrounded the pond. The fall evenings were peaceful. They stopped talking and the only sound they could hear was their boots crunching in the snow.

"Okay, here's a joke." Destrey cleared his throat, breaking the silence. "I used to be addicted to soap…before I got *clean*."

Anya giggled.

"Ha ha," Lexie smirked.

"Not one of your best," Donnie said. "Most people don't see you as *clean*."

Lexie giggled.

"Oh, yeah?" Destrey tried to shove Donnie.

Mikey's friends weren't the jocks in school much to Chad's disappointment. Nor were they the brainy kids like Stanislav wished. No, Mikey knew they were the nerds in the school. Each one had been chased down the hall by the bigger kids at some point, except Donnie. He was one of the big kids.

Mikey inspected each of one his friends and smiled. Yep, they were a unique group of what most would call misfits or losers. But at least they had each other.

"Oh no!" Mikey suddenly shouted, interrupting their silent walk. They stopped and stared at him. His face was all crinkled up.

"What's the matter?" Lexie asked.

"I left the hockey stick back there on the bench."

"Oh yeah, I saw it. You left it over there." She pointed.

"I'll be right back," he mumbled as he turned to head back to the pond.

"Come on, man, leave it there. It's gettin' dark out here!" Destrey said. He adjusted his knit beanie far over his ears.

"Are you nuts? I can't just leave it out here," Mikey shouted back and started jogging away.

"You weren't so concerned about it a minute ago," Donnie smirked.

"Shut up, Donnie," Mikey said. "You guys go on home. I'll catch up."

They stood for a moment watching him jog off toward the pond. Stanislav and his sister walked on toward their block. Donnie and Chad reluctantly continued on. But Lexie and Destrey stayed behind to watch Mikey.

"He's crazy," Destrey said to Lexie.

Mikey jogged to the bench. He looked up at the full moon already high in the sky. It illuminated the entire pond. He looked down at the bench, but he didn't see the stick anywhere.

"What the—" he said. "It was right here."

Mikey closed his eyes, thinking back to how happy his father was that morning. *My dad's gonna kill me if I don't come home with that stick*, he thought. Mikey knew it was an expensive gift and that his dad didn't have a lot of money to spend. He sighed as he remembered when his dad gave it to him as a birthday gift. Mikey was hoping for a typewriter so he could write more articles like a real reporter, but no, his father gave him that hockey stick.

He bent down and looked under the bench then all around it. *He's gonna kill me I just know it,* he thought. He looked around until he was just about to give up. That's when he thought he heard something coming from the frozen pond. It sounded like ice cracking. He looked out at the surface in time to see the wind kick up some snow and scatter it across the surface. There, out in the middle of the ice, was the hockey stick.

"No way. You've gotta be kidding me," he said. "How the heck did it get out there?" He exhaled and edged across the ice with his arms spread to balance himself, being careful not to slip.

"Mikey, no!" Lexie shouted. She ran to the edge of the pond

with Destrey following her. "Stop! What are you doing?"

Mikey turned and saw Lexie and Destrey looking frantic with eyes wide and arms raised.

"Will you two calm down? We were just out here skating, sheesh," he shouted. "My hockey stick is *right there*."

"I know. But just watch your step, okay?" Lexie said as she wringed her hands. Mikey could tell all that talk about the ghosts had made her nervous.

He turned and bent down to pick up the hockey stick. But as he did, he saw something move under the ice. He squinted to see if it was a fish or something else. He bent down closer and looked into the darkness below the ice for a second or two. He saw nothing.

"Huh." He narrowed his eyes. "I could've sworn I saw something." He stood straight and turned to head back to his waiting friends.

"What's wrong?" Lexie asked.

Mikey looked up. "Nothing. It's just that I thought I saw someth—"

Just then, a hand broke through the surface right in front of Mikey and grabbed his ankle so tight, he thought his foot was caught in a trap set out for a fox. But before he could react, the hand around his ankle pulled him underneath the ice in one strong yank. Clumps of ice flew everywhere.

All that remained on the surface was the hockey stick.

Mikey could hear Lexie's scream before his head went under. But once he was under the extremely cold water, he felt his body go into shock. It was as though millions of tiny needles pricked his skin all at once. He opened his eyes and looked around. The moon's glow penetrated the surface. Then, he looked down at what held his ankle. He couldn't believe what he saw with his own eyes.

There, under the frozen pond, were four very pale children staring at him with tormented looks on their faces. The one boy let go of his ankle and floated over to him. As he approached, Mikey noticed the boy had the same hair color as he did only it was shorter. It was almost like looking in a mirror. He wore a striped t-shirt and jeans. The others wore simple shirts and jeans, too. Their hair slowly waved along with the current of the icy water as faint light from the moon above penetrated the water and danced across their gaunt faces.

Mikey began to feel his lungs betray him. As he tried to swim to the surface for air, the boy ghost slowly pointed to the dark murky water beneath them. Mikey turned to see what the ghost was pointing at but couldn't see anything. He could feel his ears burn from the cold water and he knew he would black out any second. He frantically tried to swim away, but the ghost earnestly pointed to the murky water again. But Mikey began to pass out.

The last thing he remembered before blacking out was the faces of the children under the ice.

CHAPTER 4

Alive Again

Mikey heard voices.

"Come on, Mikey!"

He turned his head to see who was speaking to him, but he couldn't see who it was in the darkness.

"Blow out the candles!" the voice said. It was a soft voice. It was a woman's voice.

"Go ahead, make a wish and blow out the candles and then we'll open all your presents," the voice said. That's when Mikey realized it was his mother's voice.

"Mom?" he tried to whisper to her, but he couldn't.

He heard voices again.

As he lay still, he realized they were his friends' voices. He slowly opened his eyes to see them staring down at him, their faces pale with fright. He frowned.

The rows of fluorescent lights on the ceiling glared behind them. Mikey squinted. The pungent smell of disinfectant mixed with stale air made him wince and he heard the sound of adult voices nearby, too.

"Mikey? Are you okay?" Lexie asked him.

He nodded and looked down at his body realizing it was covered with many blankets. He enjoyed the warmth. He wiggled his toes and was glad to feel his feet and legs again.

"You gave us quite a scare, Mike," a male voice said. He turned to see Doctor Simpson standing over him with Mikey's wrist in his hand. He looked at his watch as he took Mikey's pulse. "Your dad will be here any minute."

"Where am I?" Mikey barely said through chattering teeth.

"You're in Sherman Oaks Hospital, Mike," the doctor said. "You fell through the ice and nearly froze to death." He pried one of Mikey's eyes open and inspected it.

Mikey looked at his friends. They were nodding in agreement.

"Don't you remember?" The doctor handed the nurse a clip board.

"I can remember…the cold water, my ears burning, and—"

"Actually, Mike, you *did* die." Doctor Simpson leaned in and gently touched Mikey's shoulder. "But only for a few seconds and then the paramedics revived you."

"It was scary, Mikey!" Lexie said. Her blue eyes were wide with excitement. "I was…I mean, *we* were so concerned for you."

"How did you guys get here?" Mikey whispered.

"Oh man, it was so cool!" Destrey said. His knit beanie was off so his brown curly hair was nearly over his eyes. "We got to ride in my dad's sheriff's patrol car. The sirens were blaring and everything!"

"Yeah, but I didn't like seeing them put you in the ambulance." Chad stepped over to the bed. "You gave us a good scare, Mike."

"Did you see anything when you were dead, Mikey? Anything special?" Destrey asked as he approached. "A bright light? A tunnel? Was it spooky?"

Mikey crinkled his face in confusion.

Donnie stepped over and hit Destrey on the arm. "Knock it off, doofus. He *died*. He didn't go to Disneyland."

"Ow!" Destrey rubbed his arm. "Hey, I've heard some people say they saw a light at the end of a long dark tunnel when they had a near-death experience."

Donnie shook his head.

"It's true!" Destrey turned his head. "Ain't it, Mike?"

"Alright, kids," the doctor walked over and opened the door. "Time to wait outside in the hall until your folks pick you up. Mike needs to rest."

"But doctor, isn't the patrol car going to take us home? It brought us here," Destrey whined as they exited the room with forlorn faces. "And I have more questions to ask Mikey…"

Mikey nodded good bye to his friends as they exited the room. He continued to wriggle his toes and legs. Then, he heard his father's voice out in the hall. The door burst open to reveal his father's ashen face.

"Mikey!" His dad ran over to him. "Are you okay son?"

Mike relished seeing his dad's obvious concern for him. He had thought his father would be angry with him.

"Yep," he said.

His dad brushed Mikey's damp hair to the side.

"What happened?" he asked.

"We were practicing and I guess I skated onto some thin ice," Mikey said. "I think."

His dad exhaled loudly.

"Alright, then, no more hockey practice on that pond, got it?" his dad said.

"Alright," Mikey said, relieved that he wouldn't have to play hockey anymore.

"The ice is too thin. We'll have to find a way for you to practice at the rink."

"Dad!" Mikey whined.

"Mikey, you died! You're lucky they were able to revive you." His dad pulled up a chair and sat, leaning forward. His face looked long and tired. "No hockey tournament is worth that."

"It's not the hockey," Mikey said, pulling himself up to a seated position. "It's something else."

His dad straightened. "Huh? What do you mean?"

"I mean..." Mikey hesitated. "I saw *something*."

"You saw something? When?"

"When I was under the water."

His dad furrowed his brow.

"What are you talking about?"

Mikey cleared his throat. "Dad, when I was under the water, I saw something."

His dad leaned forward in his chair. "What did you see?"

"I saw some kids," Mikey said. His face was expressionless. "I saw a bunch of children about my age under the ice."

His dad sat with his mouth open for a second or two. He seemed to be searching for the right words to say. Mikey expected his dad to laugh or brush it off as a dream or something. He waited for his dad's response.

"You saw ghosts?" his dad asked.

Mikey's eyes widened. He nodded, astonished that his dad understood. He even thought he saw some semblance of relief in his dad's eyes.

"How did you know?" Mikey asked.

"Mikey, you were probably dreaming." His dad leaned back.

The semblance of relief was gone.

Mikey leaned back on the pillows.

"It wasn't a dream, Dad," he said. "I saw their faces clear as I'm seeing yours now."

His dad looked away. "Mikey…"

"They were real," Mikey continued.

"Son…"

"And they seemed to be trying to tell me something," he said.

His dad stood.

"And one of them looked a lot like…"

"Enough!" his dad shouted.

Mikey's body jolted from the shout.

"I knew you wouldn't believe me." Mikey crossed his arms over his tightened chest. His eyes welled up. "Nobody ever believes me."

His dad ran his hands through his own hair in frustration.

"Son, you had a near death experience. In fact, you *did* die for a few seconds," he said. "You were probably having a vision."

Mikey studied his dad's face. He wasn't convinced his father believed his own words.

"It wasn't a vision," Mikey murmured.

"Now, get some rest. I'm going home to get you some clean clothes." His dad took out his car keys.

"I know it wasn't a vision because one of the ghosts looked familiar," Mikey said. "In fact, he looked a lot like me."

His dad dropped the keys onto the floor. He stood speechless for a few seconds.

"You'll be staying here tonight and then I'll take you home in the morning." His dad picked up the keys and reached for the door.

"You're leaving me here?"

"I'll be right back. Get some rest, okay?" His dad left the room.

Mikey rolled over and sighed.

"I know what I saw was real," he mumbled to himself. "I know what I saw. *It was real.*"

CHAPTER 5

Confessions

The boiler room of the school was easy to access since the kids found the broken window in the back of the school. Years earlier, some older kids, who had long since graduated, cracked the window one time when they broke into the school to play a prank on the principal. Mikey and his friends would sneak in and hide in the boiler room down in the basement. It was their hangout in the wintertime. The only use for the boiler room was to house the large furnaces that heated the entire school, the janitors' lockers, and a few cleaning supplies stacked on metal shelves.

After Mikey was released from the hospital, he asked his friends to meet him in the boiler room. He had to tell them what he saw.

Once inside, the warmth from the rumbling furnace felt good and the kids took off their jackets and gloves. Mikey sat on a bench across from his friends.

Here we go, he thought. *What are they gonna say? Will they laugh? Will they believe me?*

"Man, what were you thinking?" Destrey asked.

"My new hockey stick," Mikey said. "I couldn't just leave it on the ice."

"And so you went after it?" Chad said. "Dude, you can always get a new hockey stick."

"You scared the heck out of us, Mike," Donnie said. He pulled a grape flavored lollipop out of his pocket, unwrapped it, and then popped it in his mouth.

"Guys," he said. "You won't believe what I saw down there."

They all looked at each other then back at him.

"You saw something in the water?" Chad brushed aside his dark blonde bangs.

Mikey nodded.

They looked at each other with raised eyebrows.

Destrey leaned in. "What did you see?"

Mikey hesitated, not sure how he would handle their reaction to his story. Could he take it if they laughed? And what if they *did* believe him? What would happen next? He knew he had to tell them what happened. He hoped beyond hope that they would believe him.

"Go on, Mikey, you can tell us," Lexie said. She scooted next to him.

He looked down at his snow boots.

"Guys, I'm only gonna tell you this once. I don't care what you think or what you say, but you can't tell anyone else what I'm about to tell you, understand?" he said.

His voice had a seriousness to it.

"Man, don't tell us if you don't think we should know." Chad crossed his arms.

"Can I trust you all?" Mikey asked.

Destrey fidgeted then looked at Lexie who looked at Chad who looked at Donnie. Then, they all turned to Stan who looked so small sitting next to Donnie. Stan adjusted his wire-rimmed glasses and nodded.

"Alright then," Chad said. "We all promise not to tell anyone outside this room what you are about to tell us. Right?"

They all agreed.

Mikey took a deep breath.

"Okay," he said. "I saw…well, I saw *them*."

No one said anything for a second or two.

"Them?" Chad looked at the others then back at Mikey. "You saw them?"

Mikey nodded. "Yes."

"Who?" Chad asked.

Destrey gasped and his eyes grew wide when he realized what Mikey was saying. He covered his mouth.

"Them?" Donnie scratched his ear. "*Them* who? Them what? What's he talking about?"

Mikey looked at Chad then at Donnie. He turned to Lexie.

"I saw them," he said to her big blue eyes.

She nodded slowly.

"I saw the children under the ice," he said.

§

Mikey sat in horror as his friends busted out with laughter so hard, that some of them fell off the benches in the school boiler room. All his friends laughed, except Lexie. She sat staring at Mikey.

"That's the funniest thing I've ever heard!" Donnie said. He rolled on the floor holding his gut.

"I'm serious!" Mikey said. "You saw me go onto the ice after the hockey stick!"

"Yeah, but—"

"And we all know the ice wasn't thin because we had just skated on it!" Mikey cringed as they continued to laugh. "And you saw me disappear under the ice."

But they didn't seem to listen.

"I knew I shouldn't have told you." Mikey stood, grabbed his jacket, and moved toward the stairway.

"Mikey don't go," Lexie said. She hit Destrey and Donnie on the legs and they stopped laughing long enough to sit back down.

Chad nudged Donnie and the two snickered.

"Hey Mikey, don't go," Destrey said. He brushed aside his curly brown hair. "We were only foolin' around."

"Yeah, come on," Chad said. "We believe you."

Then they started laughing all over again.

"He saw children under the ice!" Donnie screamed with laughter.

Mikey could still hear them laughing and making ghost sounds when he pulled himself through the window and stood in the snow quickly putting on his coat. He heard Lexie following him.

"Wait up, Mikey," she said.

But he buried his hands deep into his the pockets and huffed off.

It's no use," he said. "No one will ever believe me."

"Mikey wait!" she shouted after him. But he continued walking away. "I believe you!" he heard Lexie shout after him.

CHAPTER 6

Microfilm

A couple of days later, Mikey walked down main street thinking about what to do next. The air was cold and crisp on that sunny day, but some snow remained along the roads and in the woods. He kicked a few stones away as he walked.

This is crazy, he thought. *I must be nuts. Is it any wonder that no one believes me? Why should they? Who sees ghosts anyways except crazy people?*

He sighed.

Except, I did see the ghosts. I know what I saw and I'm not crazy. He walked with determination. *I'll go to the library and find out just exactly what happened at that pond.*

Just then, he paused when he noticed Reverend Johnson approaching. The Reverend stopped right in front of him.

"Well, hello Mikey. How are you feeling this fine morning?" He was his usual chipper self all wrapped up in an overcoat, knit scarf, and cap. "Heard you gave your father quite a scare, huh?"

Mikey looked down at his own snow boots and nodded.

"Well, I must say, I was frightened when I heard what happened." The Reverend put his hand on Mikey's shoulder. "Sure am glad you're alright now."

Reverend Johnson looked up into the clear sky.

"Supposed to snow later on this evening. Hard to believe with that blue sky and not a cloud in sight. I think we'll have snow all the way through to Christmas. What do you think?"

"Uh, yeah, I think you're right, Reverend," Mikey said.

"So, where are you headed?" he asked him.

"Um, to the library."

"The library?" the Reverend said. "Well that's a surprise. Usually kids your age head over to the drug store to buy candy and read comics on a Saturday morning," He chuckled.

"Uh, yeah, well, I have some homework to do before I get to buy candy and such," Mikey said. He started to walk away hoping the Reverend wouldn't ask anymore questions, but he stood in his way. His six-foot three-inch frame was imposing to most kids.

"So, what are you working on at the library?" He asked.

"Hey you!" came a shout from the other side of the street. Reverend Johnson turned around to see who was yelling. Mikey noticed the smile leave the Reverend's face when he saw it was only the town bum stumbling over to them, drunk as usual.

"Hey you, Rev'ren'," the bum slurred. "I know you!"

"Run a long now, Mikey," Reverend Johnson said. He gently motioned Mikey by him. "Nothing to see here."

The bum approached and, as he did, Mikey could smell a couple of weeks' worth of alcohol on the man's clothes.

"I know who you are!" the bum shouted.

"Alright, alright," Reverend Johnson said as he raised his hands to stop the drunken man from coming too close. "Let's get you some hot coffee, huh Ed?"

"Ed Stuckey," a woman whispered as she approached the scene from behind Mikey. She shook her head as though disappointed.

"Huh?" Mikey turned his head. He didn't even notice she was there.

She motioned toward the two men. "That bum over there," she said to Mikey as they watched Reverend Johnson take Mr. Stuckey by the shoulders and turned him around. "That's Ed Stuckey, former school principal. Such a shame, really. He was once such a reputable man in this town." She observed the scene for a moment, then turned and walked hastily away.

"Yeah, a shame," Mikey said as though he knew what she was talking about. *So who's Ed Stuckey?* He thought. *It's just the town bum.*

"Some nice hot coffee will do you good, Ed," the Reverend said as he turned and smiled a forced smile at Mikey.

"I know who you are!" Mr. Stuckey slurred again.

"Come on, Ed. Let's get you inside where it's warm," Reverend Johnson said. "Good-bye Mikey. Have a wonderful Saturday."

"It's you!" the old bum shouted with desperation. "I know it's you! I'm not crazy like everyone says I am. I know what I'm talkin' 'bout!"

Mikey watched for a few more seconds, and then turned to

head over to the library.

§

As Mikey walked, he pictured his father lying on the couch surrounded by empty beer cans. He would never tell his friends what he saw night after night. He didn't want them to think poorly of his dad. *I guess he's pretty tired from a long day at work when he gets home,* he thought. Yet he knew this behavior started after his mom left them. Mikey felt sorry for his dad at times and other times he was angry with him. He knew his dad was doing the best he could and probably never expected to raise a son by himself and now Mikey went and scared him by being in the hospital for a couple of days. He didn't mean to scare his dad like that. Mikey usually stayed out of trouble and made good grades in school.

He kicked up some snow as he walked. He thought his dad was doing an okay job of raising him so far, but he missed coming home to a bright, clean house and decent food.

As he approached the library, he spotted his father across the street coming out of the Sherman Oaks Townhall building. He waved.

"Hey Dad!" Mikey shouted. His dad waved back, got in his patrol car, and drove away.

Mikey pulled open the heavy wooden door to the library and entered the large four-story building. His eyes followed the exaggerated staircase in the middle of the entrance. It seemed like something out of *Gone with the Wind* or some other old movie his mom used to watch on T.V. Built in the late 1800s, the library seemed opulent to most townspeople. At least that's what the history teacher told him. Mikey didn't care. He enjoyed its warmth with rows and rows of books and large wooden tables. Dozens of people walked up and down the carpeted stairs. Some were college students, others were older people. Along the balcony of the second floor, Mikey spied students sitting at tables, reading or talking quietly by the light of small lamps. He gazed over to the main desk made of carved mahogany. Behind it stood Miss

Jennings, the new librarian. She had been promoted from assistant to main librarian over the summer. She wore her long brown hair in a tight ponytail behind her head. She peered over her dark rimmed glasses now and then while stamping dates on books.

Mikey sighed when he saw her. He always had a little crush on her.

"Shhh!" she said to a group of teens at a nearby table. "Whisper please."

"Hello Miss Jennings," Mikey said as he approached the front desk. "Can you help me with something?"

She gasped when she saw him and quickly came around from behind the desk.

"Mikey!" she said rather loudly causing several people to look up from their books. She gave him a soft motherly hug around the shoulders.

"It is so good to see you up and about," she whispered. "I am so glad you are alright. When I heard the news, I was very concerned."

Mikey felt his face grow warm.

"Thanks," he murmured. He hesitated to look into her hazel eyes because they were so cozy. He swallowed back his embarrassment. But he did enjoy her hugs.

"So what can I help you with today?" she asked.

Miss Jennings was the typical single and mousy librarian. She remained single even though many older women tried to set her up with nephews and grandsons. Today she wore a black turtle neck, bead earrings that hung low, and a long denim skirt. Mikey always thought she was pretty and probably a good match for his single father. He knew they went to high school together a long time ago. She was tall, thin, and angular with willowy long arms. But he wasn't sure his dad would like her. She didn't look a thing like Mikey's mother, which was fine by him.

"Well, I need to research something that happened a long time ago," he said.

She grabbed a few books and began walking down an aisle. "Oh? Sounds intriguing. I know you enjoy reading old newspaper articles. What did you need to research?"

"That bus accident that happened in 1961," he said as he followed.

Miss Jennings stopped walking and turned around. Her brow furrowed. She suddenly looked like someone had told her a friend had died.

"Why on earth do you need to research that tragic event?" She adjusted her glasses and placed the books onto a cart. She wheeled the cart down the aisle with Mikey following her.

Tell her about the ghosts, he thought for a second. *She'll believe you. Tell her.*

"Um, well for…school," Mikey said. He helped her push the cart.

"Why thank you, Mikey. So this is for a school assignment, huh?" Miss Jennings said. "I know all the school projects assigned this semester and I don't remember any of the teachers saying anything about—"

Mikey stopped the cart. Miss Jennings looked at him with that serious concerned look that only adults seem to have.

"Okay, so it's not for school," he confessed. "It's about…"

Just tell her about the ghosts! He thought as he searched for the right words. He didn't want to lie again.

"It's for me... It's personal," he said. Well, it was the truth.

She squinted. "Personal?"

And then her eyes grew large as she remembered how Mikey's uncle, his father's younger brother, was on that bus.

"Oh, I understand," she said. "Come this way. And please be quiet."

Mikey turned and quietly followed closely behind the librarian.

Miss Jennings led him downstairs to the research department. This was Mikey's favorite part of the library. He sometimes read through the periodicals pretending to be a reporter like Carl Bernstein or Bob Woodward, researching an article for the newspaper. The area was filled with some college students writing papers and flipping through stacks of books. They looked up from their work periodically to see what was going on.

She finally guided Mikey to where some interesting machines lined the walls.

"Here's our microfilm projectors," she explained. Then she retrieved a couple of boxes of microfilm from the large drawers. "You remember how to load the film into the projectors, right?"

He nodded. She watched him load the film so he could scan

through hundreds of pages of newspapers from the year 1961.

"I'll leave you here for one hour, okay?" she said. "After that, you'll need to let others use the machines."

"Okay, thank you Miss Jennings," Mikey said. She smiled warmly then started to walk away.

"By the way, Mikey," she said. "How's your father?"

Mikey grinned. "Um, he's okay, I guess."

"Good. Please tell him I said hello, okay?" She turned to walk back up the stairs.

"Sure!"

"Shhh!" said a woman in the aisle next to him.

Mikey turned to view the microfilm. He casually read through all the newspaper headlines from long ago. He chuckled at some of the advertisements. They were drawings instead of photographs.

"Lucky Strike cigarettes. You can't get lucky without them!" he read. The ad was a drawing of a man dressed in a nice suit holding a cigarette. Behind him was an attractive young woman leering at him longingly. "Oh brother," Mikey said. Then he went on to the next ad.

A drawing of an attractive woman from the waist up appeared. She wore a girdle and nothing else. She coyly covered her nude torso with her arms as she winked.

"The new sleek line girdle. So slim and sleek, he'll think you're a new woman," Mikey laughed out loud at that one then quickly covered his mouth. He looked around to see if anyone noticed.

He turned the knob and saw the next advertisement. It was a drawing of a family: a young boy, his father, and his mother, they were laughing while standing together in a grassy front yard. The boy held his mother's hand and she looked down on him in a loving way. Mikey concentrated on the woman's face. She was young with her brown hair tied in a ponytail. She wore a floral print dress. Her smile was sweet and almost sympathetic.

Mikey leaned back and looked down at his shoes for a moment, then turned the knob again. He looked at the screen and sat straight up in his chair with eyes wide open when he came upon the next heading.

"TRAGIC BUS ACCIDENT IN SHERMAN OAKS LEAVES THE TOWN SHOCKED AND IN TEARS," he read.

"That's it," Mikey said.

A few blurry black and white photographs of the pond appeared. He could see the back end of the school bus being towed out of the water by a large tow truck. He spotted local law enforcement in the photograph.

"Four local middle school students reported missing were found on the bus. All had drowned," Mikey read. He quietly read out loud the names of the dead pausing when he read his uncle's name. "Kevin Thompson."

"They all were 12 years old," he murmured. "Just like me."

He studied the photographs for a moment then turned the page. He gasped at the sight. School photos of each victim appeared on the screen.

"Wow," came a voice from behind him. "Your uncle looked a lot like you, Mikey."

But Mikey couldn't speak. He just stared at the photograph. All the blood drained from his face.

"Mikey?" Lexie asked. "You alright?" She tapped his shoulder.

He jumped from the touch. He turned to see a frightened Lexie. She studied his wide eyes.

"That's them," Mikey whispered. He studied each face on the screen. "That's *them*. I saw each one of them that night in the water."

Lexie leaned in and looked at each photograph carefully. The children had shorter haircuts and one boy wore dark rimmed glasses. They were smiling that fake school picture smile. Kevin Thompson wore the striped t-shirt.

"How sad," Lexie'S eyes became shiny with tears. She covered her mouth. "This is just so sad. Who could do such a thing?"

"They look like everyday kids," Mikey said. Then he turned to Lexie.

"By the way, what are you doing here?"

"I ran into Reverend Johnson who told me you were in here," she said. "I didn't mean to scare you. I figured you were researching for another article."

"You didn't scare me," he smirked like he was aggravated. He pushed his chair in closer to the screen. "You probably came here to laugh at me?"

"No, of course not," she said. "I believe you, Mikey."

He pursed his lips as though he didn't buy into what she said.

"The bus driver," Lexie said. She pointed to the words on the screen. "Seems that the bus driver went psycho and drove the bus into the water. He escaped though. Says here no one ever found him. He was last spotted in the next town hitchhiking."

"Look!" Mikey shouted.

"Shhh!" came the voice from the aisle next to them.

"Sorry. Look here," he whispered. He and Lexie focused on a photograph of the bus driver. It was taken from his employee identification card found in his locker at the school. "He looks...*familiar.*"

"You think so?" Lexie said.

"Yeah, but I can't place him." Mikey squinted his eyes and concentrated on the photograph.

"You're crazy," came a shout from behind them.

They jumped then turned to see Chad, Destrey, and Donnie standing behind them. Donnie had a lollipop in his mouth as usual.

"What are you guys doing here?" Mikey frowned. "Came to make fun of me did you?"

He stood and began to roll up the microfilm.

"Hey Mikey," Chad said. "Come on, no hard feelings huh?" He jerked his blonde bangs away from his eyes.

But Mikey ignored them.

"Come on," Destrey said. "Don't be like that. I really want to look at the photographs."

"You would be amazed at how the children were just regular kids like us," Lexie said. "Show 'em, Mikey."

He sighed and turned the knob until the photographs appeared again.

"Wow," Destrey said. "They were just regular school kids."

"Your uncle looks—" Chad started to say.

"A lot like me, I know." Mikey stood back with his hands in his pockets.

He watched his so-called friends continue to review the headlines. They stopped when they got to the bus driver's photograph.

"Does he seem familiar to you?" Lexie asked them.

"Look how old he was back then. He's probably dead by now," Donnie said.

"Yeah or living in Mexico. I hear escaped convicts or murderers head down south to hide from the cops," Chad said.

"I dunno," Destrey said. "He sorta does remind me of somebody."

The man in the photograph had darker hair with some grey on the temples. He had a thin mustache and wire rimmed glasses. His face was bent downward in a strange frown.

"Hey kids," said a voice from behind them. "We need to use the machines."

They turned to see a couple of college students holding numerous books and folders staring down at them.

"Come on, guys," Mikey said. He quickly took the film out of the machine.

As they exited the library, Mikey still seemed a little out of it after seeing the faces of those children again. They decided what he needed was a cup of hot chocolate over at the drug store.

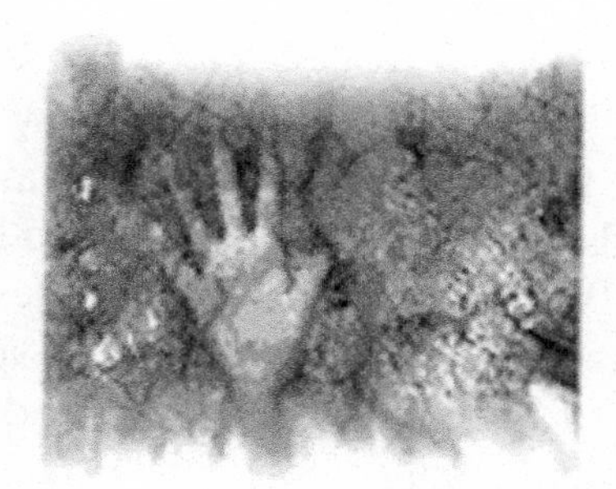

CHAPTER 7

Sledgehammer

"Come on, Mike," Chad said. "You can't stay mad at us forever."

The pipes in the boiler room burped and hissed as though reminding the kids they shouldn't be there so late at night.

"Yeah, Mike. What about the tournie?" Destrey said.

Mikey thought long and hard about the situation. He knew he didn't have a lot of friends to begin with and he remembered how much the tournament meant to his dad. He knew he'd have to trust just one more time.

"I guess," he sighed.

"Hey, that's it!" Donnie leaned over and shoved Mikey. Because Donnie was a good twenty pounds heavier, Mikey went backwards over the bench and landed on the tile floor.

Donnie quickly retrieved his friend. "You okay, Mike?"

"Yeah, yeah," he said as the others chuckled and chewed bubble gum.

"Dead kids, huh?" Chad asked. "You really saw them?" He took out some cards from his pocket and began shuffling them.

Mike carefully nodded as he sat on the bench across from the others. He still wasn't sure they really believed him.

"Well, what are we supposed to do now?" Destrey asked. He blew a big pink bubble.

"What do you mean *we*?" Mikey said. "This has nothing to do with you guys."

"Ah now, come on Mikey," Destrey said. "You gotta let us help."

"Yeah, Destrey loves this sorta stuff," Donnie said. He worked hard on the wrapper of a piece of Bazooka gum. "Ya gotta let us help you."

Mikey frowned.

"Look, this happened to me," he stood and walked to the doorway. "I don't need your help."

Chad handed Donnie the cards and walked over to Mikey.

"You're always doing this stuff," he walked past Mikey.

"What stuff?"

"This loner stuff," Chad said. He opened the door and headed up the stairs.

"What's that supposed to mean?" Mikey followed him.

"Look, if you want to go through this all on your own, go ahead." Chad sighed with frustration.

Mikey followed him out the window and into the snow.

"But don't you think you should trust your friends?" Chad asked.

Before he knew it, they had all surrounded him there in the cold night.

"So, you're saying you believe me?" Mikey asked.

"Yeah, sure," Chad said. He motioned to all of them as they stood there.

"You don't sound convincing," Mikey smirked.

"Well, we didn't see the ghosts like you did," Chad said. He walked over to Mikey. "But we believe you saw them."

"Yeah, let us help you out," Donnie said.

"No more laughing at me?"

They all shook their heads.

I know I'm going to regret this, Mikey thought.

"Shake?" Chad put his gloved hand out.

Mikey studied it for a second or two then shook it.

"Deal," he said.

Destrey jumped in between the two. "Okay, so what's the plan?"

Mikey looked at Destrey as though he was crazy.

"I dunno," he said. "I haven't thought about it yet."

They began to walk down the street toward the neighborhood. A light snowfall began.

"Well, we've got to have a plan!" Destrey followed along.

"I guess we could ask around town. Interview them like the reporters do. You know, like Woodward and Bernstein?"

Destrey looked up at Donnie who shrugged and shook his head.

"The two famous reporters from the Washington Post that investigated…nevermind. I suppose we could talk to some people who lived here back then. I can talk to my dad," Mikey said.

"Really?" Chad said as though surprised that his friend would talk to his father about something so personal.

"Yeah, why?" Mikey asked.

Chad shrugged. "Nothing," he said. "It's just that…"

"What?"

"Nothing."

"I can talk to my neighbors," Lexie said.

"Yeah, I guess that's what we should do first. Ask around and see what people remember," Mikey said. "We'll ask the journalistic questions…who, what, where, when, why, and how."

"How what?" Destrey asked.

Mikey rubbed his forehead in frustration.

"But we've got to be quiet about this," Donnie said. His face was crinkled up as though he was in pain.

"What do you mean?" asked Chad.

"If anyone at school finds out about this, we're dead!" Donnie said. He kicked a stone to emphasize his point. "You know? The big kids will tease us and make fun of us at school."

"Yeah," Lexie sighed. "He's right. They'll make fun of us…even more than they already do."

"They think we're losers enough already," Destrey said. "We don't want to give them any more ammunition."

"Okay, then we'll have to keep this a secret just between us. Got it?" Mikey asked as he turned around. They all agreed.

He felt better talking about it. To hear his friends talk made it seem more real. As they walked, Mikey couldn't help but notice the townspeople walking near them. He began to closely inspect each man as he approached. *Could he be the former bus driver?* Mikey thought. Then, he turned and saw another man approaching. *What about him?* Mikey shook the thought out of his head. He didn't like feeling so suspicious of the townspeople, but he couldn't help but feel something inside. He couldn't help but think that maybe the killer was closer than they thought.

They kept talking and bouncing ideas off each other until they turned the corner and disappeared down the block.

§

Reverend Johnson stood outside the quaint Sherman Oaks Church preparing to shake hands with members as they left the Wednesday night church meeting. He took a deep breath in. The air was crisp and smelled of snow.

"A good meeting, Reverend," Richard Chapman said. He shook the Reverend's hand firmly.

"Thank you, Rich. Always good to see you and Mabel here on Wednesday nights," Reverend Johnson said.

"We wouldn't miss it," Richard said.

"The coffee was a little stale, though," Mabel said as she exited. "And I miss the Bible studies we used to have on Wednesday nights with Reverend Ellis."

Reverend Johnson smirked. "Alright, Mabel. I'll look into fresh coffee for next week."

"Now all we do is sit and talk. Why is that?" Mabel asked. But the Reverend ignored her and gently led her down the steps without answering her. "Talk, talk, talk. That's all we do anymore. I miss the Bible studies."

One by one the church members emptied into the parking lot. Reverend Johnson walked to his car and put a large cloth bag in the trunk. Right before he closed it, someone called his name from behind.

"Almost forgot the sledge hammer you asked for, Reverend," Richard said. He handed the large hammer to the Reverend who set it in his trunk and quickly closed it.

"Why thank you, Rich. I'll have it back to you in no time," he said.

As Richard walked away, he turned around and asked. "So, what are you using it for again?"

"Thought I'd take out a wall in my house. Make the living room a little larger, you know?" Reverend Johnson said as he got into his car.

He waved goodbye and pulled out of the parking lot. As he drove, small snowflakes fluttered down onto his windshield. He watched them in flicker in the headlights as they fell.

After a few minutes, he turned down the back-road heading toward the pond. He slowed down and turned off the headlights. He drove slowly near the edge, put the car in park, and sat for a few minutes enjoying the solitude and the idea of getting rid of some loose ends. All he could hear in the night was the low humming of the furnaces from nearby homes, a few owl hoots, and the soft whisper of falling snow.

Satisfied no one had followed him, he got out of his car and went to the trunk. He retrieved the sledge hammer and walked to the frozen pond. He carefully walked out onto the ice about twenty feet away from the shore, making sure of each step. He turned his head left, then right to see if anyone was close by, then rammed the hammer into the ice making a hole the size of a bowling ball. The echoing sounds sent a few birds into the air. He stepped back making sure cracks in the ice didn't spread beneath his feet. The ice seemed to be about four or five inches thick.

He repeated the forceful blows until he made a larger hole into the ice. He wiped the sweat that had formed on his forehead, tried to catch his breath, and then headed back toward his car. He set the sledge hammer down and took the large cloth bag out of his trunk.

"I'm gettin' too old for this." He grunted as set the bag down. He stood still again listening for any unusual sounds. Satisfied that he was alone, he dragged the bag to the hole in the ice, and then bent over it. He unzipped the bag and winced from the smell of rotting meat.

"This is it, Ed Stuckey," he said to the dead body inside. "Your final resting place."

He made sure the cinder block was inside the bag. Slowly and carefully, he shoved the body into the waters making sure not to slip in himself or crack the ice. He watched the body sink deep into the inky black water below. A few bubbles rose to the top. "So long and good riddance."

He grinned as though cherishing the sight, and then he stood and stretched his back. Finally, when the dead body was out of sight, he turned to head back to his car. As he took a couple of steps, he heard the ice crack. He looked down and noticed a crack spreading underneath his boot.

"Oh great," he sighed. He carefully lifted his foot and stepped as lightly as he could, hoping not to join his victim in the icy waters that night.

He took another step. Another crack appeared. He lifted his foot off the ice and started to put it down, but when he did, something crashed through the ice and grabbed his ankle. He yelped and tried to move his leg, but whatever it was that had hold of him, it had a vice-like grip. He fell to the ice and looked at his ankle, but couldn't see, so he reached into his pocket and pulled out a small flashlight. His cold hands fumbled with it until he turned it on. And once he did, he shined the light on his ankle.

To his horror, he saw what had a hold of his leg. It was a hand that held his ankle with a solid grip.

A death grip.

"What the devil?" his eyes widened. He yanked his leg, but the grip was too powerful. That's when he noticed something about the hand. It was a small hand.

A *child's* hand.

As the panic rose inside him, he yanked his leg so hard that it finally came free. He scurried along the ice, hearing it crack more and more from his weight. He could hear pounding on the ice, but the sound wasn't from the surface. No, the pounding came from underneath the ice as though someone or something was trying to break out. He tried to stand, but the surface was slippery. He frantically crawled on his knees toward the edge of the pond, but right before he reached the edge another arm crashed through the ice and grabbed his tweed jacket.

"No!" he shouted and grabbed the arm. It was thin, wet, and frozen stiff. He yanked on it, but the child had a powerful grip on his jacket. He continued to struggle and crawl away as fast as he could until he heard the sound of fabric ripping. Finally, he was free. He stood up and ran the rest of the way to the edge of the pond, scrambled for his keys, then opened the car door. He threw his flashlight onto the front seat and sat down clutching his chest, desperately trying to catch his breath.

From the driver's seat, he could see the arm still protruding out of the ice. It seemed to be holding something in its grip. He sat, shivering, watching it from his car. Then, the arm slowly sunk down into the water and disappeared below. He could hear himself gasping for air. He pushed open his car door when he realized he needed to place the sledge hammer into the trunk. He never moved his old body as quickly as he did that night. Seconds after slamming the trunk shut, he started the car and spun it out of there sending ice and mud flying behind his car into the silent night.

CHAPTER 8

Ghost Story

"Burgers again?" Mikey asked as he sat down at the small metal dining table. It creaked and wiggled every time he leaned on it. He knew it must have been circa 1955 or sooner. He hated that table and wanted the large wooden table they had before…before his mother took it with her when she moved out.

His father made some clanging noise from the kitchen that sounded like plates being set on the counter.

"What'd you say?" his dad asked from the kitchen.

"Oh boy, burgers again!" Mikey said with fake enthusiasm.

His father came out with a couple of sodas and plopped them down on the table.

"That's what I thought you said." He popped open one cream soda can. Mikey watched him pour out the drink into the tall plastic cups. Mikey inhaled. The soda smelled delicious. Then he stepped back into the kitchen and returned with burgers on the plates. No fries, no ketchup, no nothing special. Just a couple of hamburgers. He sat down across from his son.

Mikey sighed.

He leaned his chin on his hand and remembered the backyard cookouts they used to have when his mom was home. Grandma and grandpa would come over and there was food everywhere: potato salad, French fries, his mom's homemade apple pie. It was fantastic! He closed his eyes and could almost smell the meat grilling. The smell reminded him of summertime, his most favorite time of the year. He could see his dad standing at the grill flipping the burgers over with a big smile on his face and that goofy white apron tied around his waist. No freezing cold ice storms, no snow, no hockey. Just fun times with his friends and family. Mikey licked his lips and opened his eyes again.

"Go ahead and eat up, I've got some work to do in my office," his dad said as he got up from the table and returned to the kitchen.

"Yeah, I've got some work to do, too," Mikey said.

"Yeah?" his dad asked.

"Uh, yeah. Another news story I'm working on for the school paper. It's gonna be big," he said as he pushed his hamburger with his finger.

"Really?" his dad said as he sat down again.

"Uh, huh. But I need to do some research. I, uh, have to ask some questions."

"Well, that'll be interesting."

"Dad?" Mikey said. He took a deep breath in before he spoke again. He couldn't believe he was actually going to talk to his dad about the pond.

"So no practice for awhile, huh?"

You can do this, Mikey. You can do this. He thought.

"Um, yeah I guess the ice is getting too thin," Mikey said. "Um, uh, Dad?"

"Well, another storm is coming and the ice will harden again."

"Yeah, I guess." Mikey took another bite of his burger.

Change the subject, he thought. *Change the subject.*

"Dad, can you tell me about what happened to—"

"That's the thing I like about hockey." He rubbed his hand along the table. "The challenge."

Mikey took another bite and chewed while his father talked.

"You know?" His dad took a bite of his burger then made a sour face as though it didn't taste all that great. "I like my burgers grilled rather than fried."

Me too, Mikey thought.

"The ice, the skill, the balance, the stamina it takes to win. You know what I mean?" his dad said. "So exciting."

"Uh huh." Mikey nodded and sighed. He thought about what was underneath the ice.

Yeah, well if you only knew what was underneath that ice, he thought. *You'd realize what's hidden is sometimes more important than what's happening right in front of you.*

"Dad?"

"Yeah, son?"

"Um…uh." He swallowed. *You can do this,* he thought.

"What is it?"

"Um…can you tell me what happened to Uncle Kevin that one

day?" he asked. He sort of winced as he waited for the answer.

His father sat still for a moment.

"What? Uncle Kevin?" he asked. "Why?"

Mikey shrugged. "I dunno. We haven't really talked about it much and I just wanted to know about it," he said. He hoped his dad wouldn't figure out he was being interviewed for a case.

His father looked at him through squinted eyes. He sighed loudly as though frustrated. "Mikey," he said. "This has nothing to do with what happened the other night, does it?"

Mikey didn't answer, but looked down at his plate and pushed his burger around with his finger. He grabbed it and took a big bite hoping to get rid of the yucky taste of regret from his mouth. He knew he never should have said anything.

His father leaned on the table.

It creaked and wiggled.

"Son," he began. "Why do you want to hear that story? It'll just give you nightmares."

Mikey swallowed. "It's that bad, huh?"

His father rubbed his tired eyes.

"No, I mean, it's just a story about a bunch of kids who died. You don't need to hear that right before bed time. Now finish your dinner and do your homework, okay?" He started to walked off.

Mikey leapt out of his chair and ran over to his dad.

"But Dad, I really want to know," he said.

His dad hesitated then looked up at the stairs. His eyes returned to his eager son. Maybe it was best for him to hear about it now—especially from his own father and not secondhand stories from townsfolk.

"For this article you're writing?" he said. He took a swig of his soda and pulled out a chair.

"No," Mikey said, "for me. I really want to know."

"Oh alright." He scratched his head. "Uh, let's see…" Mikey could almost see his father review images one after another in his mind like the microfilm machine at the library. "I remember that my little brother didn't come home after school that night. He and his gang of friends went to the pond. Apparently, they were followed by the school bus driver. Some say he was a kid killer, you know?"

"Was that true?"

His dad shrugged. "Just some rumors started by kids at school. I never took the bus. I always rode my bike or walked to school, so I never met the guy. But my brother Kevin took the bus and said the bus driver gave him the creeps."

Mikey nodded.

"Anyway, all we know is that for some reason, the bus driver talked the kids into getting on the bus. Then he drove it full speed into the pond. Some neighbors heard the crash and screams from the—" His voice trailed off. "Children."

"Dad?" Mikey asked. "You okay?"

"Yeah," he said. He took another gulp of soda. "Just thinking back to it."

"I read that the kids were 12," Mikey said. "My age."

His dad nodded. "Yeah. Kevin was just a little kid."

"And they never found the bus driver?" Mikey asked.

His dad shook his head.

"Nope. Witnesses say he was picked up by a hitchhiker and left town. He was never seen again. Back then, we didn't have the media coverage on such cases like we do now. Heck, I don't even know if the FBI was involved. He was able to get away scott-free."

"I see," Mikey said with a faraway look in his eyes.

"Your grandparents, my mom and dad, were, uh, in shock. Their lives were shattered. Our home was never the same again," he said. "We set a present out for Kevin at Christmas time for years until, finally, my parents realized he wasn't coming back."

"Wow," Mikey sighed.

"They blamed me," he said right before he took another gulp of soda.

Mikey winced. He wasn't sure he heard his father right.

"What?" he asked.

"They blamed me for what happened."

"But, why? You weren't there. You had nothing to do with it," Mikey said.

"That's the point. *I wasn't there.* I was supposed to take my dad's car and pick him up at the school, but I was with my friends. I completely forgot. So when Kevin didn't turn up for dinner, my dad lost it."

Mikey watched his father's face. He could see in his eyes that he was back there in 1961 again in his parent's living room.

"The old man just lost it, you know? And then the cops came and told us what happened." He finished the soda and crushed the can. "The old man had to go identify the body."

Mikey swallowed hard. His head started spinning. *Identify the body,* he thought. He tried to fathom what those words really meant. *The body…of a 12 year old kid.*

"I never—I mean *they* never forgave me for that," he said. He rose up and walked to the kitchen. Mikey could hear him crack open a can. When his dad returned, he was drinking a beer. "Nope. They couldn't forgive me for that one. I messed up a lot as a kid. You know, staying out late, drinking beer, that sort of stuff is easy to forgive. But not this."

"Sorry, Dad," Mikey said. His throat was dry. He drank some soda.

"There were a lot of stories floating around after the accident," he said.

"Stories?" Mikey asked. "What sort of stories? You mean *ghost* stories about the pond being haunted?"

"Yeah. You've heard 'em?"

Mikey nodded.

"You know, I went out to that pond once," he said.

"Really?"

His dad took another sip of beer and nodded.

"Yeah. It was years later. I don't know what I was looking for, but something made me go there." He scratched his head.

Mikey leaned in to listen.

"I went out there at night and stood in the middle of the pond, drinking a beer," he said. "Remembering my brother…remembering all the times I played hockey on that ice. I stood there remembering all the good times and wondered how things got so bad."

Mikey looked away. His dad took a large gulp of beer. He wiped his mouth.

"We played hockey on that ice every winter," his dad's voice was above a whisper as he remembered. "One year, we went to the championships. I was teaching my brother how to play. The kid was pretty good."

"What happened?" Mikey asked.

His dad sat silent for a few moments staring at the wall. Then, he looked at his son.

"Huh?"

"On the ice that night, when you were alone, with the beer, what happened?"

His dad crushed the empty beer can in his hand and left it on the table.

"You mean, did I see a ghost?"

"Yeah," Mikey said with wide eyes.

"No. Nothing happened." His dad frowned.

Mikey sat back, disappointed.

"Listen, I don't want you reading about that stuff anymore, okay?" his dad said as he pushed the chair back and stood. "It'll give you nightmares. Now finish supper then go do your homework." His dad picked up the crushed beer can and turned to head into the kitchen. He slammed the beer can onto the counter and pounded his fist down hard. Mikey jumped, startled from the sound. "Nothing happened." Mikey heard his dad mumble.

Then, his dad walked off toward the stairs. His six-foot-two inch body looked heavy as he walked on each step. He seemed to have the weight of the world on his shoulders. Mikey sighed. He never had a brother or a sister. He had no idea what it was like to lose someone close. Well, his mother left him, but she didn't die. He sat there at the table and tried to imagine what it must be like to be told your little kid brother is dead. He shook his head.

And then he wondered what it would be like to be blamed for it. He shivered.

Over in the corner of the family room was a small table. On it was a picture frame. Mikey walked over and picked it up. He had looked at that photograph so many times all his life. It was one of three his mother left behind. Mikey studied it carefully. Now he knew. Now he understood. The photograph was of his grandparents and his father who must have been about twenty years old.

Mikey always wondered why his father wasn't smiling in the photograph. None of them were smiling.

Now, Mikey understood why.

He walked over to his school bag, and took out notebook. He started to write down some things his father said about the accident. But all he could think of was that look of sorrow in his dad's eyes. He pushed the notebook aside and took out his math homework. It was hard to concentrate on arithmetic that night, but he tried.

CHAPTER 9

Nightmares

Mikey knew he was dreaming because he was flying over the school again. He could see the roof tops and the town road heading north into town. He flew high above the trees, nearly missing the telephone wires and a few sparrows. He swooped down low and felt his stomach turn a little like he was on a roller coaster. Then, before he knew it, he was standing at the frozen pond. It was a clear afternoon and the snow glistened in the sunlight. He looked down at his feet as they ambled slowly across the frozen surface. He put his arms out to help balance himself.

He bent down and smoothed away some of the snow so he could see into the ice, but it was too thick. All he could see was more ice.

An arm broke through and took hold of his hand pulling him into the icy waters. He felt his whole body jerk as the cold enveloped him. He didn't want to open his eyes, but something told him to. When he did, he saw those faces again. Kevin Thompson stared at him. He wore the same shirt in the dream as he did in the photograph Mikey saw at the library. Again, like in slow motion, Kevin pointed toward the darker water beneath them as though he wanted to tell Mikey something. But Mikey shook his head. Mikey took out his notebook and started to scribble down what he saw, but the water made the paper soggy.

Kevin's face turned angry. He pointed again, but all Mikey could see was darkness.

"I can't see anything!" he shouted. But the children under the ice kept pointing. "What do you want me to see?"

"Mikey?"

He heard a distant voice.

"I don't know what you want me to see!" he shouted again.

"Mikey!" the voice said again.

Before he could say anything else, Kevin came at him quickly, reached out, and forcibly pulled Mikey's body down into darkness.

Mikey jerked up and looked around. He knew he was awake.

His neck and face were hot and sweat dripped down his forehead. He blinked a couple of times to focus his eyes, and to his horror every student in Mrs. Novack's history class was staring at him with wide eyes. Mrs. Novack , a portly woman with curly hair and big brown eyes hidden behind her wire-rimmed glasses, stood with her hands on her wide hips and concern on her face. He tried to grin, but his cheeks hurt. On his desk was his notebook, wet with drool.

"Mikey! Wake up. Are you alright?" she asked.

He wiped his forehead and nodded.

"You were shouting out in your sleep," she said. With that all the students began laughing and pointing at him. He sunk back into his chair.

"I'm okay," he said.

Mrs. Novack chuckled a little under her breath. "Who were you talking to in your dream? It sounded pretty intense."

One boy stood up and placed his hands on both sides of his face. "What do you want me to see?" he mocked Mikey by imitating his voice in the dream. The class roared with laughter.

"Okay, class, enough wasting time. Time to get back to work." Mrs. Novack clapped her hands to try and get the class to quiet down. "Mikey, no more sleeping in my class, understand?"

Mikey cleared his throat.

"Yes, ma'am," he said.

§

Mikey entered the cafeteria and picked up a plastic tray for hot lunch. He stood in line behind some girls who giggled when they saw him. He sighed and looked away, but the giggling continued as the line moved forward.

Here we go, he thought. *I suppose at some point people at school would find out.*

"Pizza?" the lunch lady asked. She wore the usual pale blue uniform, a hair net covered her hair, and she had bright red lipstick on her mouth. She chewed her gum like a cow chews cud. She stood with a bored look on her face as she waited for Mikey's answer.

"Well? We don't got all day," she said.

"Uh, yeah, sure," he said.

She plopped a slice of pizza that look like it was made of cardboard onto the larger space of the tray. Then she scooped up some lettuce and one cherry tomato and set that down into one of the smaller compartments of his tray. Finally, she placed a chocolate brownie into the remaining compartment and looked down at him with those dull grey eyes.

"Next," she said, chomping on her gum.

Mikey sighed then continued on to the milk. Chocolate and regular milk, in small cartons, were stacked on a table. Chocolate was for good days, but he knew today was a regular milk day. He grabbed a small carton of milk, and a napkin, and headed to the cash register where another bored lunch lady stood collecting the forty-five cents for each lunch.

Mikey dug into his pocket for the lunch money and handed the coins to her as she yawned.

"Next," she ordered without even looking at him. He picked up his tray and headed to the lunch tables and benches that filled the cafeteria.

"There he is!" One of his classmates pointed to him. All the kids sitting at that table turned their heads to see an embarrassed Mikey standing there. They sucked on the straws sticking out of their milk cartons and grinned.

"Tell me what you want me to see!" the boy said, repeating what Mikey had shouted in his dream. He used a dramatic voice and hand gestures for effect. "Just tell me what you want me to see!"

All the kids at the table began laughing as Mikey quickly walked away and found a seat at an empty table. He could hear more kids laughing behind him. He didn't bother trying to find his friends. He just sat down as quickly as he could so he could disappear.

Maybe the floor will open up right underneath me, he thought… *And swallow me whole.* He picked up the pizza slice then put it back down again, choosing instead to open his milk carton to take a big gulp of milk. He turned his head and saw Lexie sitting off to the side alone at a table reading a history book because she was weird like that.

"There he is!" came another shout from next to him. He swallowed the milk and gathered his tray to head over to Lexie's table. The three girls laughed and pointed at him while he walked. "He's the boy caught dreaming in class!"

They kept giggling, so Mikey walked faster until he plopped down next to Lexie, spilling some of his milk.

"Hey!" she said with a furrowed brow. "Don't splash my book with your—"

She turned her head to see Mikey sitting next to her. "Oh hey, Mikey!" she smiled away her anger. "Where's the others?"

"I don't know," he said, and he took another gulp. Lexie could see the girls standing off to the side, still giggling.

"What's their problem?" she asked.

Mikey looked at her. "You mean, you didn't hear?"

"Hear what?"

"About what happened in history class," he said.

Her face became sad. "Oh yeah, the whole school knows."

He sunk even lower.

"Come on, Mikey." Lexie grabbed his arm and forced him to sit straight. "So you were dreaming in class. So what? It's no big deal. Mitchell Brock sleeps in class every day and no one makes a big deal out of it. "

"Yeah, tell them that." He pointed to the girls as they walked off.

"Who cares about those dumb girls anyway." Lexie shot them a harsh look. "Come on, just eat your lunch so we can go to recess."

Just then, Donnie and Destrey came to the table, plopped down across from Mikey without saying a word.

"I suppose you heard all about it?" Mikey asked, but he noticed they were staring at something behind him.

He slowly turned around to see three big eighth graders approaching the table. They each wore a smirk on their faces. Mikey swallowed because he knew what was coming.

"Hey doofus," one said as they walked up. Mikey ignored them.

"I said, hey doofus." He kicked the bench underneath Lexie and Mikey.

"Hey! Knock it off!" Lexie said.

"Pipe down, princess," the boy said. "I wanna talk to this doofus who yells in his sleep." The boys with him laughed. Donnie and Destrey looked down and chomped on their pizza slices.

This is going to be a long day, Mikey shook his head.

"Just go away, you morons." Lexie turned around and went back to reading her book.

"Hey doofus, talk in your sleep again for us," the boy said. Mikey ignored him. He looked at his frightened friends.

"You gonna write about your dream for the school paper?" the boys laughed.

"Let's get outta here." He stood to leave. Lexie, Donnie, and Destrey followed suit.

As Mikey and his friends walked off, the obnoxious eighth graders continued to mock him. He could still hear the boys laughing even as he walked out the cafeteria door.

"This is why we have to keep it quiet," Mikey said as they walked to the playground.

"Yeah, well, don't fall asleep and dream about the ghosts in class anymore," Donnie said.

"Gee, hadn't thought of that," Mikey said. "I'm sure glad we have you around to do all the thinking for us, genius."

Destrey chuckled so Donnie shoved him. The four of them headed to the tetherball courts on the playground.

§

"That's all everyone was talking about at lunch today! Man, it was so funny!" Destrey shouted as he, Donnie, Chad, and Lexie walked home from school with Mikey. "Mikey was dreamin' in class. That's what everyone was saying."

"Yeah, well…I didn't see you laughing with those eighth graders." Mikey clutched his book bag as he and the others walked home from school. "As a matter of fact, you were scared speechless when they came over. I'm just so glad I was such wonderful entertainment for everyone today."

"Sorry, Mikey," Lexie said in a small voice.

"It's okay," he said. "We were known as losers before. Now it's just solidified."

"So, what was Kevin Thompson trying to tell you?" Chad

asked. “You know, in the dream?”

Mikey rubbed his face.

“Man, I don’t know. All I know is that every time I go to sleep, I see those faces now. I hardly slept at all last night,” he said.

“They must be trying to tell you something,” Lexie said. “We’ve got to find out.”

“Why?” Mikey asked. “Why can’t we just leave them alone? Why can’t we have everything like it was before all this happened?”

“Because!” she shouted as they crossed the street. “Those kids were murdered. And they chose you. They want to tell you something. It’s your uncle, Mikey. He must have something to tell you!”

What on earth would they want to tell me? Mikey thought. *Don’t they know I’m the town loser?*

“Yeah,” Destrey said. “My old man told me that people have gone missing and that some suspect those ghosts probably did it.”

They all crossed the street and walked on toward the park.

“Your old man said this?” Donnie asked.

Destrey nodded.

“Yep, he said ever since the accident, people claim the pond is haunted. He said that’s why none of the adults want their kids playing on or swimming in the pond. And that’s why so many people moved away.”

“Your old man is a sheriff’s deputy,” Donnie said as he kicked some snow.

“I know,” Destrey said. “What’s your point?”

“And he believes in ghost stories?”

“Shut up,” Destrey said.

“My parents didn’t even know about the accident,” Lexie said, adjusting the red knit cap over her long blonde hair.

“That’s because they’re new here,” Destrey said. “My mom and dad have lived in Sherman Oaks all their lives. My dad said after the accident, a whole lot of people left the town because they couldn’t take it anymore.”

“They couldn’t take what anymore?” Donnie asked.

They stopped at some picnic benches in the park and plopped down to hear the story.

“Well, my dad told me that after the accident happened, news people were all over the place asking questions. They had no peace and quiet," he said as he took off his gloves.

"Oh, so they were on TV?" Donnie said.

"No, but they were in the newspapers every day," Destrey said. "And some people said that when you walked by the pond at night, you could hear a child crying off in the distance," he said.

Donnie rolled his eyes in disbelief.

"Yeah right," he smirked.

"No really! And then my dad said that an old woman disappeared after being seen walking by the pond. After that, on Halloween night, a boy disappeared. He was last seen walking by the pond," Destrey explained.

"Really?" Lexie rubbed her arms. "That gives me the chills!"

"Ooh! I have goosebumps!" Donnie teased. Lexie slugged him in the shoulder.

"We'll have to look it up at the library," Mikey said. "Maybe that's what they're trying to tell me."

"Yeah, so I think we should try and commune with them," Destrey said.

All the kids cocked their heads in confusion.

"Huh?" Donnie said. *"Commune?* What does that mean?"

Lexie looked at her Princess wrist watch. "I've got to get home. I think we should talk more about it later." She stood. "Bye Mikey. I hope you get some sleep tonight."

"Thanks," he said as she walked off.

"Bye Mikey," Donnie mimicked Lexie's voice. He batted his eyes and made kissing sounds with his lips. "Have a good night's sleep!"

"Shut up," Mikey said. He slugged Donnie in the arm. He turned to Destrey. "What do you mean by *commune*?"

"I read about this once in Life magazine. There are people who talk with ghosts, you know, to find out what happened to them and how they died and stuff," Destrey said. "I think we should try it."

"How?" Donnie sat down. "Just how the heck do you commune with ghosts?"

"I dunno. Maybe we should all meet at the pond tonight and talk to them through the ice," Destrey said.

"Man, I am not going to stand out there on the ice at night talking to ghosts." Donnie stood to leave. "You're crazy if you do that! I don't want to end up under the ice like Mikey."

Mikey was tired of talking about it. He rubbed his temples. All he wanted was some sleep.

They all stood to walk home. He thought about the things Destrey had told him while they walked.

"So people really disappeared, huh?" he asked.

Destrey nodded. "Supposedly."

"And most of the town left after the accident?"

"Yep."

"Why didn't your family leave?" Donnie asked Destrey.

"My mom and dad were just married. They didn't have any kids yet, so they didn't have to fear losing a kid or anything like that," he said. "Most of the families that left had kids at the school or kids on that bus that night. My dad said those families just couldn't handle it. You know, the loss and such."

Mikey thought about his dad's family and how torn apart they were after it happened. They were one of the families that left soon after the accident.

"Yeah, my grandparents left this town," he said in a low voice.

"But your mom and dad came back, huh?" Destrey asked.

Mikey nodded.

"Yeah. My dad said he always wanted to raise a family here so they moved back soon after I was born. But my mom never liked it here. At least that's what he tells me."

As they passed the church, they saw Reverend Johnson sweeping the steps.

"Hello, boys!" he shouted as they walked by. They waved back. "How was school today?"

Mikey was just about to say something when they heard a siren. They all turned around to see what was happening and saw Mikey's dad drive past at a high speed toward the pond outside of town. Behind his car were two more patrol cars and an ambulance.

"Oh my," said the Reverend. "I hope it's nothing serious."

"Mikey, that was your dad!" Destrey said. "Yeah, let's go!" Mikey ran off after the cars.

"Be careful boys!" Reverend Johnson shouted after them. "And don't get in the way!"

CHAPTER 10

Old Man Stuckey

"Come on!" Mikey waved to the guys. "This way!" He knew a shortcut through the woods. The guys followed him huffing and puffing while pushing low hanging tree branches out of their way. They could hear the sirens and the crunching of the tires on the snowy roads leading toward the pond. Then, they came to the clearing and saw all the cars parked by the far side of the pond. The woods were mysteriously still. No wind was seen moving the bare tree branches. Just eerie stillness.

Mikey carefully peaked out behind the bushes. He spotted his father and his deputies walking toward something lying on the ice.

"What is it?" Destrey whispered.

"Not sure," Mikey said. "Let's get closer."

They left the bushes and made their way toward the scene keeping close to the trees so they wouldn't stand out. They were so close; they could hear the voices of the sheriff and his men.

"Have Deputy Jones take her into town and I'll stop by her house later on to question her," Mikey's dad said to Deputy Rogers.

"Okay, Sheriff," Deputy Rogers said. He slowly walked with his arm around a woman's shoulders supporting her. Mikey could see she was obviously distraught.

"Hey, that's your dad, Destrey," Donnie said. Destrey leaned in and noticed it was his father walking over to his patrol car.

"I wonder what he's doing here, He's usually back at the office taking calls. I'll have a full report tomorrow morning after I talk to him tonight," he said.

"Shhh," Mikey said. He wanted to hear what his father was saying.

The Sheriff and another deputy made their way over to the dark lump on the ice along with the paramedics. They all bent down and spoke in hushed tones.

"Looks like it is old Ed Stuckey," Mikey's dad said.

"What?" Mikey said. He turned to the others. "Did you hear

that?"

They nodded with wide eyes and mouths agape.

"I'll take a few photographs before you take the body. Is Martin at the coroner's office coming?" his dad asked the paramedics. They nodded.

"Stay here and give me a hand, huh Dave?" Mikey's dad asked deputy Rogers. He was the new young deputy who had arrived in town recently.

"No problem, Sheriff," Dave said.

Just then, the coroner's station wagon pulled up. Mikey watched his father retrieve the camera from the trunk of the patrol car. He spoke with the coroner for a few minutes before heading back to Mr. Stuckey's body.

"I swear, I just saw old man Stuckey the other day," Mikey said. "He was yelling at the Reverend."

They watched as the Sheriff took some photographs and the coroner pronounced Mr. Stuckey dead. His lower body was in the ice while the upper half was on the surface. As the paramedics lifted him up and pulled him out of the frigid water, the kids could see his body was frozen stiff as wet laundry left out on the clothesline in January.

Donnie shook his head and scratched his hair. "This is just too strange," he said.

"Do you think they did it" Destrey asked. "Do you Mikey? Do you think the ghosts killed old man Stuckey?"

Mikey knew what Destrey was saying, but something inside him didn't think the children under the ice would do such a thing. Why would they want to harm an old drunk like Mr. Stuckey?

"He was their Principal when it happened, remember?" Chad said.

Mikey turned his head to look at him. "What? Oh yeah. I forgot."

"You're right!" Destrey said to Chad. "Maybe they were angry at him or something."

Mikey did think it was strange, but maybe the children were angry at Mr. Stuckey and wanted revenge. But the old man had lived in the town for so long.

"Yeah, but, why would they kill him now? He's lived here for so long. Why now?" Mikey asked. "It doesn't make sense."

The boys watched as the Sheriff and his deputy placed yellow caution tape around the scene to keep bystanders away. Some neighbors bundled up in coats and scarves had already gathered at the scene and Mikey's dad tried to move them along. Mikey watched some of the neighbors walk off. As he watched them, he noticed something in the trees directly across from him. He squinted and tried to focus on what it was. It looked like a boy standing among the trees looking directly at him. Shadows covered his face.

Mikey stared at the boy for a moment. Then, he felt all the blood leave his face.

"Guys…" He slowly pointed at the trees across the way as though in a trance. "Look!"

The boys jumped from the shout and followed Mikey's finger as it pointed to the trees.

"What is it?" Donnie said. He searched the trees but didn't see anything.

Mikey kept an eye on the boy in the trees. He realized it was Kevin Thompson's ghost staring back at him.

"There! In the trees! See it?" he asked. He walked out of the woods and stepped toward the pond.

"Mikey, get back here! Your dad will see you!" Destrey tried to grab Mikey's shirt, but it was too late. It was as though Mikey was in a trance being pulled by something across the way. Something that they couldn't see.

"It's him!" he said. "It's Kevin."

Chad looked and tried to focus in on the area, but he couldn't see what Mikey was talking about. "Where?" he took a few steps out of the trees too.

"I see him!" Mikey said. "There! In the trees!"

The other boys ran out of the woods to get a better look.

Chad watched in confusion as his friend stared at the myriad of bare trees on the other side of the pond. Mikey raised his hand and slowly waved. To his amazement, the ghost dressed in a striped shirt and jeans waved back.

"Did you see that?" he turned to ask Chad.

Chad raised an eyebrow when he saw Mikey's pale face. "Uh, no. I don't see anything but trees, Mike."

"He's wearing the same shirt." Mikey turned his head, "the

same shirt we saw in the photographs at the library."

"What?" Chad said. He searched the trees again but saw nothing. He studied Mikey's frightened eyes. "Mikey, what are you talking about? There's nothing over there, man."

Mikey's eyes were glossy now. He pointed.

"Yes, there is! Right over there." He turned to see his friends' contorted faces as they tried desperately not to laugh.

Mikey narrowed his eyes as his heart filled with anger.

"I knew it," he said. "I knew you guys didn't believe me."

He turned to leave.

"Hey! Boys!"

The boys jumped from the shout of Mikey's father approaching them. Destrey grabbed his chest.

"Mike, what are you boys doing here?" he said as he walked up.

But Mikey continued to watch the ghost of Kevin Thompson as it turned and walked off deeper into the woods.

"Mikey, answer me!" His father touched his shoulder and made his son jerk with fright. Suddenly, a cold wind blew across the pond and bent the trees.

"Huh?" Mikey said. He could see his father's eyes were full of concern. "Oh, sorry Dad."

"Hey, you boys ought to get home now," he said. "There's nothing you need to see here."

"What happened, Sheriff Thompson?" Destrey asked while peeking over toward the scene.

Sheriff Thompson tipped his tan felt cowboy hat back and looked at the scene.

"Well, looks like old man Stuckey drowned or froze in the pond the other night," he said. His voice sounded sad.

"Foul play?" Destrey folded his arms across his chest.

The Sheriff chuckled. "Uh, we don't know yet *detective*," he joked. "But I'll let you know as soon as possible. Come on, fellas. You should head home now before your parents start flooding my office with phone calls asking where you are."

"So was he murdered?" Donnie asked.

"We'll need to wait for the coroner's office to determine that, son," Sheriff Thompson said. "I think he was probably drunk and wandered onto the ice and fell through the cracks, hit his head, or something."

“How sad.” Destrey put his hands in his pockets. “He wasn’t a bad person. He was a nice drunk.”

“Yeah,” Donnie said. “Never harmed anyone.”

“Alright, guys. See you later.” The Sheriff zipped up his jacket. “It’s getting cold out here. You had better head home.

“Aw, come on,” Destrey whined.

But the Sheriff turned them around and gave them a gentle push toward the woods. “Go straight home, understand?”

They nodded as they left. Mikey stayed behind.

“I don’t know what Mike was staring at,” he heard Chad say as he walked off.

Then, he hesitantly turned toward his dad.

“Sorry,” Mikey said.

“No harm done. I would’ve come out here too when I was your age. I loved this sort of stuff. I guess that’s why I went into law enforcement. Come on, I’ll give you a ride home,” his dad said.

CHAPTER 11
Unanswered Questions

As usual, Mikey rode in silence next to his father. Yet this time, he stared out the window trying to build up enough courage to tell his father what he saw in the ice. Every time he tried to speak, something deep inside would stop him. As the trees passed by the window, he couldn't help but imagine the ghost of Kevin staring back at him.

Why was he there? Is Lexie right? Did he choose me? What was he trying to tell me? Did he have something to do with old man Stuckey's death? I hope not. His head was spinning.

He listened as his dad fiddled with the radio. *Maybe I should tell Dad what I saw. He probably won't believe me either,* he thought. He crossed his arms over his chest. *No one believes me.*

He turned to look at his father while he drove the patrol car. His father's face looked long and lean. He had lost a lot of weight. Mikey knew his dad was drinking more than he ate. He wished there was something he could do to make his father happy again. Ever since his mom left them, Mikey's dad became more and more of a recluse. Mikey thought of Miss Jennings.

"Dad," Mikey said as they pulled up to a stop light.

"Yeah, son," his dad said as he pulled out a toothpick from his pocket.

"Do you ever think about dating?" Mikey asked.

"No." His father chuckled and looked at him. He had the toothpick dangling between his lips. "Do you?"

Mikey smirked. "No…"

"Is there a girl you like?"

"No, I'm not talking about me. I mean do *you* ever think about dating someone?"

"What?" his dad said. "What made you ask me that?"

"Well, I was just wondering. I mean, the divorce was over four years ago. Don't you think you're ready to, you know, move on?" Mikey asked. He had never said anything like this before to his father. He could feel his stomach knot up. He swallowed hard.

"Son," his dad sighed. "Oh, I don't know. I guess I don't think too much about things like that anymore."

Just then, Mikey sat up straight. He noticed Miss Jennings approaching the cross walk. She walked right in front of the patrol car, her long hair flowing in the breeze.

"What about Miss Jennings the librarian?" Mikey said as he pointed to her.

His dad lowered his sunglasses and watched Miss Jennings walk by the car. Mikey could see his dad's eyes following her form as she walked.

"What about her?"

"Don't you think she's, you know, *pretty*?" Mikey asked. His dad looked over at her and moved the car forward. He watched her walked for a few more seconds, pushed his sunglasses back over his eyes, then drove off.

"Yes, she's very attractive," he said.

"Well?"

"Well, what?" his dad said. He chuckled under his breath as though he knew what his son was up to. "You think I should ask her out on a date?"

"Yeah!" Mikey shouted out. His dad let out a hearty laugh.

"Well, son, I don't think a prim and proper lady like Miss Jennings would want to have anything to do with—"

"She asked about you the other day at the library," Mikey cut him off.

His dad's face looked surprised. "She did?"

"Yeah. She asked me to tell you she said hello," Mikey smiled with satisfaction.

"Huh," his dad said. Mikey could tell his dad was seriously thinking about the prospect. "I'll be darned."

"Yep. I think you should really consider asking her out on a date…or for some coffee or something," he said. "I don't know, whatever it is you old people do."

"You know she and I went to high school together," his dad said as they turned into the driveway.

"Really?" Mikey said with mock surprise as though pretending not to know.

"Yeah. She was pretty quiet back then, too. I was one of those loud obnoxious kids who made a lot of trouble," he said.

"Well, I'm sure she sees how you've changed since then," Mikey said as he got out of the car. "Promise me you'll think about it?"

His dad laughed as he took off his gun belt and slung it over his shoulder. "I promise. Now go get started on your homework. I'll start dinner."

Mikey shuddered at the thought of his dad's cooking. Then, he hustled upstairs thinking more about his dad and Miss Jennings. Mikey thought his dad was still a good looking guy for being so old. *What is he now? Thirty-two or something like that?* He thought. He was convinced Miss Jennings would think so, too. He entered his bedroom and then tossed his books onto his bed. *She's just what he needs to get his mind off of work and drinking*, he thought.

Mikey looked around his bedroom walls. He had a JAWS movie poster above his bed, a Rocky poster, and poster of "The Fonz" from the "Happy Days" television show, as well as a few hockey posters along the other walls. Some of his articles that made it into the school newspaper hung on the walls near his bed. He remembered how Miss Jennings helped him do research for those articles. He walked over to his dresser then opened up the top drawer. Inside, hidden underneath his socks, was a framed photograph of a man, an attractive woman, and a little boy playing together at the park on a sunny spring day with flowers all around them. He looked long and hard at the photograph. He had found the picture in a magazine, tore it out, and framed it. He rubbed a speck of dirt off the glass and carefully polished it with his shirt sleeve. He smiled and gently placed it back into the top drawer.

Then, he took out his math book and started completing his addition exercises.

§

After dinner was finished and all the dishes washed, Mikey sat on the couch waiting for his dad to fall asleep in the easy chair. It didn't take long for the fifth can of beer to finally knock him out. His snoring resonated throughout the darkened house.

Mikey tiptoed to the coat rack and slipped on his jacket, gloves, and knit cap. Then, he quietly snuck out the front door, making sure he could still hear his dad's snoring on the other side. When it was safe, he ran down the street toward the school.

He stopped a few times when cars approached and hid behind a bush. When all was clear, he continued his run to the back of the school. He entered the back window and hopped inside. He looked around, careful not to make any noise. It was quiet inside the basement of the school. Not even the janitor was around.

Mikey opened the door that led to the boiler room and slowly headed down the steps. He could feel the heat from the furnaces so he removed his jacket and shoved his gloves in the pockets.

"Hey," he said. He heard his voice echo. "Anybody here?"

"Yeah, over here," came the answer. He recognized Chad's voice.

When Mikey turned the corner near the lockers, he saw the gang sitting by the furnace. They were playing some sort of card game. All their jackets and scarves were piled up on one of the benches.

"Okay, so we need to discuss our plan of action," Mikey said as he removed his knit cap, jacket, and gloves. He tossed them onto the pile and sat down on a bench nearby.

"Mikey, you okay?" Chad turned his head and placed his hand on Mikey's shoulder.

He could see in his eyes that Chad was concerned. Then, he turned to see the same look on the faces of his friends. He knew then that the others were obviously concerned about him, too.

"Yeah, why?"

Destrey looked at Chad who looked at Donnie.

"Seeing ghosts during the day, Mike," Chad said. "That ain't normal, ya know."

Mikey exhaled loudly. *Here we go,* he thought.

"Look, I know it sounds nuts," he said. "But I know what I saw. I need to know if you believe me or not."

They sat silent.

"Because if you don't, then you need to stay out of my way. Got it?" he said with a certain defiance in his voice.

They nodded.

"If you don't want to be a part of this, that's fine," he said. "Then you need to go because I have to think of a plan of some sorts and I don't have time for horsing around."

He walked over to his jacket and took out a pad of paper and a pencil from the pocket.

"I've gotta find out more about the ghosts and the bus driver," he sat down and began scribbling something onto the paper.

Chad looked at the others who had contorted faces as though extremely confused.

"It's hard for us, Mike, because we never saw any ghosts before," Chad said as he sat down next to his friend. "But we trust you. Right guys?"

Destrey looked at Donnie then sat down on the other side of Mikey.

"Yeah, I believe you, Mike."

Donnie looked up at the ceiling and let out a long, obnoxious whine.

"Oh geez," he said. "Ghost stories?"

"The door's that way," Mikey said without looking up from his pad of paper.

"Oh alright," Donnie whined. He sat down across from the others. "What are we going to do now?"

"I still think we need to commune with the ghosts somehow and find out what they want," Destrey said.

"And we need to know if they killed all those people." Lexie took off her cap and patted down her hair that rose up with static electricity.

"Yeah. I mean, if they're murderers, I don't want to have anything to do with them," Donnie said.

"I don't think they're murderers," Mikey said. "I think they need our help."

"So what happened at the pond again?" Lexie asked. She took off her mittens and shoved them in her pockets.

"Old man Stuckey's body was found sticking out of the ice as though he was trying to escape," Destrey said. "I'm tellin' ya, he was running for his life!"

"Or, his body could have been dumped there by the murderer," Mikey added.

"How sad. Poor Mr. Stuckey," said Lexie, warming her hands by the furnace.

"I know. Makes me wonder who killed him," Chad said.

"All I know is that I saw the ghost of Kevin Thompson standing at the other side of the pond staring at the scene," Mikey said. "And I think he wants to tell me something."

They heard a loud crash coming from above.

They froze silent. Mikey put his finger to his lips. He pointed to the stairs and slowly walked over to the doorway. Chad followed.

They leaned on the door listening.

The others waited.

Mikey shook his head and walked back over to the bench.

"Probably the janitor's cat," he said.

"What about the hockey tournament?" Stanny asked. He had a frown and looked frustrated. "How are we going to practice?"

"Sorry, Stan," Mikey said. "But I think our part in the tournament is over."

Stanny groaned. "No!" He got up and walked away toward the lockers. He kicked one.

"Shhh!" Lexie said. "Someone might hear!"

"Sorry, man," Chad said. "We've got bigger issues now than a lousy hockey tournament. Besides, the ice is melting anyway. It's too thin to skate on now."

Mikey felt bad for Stanny. He came from Russia with his family and hockey was his life. He dreamed of one day going to the Olympics on the U.S.S.R. hockey team, but then they moved to America. Stanny came back and sat down.

"It isn't fair," he whined.

They all discussed a possible plan while enjoying the warmth of the furnace.

"Do you really think it is ghosts?" Stanny asked.

"Yes," Mikey said.

"So, we have a few questions to answer," Chad said. "First, whatever happened to the bus driver?"

"Yeah," Destrey said. "We've got to find out."

"Second, maybe Kevin's ghost is trying to help us solve the mystery," Mikey continued.

"And?" Lexie asked.

"And we need to find out from the children under the ice who killed old man Stuckey," Mikey finished.

"If they did it, would they really tell us?" Destrey asked.

Mikey looked at his watch. "I don't know, but it's getting late. How about we all head to the library after school to do more research?"

They all agreed and headed up the stairs. Once outside again, the cold air hit them hard. Lexie started shivering.

"I can't wait for spring. I sure hope we get this mystery solved before summer so we can all go swimming in the pond again," she said.

They could hear their feet crunching in the snow. As it melted and refroze, it became hard and crunchy.

"Me too," Mikey said. "I'd like to be able to tell my dad what really happened to his brother and help him catch the killer."

"You'll make a great newspaper reporter someday, Mikey," Lexie said. She smiled at him warmly.

"Okay, you two," Donnie said as he walked between them. "Knock it off. Let's keep this G-rated." He shoved Mikey.

Mikey felt his face turn red.

"See you all later," he said as he ran off down the street. He looked back to see Lexie waving at him. He waved back then ran back to his house. He slowly opened the front door and heard his father's snoring. His dad was still sound asleep and lit only by the blue hue of the television. Mikey stared at him for a second or two. The Tonight Show with Johnny Carson was on and the audience was roaring with laughter about something. Mikey quietly began to pick up the empty beer cans, turned off the television, put a blanket on his dad's legs, and then headed up stairs to bed.

He flicked on the light in his bedroom and sat down on the bed. He felt some anger rise in his belly and into his throat. *How could my mom leave him?* He thought. *He's not such a bad guy. He never hit me and he has always worked hard.*

Mikey took off his sweatshirt and threw it on the ground. Then he changed into his pajamas and laid down on his bed, staring at the ceiling and thinking more about it. *Maybe she didn't leave because of him,* he thought. He rolled over and turned off the light. *Maybe she left because of me.*

CHAPTER 12
Research

The next day after school, Mikey met up with his friends and headed over to the library to conduct more research about the accident. Once they entered, Mikey waved to the ever-present Miss Jennings as she stacked more books into her cart by the front desk.

"Here to use the microfilm machines again?" she asked. Her smile made him feel at ease. She wore her brown hair in a bun at the nape of her neck. Her silver earrings sparkled.

"Yes." He waved all his friends over. "Is that alright?"

"Of course," she said and she led them down the stairs. "You're an expert by now. By the way, I read that article you wrote about how the war ended. It was impressive. I'm glad it made it into the school newspaper."

"Uh, thanks." Mikey reached up and scratched his hair. He didn't want to blush, but he felt his face get warm.

"It just might win an award!" Lexie chimed in.

"Really?" Miss Jennings said. "Wouldn't than be exciting?"

Mikey simply shrugged and walked ahead.

Once they made it to the machines, Miss Jennings helped them hook up the film. They all removed their coats and stacked them on a nearby table. Then they reviewed newspaper clippings from the year 1961. Every once in a while, Mikey could hear Donnie whine that nasal whine of boredom, or Destrey sigh from frustration, yet they stayed with him and went through all the newspapers from that year. He smiled to himself. It felt good to have someone believe him again.

"Find anything yet?" Mikey asked.

"Well, here's something," Lexie said. They all scooted their chairs over to her machine. "Looks like this woman was interviewed by the police a few months after the crash. She was the principal's secretary."

"Maybe we can contact her?" Destrey asked. "What's her name?"

"Says here it's a Delores Stevenson," Lexie said. "Do you think she's still around?"

"We'll have to ask around and find out," Mikey said.

"Here's what I found," Donnie said next. They all scooted their chairs over to his machine. "Seems some of the parents did want to sue the school district. Looks like Principal Stuckey was one of the names on the lawsuit."

"So they were going to sue him for what happened?" Stanny asked. "That is not fair. He did not drive the bus into the water, did he?"

"No." Mikey folded his arms. "But says here they blamed him because he hired the bus driver and didn't require any references or anything."

"Any *what*?" Donnie asked.

"References," Chad chimed in. "It means Principal Stuckey didn't check the bus driver's past. He didn't ask his previous employers anything about the man."

"Oh, so no one knew about his past, huh?" Donnie said.

They sat still for a moment pondering in all that they had read.

"I think we should print out that interview with the secretary," Mikey said. "Let's ask Miss Jennings if that's possible."

He took out the film roll from the machine and placed it back in the box. He took it over to Miss Jennings while the others watched. When she had a moment, he walked up to her.

"Do you think you could print out a section from this film?" he asked.

"Sure, Mike." She took the film. "I'll see what I can do."

Mikey turned to see if the others were still watching. When he saw they were all busy with something else, he looked at Miss Jennings.

"And could you also print out an advertisement from this strip of film?" he asked as he handed her the box.

"Sure," she said.

"It's, um…of a husband and wife and their son standing on a front lawn," he said.

Miss Jennings cocked her head as though confused. "Uh, certainly. I'll find it."

Mike smiled then returned to his friends who were discussing the ghosts.

"This is getting more and more interesting." Destrey had an inquisitive look in his eyes. "I'll have to ask my dad more about the lawsuit against the school district."

"Yeah. I guess that explains why so many people left the town after the accident, huh?" Lexie said as Mikey approached them.

"She said she'll find the section and print it out for us by tomorrow. Let's go home now," he said.

§

Once outside, the sunlight was bright and the cold air felt brisk compared to the stuffy air inside the library. They walked down the steps and headed toward the main street.

"So what are you gonna be for Halloween next week?" Destrey asked no one in particular.

"Halloween?" Lexie asked. "How can you think of such a thing right now? We're trying to solve the murders of four kids, ya know."

"Halloween's next week?" Donnie asked. "I completely forgot."

"I think I'll go as The Bus Driver!" Chad said as he jumped out in front of Lexie with his arms up. "Arrrgghhhh!"

She stopped and gave him a stern motherly look.

"That's *not* funny," she said. She flipped her blonde hair over her shoulder.

Destrey and the others joined in the laughter. But Mikey wasn't laughing. That's when they remembered his uncle was one of the kids on that school bus.

"Oh, sorry, Mike. Just funnin' around," Chad said.

"No big deal," he said. He honestly had forgotten Halloween was coming. "Besides, it's so cold out we have to wear jackets over our costumes anyway. No use wearing one."

Just then, he saw his father pull up next to the curb and step out of his truck.

"Hey guys," he said. "Headin' home now?"

"Yeah," Mikey said. "We were just at the library."

"Mikey!" They all turned to see who was calling after him. It was Miss Jennings, running out with a paper in her hand. "Here's the copy of that article you wanted."

"Gee, thanks Miss Jennings," he said as he took it.

"And that advertisement." She handed him the paper.

Mikey quickly took it and folded it in half so no one could see what it was. He shoved it into his pocket, and then he looked at his father and back again at Miss Jennings. "Uh, Dad, you know Miss Jennings, right?"

"Lisa." His dad held out his hand to shake hers. "Nice to see you."

"Good to see you again, Doug, I mean Sheriff, I mean…" she said with a giggle. Mikey noticed her smile was different. She seemed to beam. She quickly smoothed out her hair and removed her glasses. She fiddled with them as she spoke.

"So, how have you been?" she asked Mikey's dad.

"Uh, great. You know, busy as usual," he said. "How are things at the library? These kids giving you a hard time?"

"No, not at all. In fact, I've been seeing them more often. They're doing some good research." She smiled at Mikey and touched his shoulder.

"Well, that's good," Mikey's dad said.

"Uh, didn't you two go to high school together, Dad?" Mikey said.

His friends stood around watching the scene. They seemed fascinated as though watching monkeys interact at the zoo.

"Yes," Miss Jennings said. "Your dad was a hockey star."

"*He was?*" Mikey asked.

"Well, I don't know about that," he said shyly. "Hey, didn't you tutor me once?" he asked Miss Jennings. "In history or math or something?"

Mikey's head went back and forth like he was watching a tennis match. He enjoyed seeing his dad so relaxed. *This could work*, he thought.

"Yes. Your senior year. I think it was English composition? I had to help you write that research paper so you could pass the class and play in the State Championships, remember?" she said.

"You went to State?" Destrey asked.

"Cool!" Chad said.

"Yeah, well, that was a hundred years ago," the Sheriff said. Then he stood straight when he realized all the kids were staring at him. "Hey don't you all have somewhere to go?"

All the grins left their faces and they said good bye to Mikey. "See you tonight," Destrey shouted. Mikey cringed.

"Tonight?" his dad asked. "What's tonight?"

"Uh, nothing. I meant tomorrow. See you tomorrow, Mikey!" Destrey corrected himself as he crossed the street with the others.

Mikey waved and gave Destrey the evil eye.

"Come on, Mikey, let's head home," his dad said as he opened the passenger side door of his pickup. Mikey hopped in and his dad closed the door. Then he walked over to talk to Miss Jennings. Mikey noticed how close his father stood to her.

He leaned close to the window to hear what they said.

"Would you want to get a cup of coffee with me sometime?" he asked. Mikey saw Miss Jennings smile that cozy smile again. She awkwardly touched her hair.

She nodded yes.

"Hey great. I'll come by the library soon," his dad said.

Mikey noticed all his friends stopped on the other side of the street to stare at his father. He frowned at them. *They're gonna ruin it*, he thought. He motioned for them to get out of there, but they ignored him and continued watching his dad and Miss Jennings talk.

"Okay, well, I'll see you soon," his dad said. As he turned to leave, he didn't notice the trash can behind him. He ran right into it, spilling the contents all over the ground.

"Oh, are you alright?" Miss Jennings said. She bent over to help pick up the trash.

Mikey saw his friends laughing. He gave them a venomous look. Then, he saw his dad set the trash can right side up again.

"No problem," his dad said. "I'm okay. See you real soon."

Then he walked in front of the truck and caught his pant leg on the fender. Mikey heard a loud ripping sound and saw his dad wince from pain. Mikey's friends roared with laughter.

"Oh my." Miss Jennings put a hand to her mouth. "Are you okay? Looks like you're bleeding!"

Mikey craned his neck to see. Sure enough, his dad's thigh was bleeding. Miss Jennings leaned in to get a closer look, but his dad was embarrassed and pulled away.

Mikey covered his eyes with his hand and sighed.

"No, no," he said. "I'm alright. Really, it's just a scrape." This time he quickly got in the truck and started the engine.

"Okay, see you soon!" Miss Jennings waved and shouted as the truck pulled away. Mikey looked through the back window and saw all his friends still bent over laughing.

CHAPTER 13
A Clue

"It's seven o'clock...do you know where your children are?" Destrey said in a menacing voice. He raised his hands and wriggled his fingers. "Bwahahaha!"

"Har, har," Lexie said as they walked along the muddy road out to the pond. "You're hilarious."

The melting snow mixed with the dirt making it a slushy mess. "So what are we doing out here again?" Lexie asked.

"We're gonna make contact with the ghosts," Destrey said.

"Or try to, anyway," Chad added.

"How?" she asked.

"I don't know," Mikey said with frustration. "We're making this up as we go along. It's not like we have experience in this sort of thing."

They all came to the edge of the frozen pond. They could see their breath in the frigid night air.

"Smells like snow...again," Destrey said.

"Yeah, supposedly a big storm is coming," Donnie said as he searched the sky.

"Okay, so now what?" Chad asked. He tugged at the sleeves of his coat then put his gloved hands under his arm pits. He stepped side to side trying to get warm. "It's getting colder. Let's do something quick before our parents see that we're missing."

"What did you tell your parents?" Destrey asked Chad.

"That I was with you studying 'til eight thirty," he said.

"And they believed you?" Lexie chuckled.

"Ha ha," Chad said.

"I told my parents I'd be at Stanny and Anya's house." Lexie stared across the pond. A slight breeze scattered some dead leaves across the surface. "I told them I'd be back by eight thirty, too. We'd better hurry up."

She looked at her Princess watch in the moonlight.

"It's almost eight," she said to Mikey who took a few steps onto the ice.

"Okay, we're out here!" he shouted to no one. "What do you want to tell us?" He cupped his gloved hands around his mouth.

"Hello?"

They all stood still as his voice echoed around the pond.

"Shhh. Not so loud!" Destrey said. "We don't want anyone to come out here and find us."

Mikey turned to his friends and shrugged, not sure what he was feeling. He took a few more steps onto the icy surface using his arms to balance. A few birds shot out of the trees startling everyone.

"Look, we're here. Tell us what you want us to know." He looked into the ice and then across the pond where earlier he saw the ghost of Kevin Thompson watching between the trees. "We need your help. *I* need your help."

Silence.

Mikey jogged out to the middle of the pond, slipping and catching himself once in a while.

"Hey!" Chad shouted. "What are you doing? Are you crazy? Don't go out so far, the ice is too thin!"

"Oh crud," Donnie said. "He's gone nuts."

"Mikey, be careful," Lexie said.

But Mikey stood on the ice looking back and forth. He could see remnants of the yellow caution tape from a few days before when old man Stuckey's body was found. He slowly walked toward it. He looked down at the ice and saw a few clear patches. All he could see was the darkness below the surface gazing up at him.

"Mikey, don't go too far," Chad shouted. "We can't get to you in time if you crash through the ice!"

"He's crazy." Donnie walked over to the bench and sat down. "It's freezin' out here. Let's go. Nothin's gonna happen."

Mikey kept walking until he reached the hole where the body was found. He didn't want to get too close and crack the ice any further.

"We need your help if we're going to solve this mystery," he said to the ghosts. "What is it you want to tell me?"

He looked up at the starry sky. All he could hear was his own breathing, the breeze whispering through the trees, and a few owl hoots in the distance.

Come on, he thought. *There's got to be something you want me to know. What is it?*

He turned to his friends lined up at the pond's edge. He

shrugged in exasperation then started to carefully walk back.

"Now what do we do?" Lexie asked. She turned to the others.

"Go home, I guess," Destrey said in a defeated voice. He kicked a chunk of ice and watched it shatter.

They watched Mikey head toward them.

I don't know what else to do, he thought. *But something's got to happen if we're to—*

He heard a crashing sound from behind him. He slipped and fell to the ground.

"Mikey!" Lexie screamed.

All the kids ran onto the ice, helping each other balance on the slick surface. They reached their friend who was staring at something behind him.

"Stop!" He raised his arm. "Don't come any closer."

They all obeyed and slid to a stop. Each stood still as they realized what Mikey was staring at.

A few feet away from Mikey was a child's arm protruding from the ice. It stuck straight up, frozen solid. And it was holding something in its grasp.

Lexie covered her mouth. Her face went pale. Destrey knelt down and crawled a few inches on the ice.

"What the…" he muttered. "Is that…is that one of the ghosts?"

"Yep," Chad nodded. His eyes never left the scene. "I'd definitely say that is one of the children under the ice."

"I thought…I thought ghosts were, you know, transparent spirit-like things," Destrey said.

"Me, too," Lexie murmured.

"Holy smokes." Donnie backed up. "No way is this happening."

"Unbelievable," Lexie whispered through her hands.

"Oh man, I have to go to the bathroom," Donnie whined.

"Shhh!" Chad said. "Dude, come on. Man up."

"Wow, Mikey," Destrey said. "You were right."

Mikey couldn't move. He tried but couldn't.

"You were so right. What is it holding?" Destrey slowly approached Mikey.

"I…I don't know," Mikey answered. His eyes were wide open and so was his mouth. He tried to swallow then he began to crawl toward the hand.

"Be careful," Lexie said.

Mikey watched the ice beneath his hands making sure it didn't crack.

"Oh man," Donnie said. He grabbed onto Chad's arm. "*We're all gonna die*."

Chad grimaced and yanked his arm away.

"Get a hold of yourself, man," he said to Donnie.

They all held their breath as Mikey inched his way over to the hand. As he approached, he could see what was in the grasp of the child's hand.

"It's a piece of cloth," he said to the others.

Destrey and Chad looked at each other.

"A piece of cloth?" Destrey asked.

Mikey finally made it close enough to grab the cloth. He focused on the small thin arm protruding from the ice. It was a pale grey and yet as solid as his own arm. He peered into the ice below and saw Kevin's ghostly face again. His brown hair swished in the murky water current and his sad eyes blinked. But this time, he saw more children with Kevin. Mikey leaned forward keeping his eye on the ghosts the entire time. He wasn't sure if they would pull him under the water again or not.

Finally, Mikey had the damp cloth in his hands. The fingers holding it opened up and released it then the arm slowly sunk back into the water. Mikey nodded toward Kevin's ghost as it disappeared into the inky darkness.

As fast as he could, he crawled back and stood up to meet the others. Lexie exhaled when Mikey made it back safely.

"Thank goodness," she said. She studied the cloth in the moonlight. "What is it?"

"Some s-s-sort of piece of cloth," Mikey said, shivering. He couldn't tell if he shivered from the cold or from fright.

"Cool," Chad said. "This is too cool, Mike!" He grabbed his friend's arms and shook him with excitement. "They *are* trying to tell us something."

"Yeah, I know, I know," Mikey said as Chad shook him.

"Maybe it was part of the bus driver's clothing?" Destrey said as he inspected it. "I bet that's what it is."

"I don't know," Lexie said as she turned it over. "Look, it has a lining like a man's jacket."

Suddenly, they heard another crack and all of them jumped.

They screamed and ran for the edge of the pond. Once they made it safely to the edge, they all bent over and tried to catch their breath.

"Oh man, I thought we were gonna die," Donnie said. He grabbed his heaving chest. "I think I'm having a heart attack." He took out a grape flavored lollipop from his jacket pocket, unwrapped it, and quickly popped it into his mouth. It seemed to calm him down.

"I've never been so scared," Lexie said. Her face was beet red.

"Can we go home now?" Destrey said.

Mikey stared out at the pond watching the leaves scurry along the surface. For the first time, he felt good. He felt some hope. For the first time in a long time, he felt as though all this was happening for a reason. It all made sense now. Or so he thought. But why him? Why now? Why not his father or someone else who was involved? He didn't have all the answers yet, but he felt he had a purpose.

"Come on, guys," he said as he inspected the piece of cloth. "Let's go home."

CHAPTER 14

Detective Williams

Mikey and his friends hardly concentrated on school that next day. All they could think and talk about was the cloth in Mikey's pocket. When he announced they would take it to his father, they felt relief and fear at the same time.

"What if he doesn't believe us?" Destrey said as they walked along the sidewalk to the Sheriff's office after school.

"Well, I'm *not* gonna tell him his brother's ghost handed it to me," Mikey said. "If that's what you mean."

"What are you going to say then?" Destrey asked.

"I'm just going to tell him we found it by the pond. That's all."

They finally reached the doorway of the office. Before he opened the door, Mikey looked at his nervous friends.

"Let me do all the talking, got it?" he said. They all nodded.

When they entered, Mikey saw his dad talking to a short stocky man in a three piece suit.

"Hey Dad," he said as he approached.

"—and that's all we'll be doing for now," said the man before he looked down at the twelve year old boy standing near him. "Who's this?"

"Oh, this is my son, Mike. Mike, this is detective Williams. He's here from Highland to conduct the investigation," he said, pointing to the man. Mikey reached out his hand and shook the detective's hand. His father taught him to always shake a man's hand firmly. It shows confidence.

"Nice firm handshake. I like that," Detective Williams said. "Nice to meet you, Mike." He was a shorter black man with closely cropped hair and a thick mustache. He had a nice, friendly grin that made Mikey feel that he could be trusted.

"From Highland, huh?" Destrey said. "The big city." He nudged Donnie who gave him a look like he could care less.

"Hey Dad," Mikey said. "I've got something to show you." He reached in his pocket and pulled out the cloth. He showed it to his dad.

What is it?"

"We found it by the pond," Mikey said.

"Where at the pond?" his dad asked. His dad took it.

"Near where old man Stuckey's body was found. It looks like it came from a man's jacket." Mikey pointed to the piece of cloth.

"It sure does." He handed it to the detective. "What do you think?"

Detective Williams looked at it closely and turned it over several times.

"You say you found it by the body? I'll need to take this back to forensics and have them analyze it then," he said.

"Yes sir," Mikey said.

"What were you doing out there?" his father asked.

Mikey panicked. He didn't have an answer.

"Uh, we were looking for my gloves," Lexie chimed in. "And Mikey was kind enough to help me out."

Mikey smiled. His dad frowned.

"You know I don't want you out there messing around, right?" he said.

"So, what happened to old man Stuckey?" Mikey decided to change the subject.

"Well, Detective Williams here is on the case. Seems the old man didn't die of natural causes. It's been ruled a homicide," his dad said.

Donnie gasped. They all looked at him.

"We're about to make a public statement to alert the community. So, no more staying outside passed six o'clock in the evening and all parents must accompany their kids this Halloween night, got that?" He looked at each of the kids.

"Awww," the kids groaned with sad faces. All except Donnie.

"So, there's a killer out there," Donnie whispered. His eyes were wide with fright.

"Now don't panic or anything like that," the detective said. "We'll find him no problem and you all can go back to playing outside again."

"Can we help?" Mikey asked.

"I don't know, can you help?" he asked.

"I saw old man Stuckey not too long ago," Mikey said.

The detective cocked his head. "You don't say. Where was

this?" he asked as he took out a small notepad and pencil.

"It was in the town square a couple of Saturdays ago," Destrey said as he walked up to the detective and peeked at his notes. "He was drunk and walking towards him as he talked to the Reverend."

Mikey shoved Destrey aside and gave him a stern look.

"I can tell him what happened myself," he said to Destrey. "Yeah, and old man Stuckey yelled at the Reverend."

"Oh yeah? What did he say?" the detective asked.

"You wear a gun, mister?" Destrey asked the detective, interrupting Mikey.

"What? Oh, yes. I wear a gun." Williams opened his suit jacket to reveal a gun in a shoulder holster.

"That's not a big gun like Dirty Harry used in the movie." Destrey smirked as though disappointed.

"In *what* movie?" Donnie asked.

Destrey gave him a harsh look. "In *Dirty Harry*, you dolt," he said. Then he turned to the detective.

"Uh, no. I don't use a big gun like that," he said. "So what did Mr. Stuckey say to the Reverend?" He turned toward Mikey.

"Doctor Stuckey," Destrey said, interrupting again.

"*Doctor* Stuckey?" Detective Williams gave a quizzical look to Sheriff Thompson.

"He was the school principal years ago. He had a Ph.D. or something to that effect," the Sheriff said.

"An EdD, to be exact," Destrey said with pride in his voice. "That's what my dad told me. You wouldn't know that about Dr. Stuckey since you come from the *big* city." He crossed his arms with satisfaction.

Mikey shoved him and mouthed, "knock it off" to him.

Williams scribbled in his notepad. "Interesting."

"He looked at the Reverend and said something like, 'I know you!'" Mikey pointed for effect.

"What did the Reverend do?" Detective Williams asked.

"He took him to the café to get some coffee," Mikey said. "To sober him up."

"Oh. Dr. Stuckey was drunk? On a Saturday morning?" he asked the Sheriff.

"He was the town drunk, unfortunately," Sheriff Thompson said. The detective nodded with a furrowed brow as though interested.

"I see," he said. "Well, kids. I will get this cloth over to forensics and let you know what comes up. I thank you for being such good concerned citizens and witnesses for me. I'm impressed. I will be in touch with you soon." He waved as he opened the door. "I'll call you soon, Doug."

Mikey's dad nodded to the detective as he left. "Come on, kids, head on home now," he said. "Except you, Mikey. I want a word with you."

Destrey and Donnie scurried out when they heard that fatherly tone coming from the Sheriff. All the kids left Mikey alone with his father.

"What were you really doing out there by the pond?" he asked. His arms were folded and his jaws muscles tensed up.

"Nothing, Dad, I promise. We were helping Lexie find her gloves and before we knew it, it was getting dark out, so we headed home," Mikey said.

His dad exhaled loudly.

"Okay, but no more being out late. There is a killer out there. Old man Stuckey was killed with a blunt instrument. The back of his skull was crushed in. He'd been dead a few days. That means someone killed him then probably held onto his body before dumping him."

Mikey's eyes grew wide. *At least the children under the ice didn't do it,* he thought. *At least, I hope they didn't do it.*

"You understand me?" he asked.

Mikey nodded. "Dad, do you think that piece of cloth means something? Could it belong to the killer?"

His dad rubbed his chin and thought about it for a few seconds.

"Could be, son. Could be. We'll find out in a couple of days."

CHAPTER 15

Halloween

A couple of days. That's torture to a kid. Mikey found that waiting for the forensics report was worse than waiting for Christmas. But it was Halloween night and he had decided to go out as a surgeon. He wore the white scrubs the nurse had given him when he stayed at the hospital. Because of the cold, he wore the scrubs over his jacket and the white cap and mask. He splattered ketchup on the white scrubs for a bloody effect. After inspecting himself in the mirror, he grabbed an empty pillow case then headed downstairs. His dad was on the telephone.

"Come on, Dad!" He motioned for them to leave. "All the good candy will be gone."

His dad nodded and waved, then hung up the phone. He grabbed his coat and keys.

"Alright, let's go," he said.

§

The neighborhood was bustling with kids of all ages. Considering how cold and windy it was that night, Mikey was amazed so many kids wanted to go out trick-or-treating. As required, all the parents followed close behind their children.

As Mikey walked, he quickly located several of his friends. Destrey wore a hobo outfit over his jacket. Donnie went as an accident victim. His head was wrapped in ace bandages stained with ketchup. He had fake scars on his cheeks. Lexie wore her Wonder Woman head piece but had to cover her entire costume with her coat. She didn't seem to mind as long as she was with Mikey. Chad decided to forgo the costume this year. He went as himself and still earned plenty of candy.

They ambled together from house to house with their pillow cases and plastic pumpkin shaped buckets full of candy. Mikey and Destrey compared loot as they walked until Mikey noticed his father had stopped walking with him.

"Hey look, my dad's talking with Miss Jennings," Mikey said. "Let's go see what they're saying."

"Ah, I want more candy," Destrey whined. "Besides, watching your dad try to impress a woman isn't all that interesting."

Donnie came up to them. "What's going on?"

"Mikey's dad is trying *again* with Miss Jennings," Destrey said sarcastically. He snorted.

"No offense, Mikey, but your dad isn't so smooth with the chicks, if you know what I mean." He nudged Destrey and the two began laughing heartily.

"Look, he's just out of practice that's all," Mikey said with a frown. He walked toward his dad. "Hey Miss Jennings."

She looked warm while snuggled in her long coat and knit scarf wrapped around her neck. She had a dark green knit cap over her long hair.

"Hello, Mikey. I was just telling your dad how surprised I am to see so many families out walking on this cold night. I hear a storm is coming next week," she said.

"Yep, a nor-easter from what I heard," his dad said. "Supposed to dump at least eighteen inches of fresh snow."

"Cool!" Mikey said. His friends came up behind him. "Maybe school will be closed."

"Yeah, well, we'll see about that. Come on, you have a few more houses to stop at, don't you?" his dad said with a wink.

Mikey got the hint and walked away with his friends.

Another hour had gone by and the kids had walked up and down at least six blocks. There were superhero costumes and Frankenstein costumes. Many kids wore their outfits over their coats as well. Finally, Mikey's pillow case was stuffed full. He slung it over his shoulder. As they headed back, he saw a group of parents had made a bonfire out of some piles of wood in the field by the park. Entire families sat huddled around the fire sitting on lawn chairs talking and drinking hot chocolate. Mikey and his friends stopped to get warm and sort through their candy.

He noticed his dad and Miss Jennings sat down together near the fire. They talked and laughed together.

"Seems they're getting along, hey Mikey?" Lexie nudged him with her elbow.

He nodded while he chomped on a caramel. "Looks that way."

"Cool!" Destrey said. He held up a chocolate bar. "A full size Hershey's bar!"

"Dang! Who gave you that?" Donnie asked as he searched through his pillow case. "I didn't get one!"

"Oh yeah, a Butterfinger." Chad ripped open the wrapper and bit off a large chunk. "Perfect!"

"You all are going to get sick if you eat too much candy," Lexie warned. She selected bubble gum and chewed it until she blew a couple of pink bubbles. "Too bad Stan and Anya couldn't come."

"Yeah, where are they?" Mikey asked. He tossed another caramel into his mouth.

"Their parents don't celebrate Halloween. Too bad, huh?" she said.

They turned around when they heard more laughter coming from Mikey's dad and Miss Jennings.

"It's kind of sad, don't you think?" Lexie said.

"What?"

"That Kevin Thompson and his friends will never have another Halloween or Christmas again," she said. Her face fell with sadness. "I can't get the image of that kid's arm sticking out of the ice out of my mind."

Mikey hadn't thought of it before. "Yeah. Imagine if this was our last Halloween…ever," he said to the other as they chewed their candy.

"Kind of depressing," Donnie said.

Mikey remembered how fun Halloween was when he was little and his mom and dad took him trick-or-treating around the block. They would each take hold of his hands and he'd walk in the middle listening to them talk about grocery shopping, or car repairs, or gossip about the neighbors. Then, they would go through his candy together and make sure he didn't eat too much before bedtime. Mikey sighed a heavy sigh as he remembered how good it was to have a family back then.

"Well, one thing we can do in their memory is solve the crime," Mikey said.

"Yeah!" Destrey shouted. "Let's do it! On their behalf, we'll solve the crime and let them finally rest in peace."

They all piled their hands-on top of one another and made a

promise.

"For the children under the ice," Mikey said.

"Yeah!" Destrey said.

Donnie blew a bubble and it popped. He winced as the gum stuck to his face. They all laughed at the sight.

CHAPTER 16

Reverend Johnson

The next morning, Mikey headed out to the corner store for the newspaper. It appeared the paperboy forgot to drop it off at their doorstep like he usually did. He probably stayed out too late trick-or-treating. So, Mikey's dad sent him on the errand. The sky was darker than it had been and he knew the storm was coming.

As he walked by the church, he noticed Detective Williams standing at the stoop of Reverend Johnson's house that was around the back of the church. Mikey decided to listen in. He carefully ran over and hid in a bush near the church.

The Reverend lived behind the church in a small white house that the town built for its previous reverend. Mikey noticed that the detective knocked lightly as not to frighten anyone inside. But no one answered. The detective stood on the front stoop waiting. Mikey wondered what questions the detective would ask the Reverend. When no one answered the knock, detective Williams knocked again with a little more force.

"Hello. Is anyone home?" he said. Then, he heard some footsteps approach the door from the inside.

"Yes, may I help you?" Reverend Johnson asked after opening the door. He stood well over six feet tall, so he towered over the detective. The Reverend had thinning white hair and surprisingly smooth skin for a man of his age.

"Reverend Johnson?" the detective asked.

"Why yes. How can I help you?"

"My name is Detective Williams from downtown. I am here investigating the death of Dr. Ed Stuckey."

Mikey craned his neck and saw the detective hold out his badge.

"I need to ask you a few questions."

"Of course, of course," the Reverend said. He glimpsed behind as though he didn't want the guest to enter his home. "My place is a mess. I was just about to head over to the sanctuary. How about we talk in there?" He closed the door behind him and walked off the stoop without waiting for a response from the detective. Neither man noticed Mikey in the bush nearby.

"Uh, sure," Detective Williams said. The Reverend wore a white collared shirt with a sweater. He didn't appear to be dressed for the sanctuary, but rather he seemed dressed to relax inside his house.

Mikey saw the two men entered through the front doors as the Reverend switched on some lights. He quickly ran over to the doors and hid behind one. He peeked through the crack between the door and the wall and listened. The butterflies in his stomach tickled. Listening in like this made him feel like a real investigative reporter.

"We're preparing for Ed's service here on Saturday," the Reverend said. "Such a shame. What a tragic accident."

"Well, it wasn't an accident," Detective Williams said. He took out his notepad and pencil.

"Oh really?" the Reverend asked as he opened a few shutters over the windows to let in some light.

"Yes, it was declared a homicide. That's why I'm here."

"Yes, of course. I understand. Well, the old man had no family around here. I could only locate a few old co-workers to come to the service. How sad is that?" Reverend Johnson sat down in a pew. The detective followed suit. "We'll have his body cremated once we get it back from the Medical Examiner."

"So, when was the last time you saw old man Stuckey?" he asked.

Reverend Johnson looked up at the ceiling as though in deep thought.

A few Saturdays ago, Mikey thought.

"Oh, let me think about that," he said. "It's been a long time, actually."

"Really? How long?"

"Oh a couple of months ago, at least."

"At least?"

Reverend Johnson nodded. "At least."

Mikey frowned. *What?* He thought. *Why did he lie to the detective?*

Detective Williams flipped through his notes. "So you didn't see him recently in town?"

The smile left the Reverend's face. He looked to the left in Mikey's direction. Mikey moved out of view as quickly as he could and held his breath.

"Uh, no. Not at all. Why?"

"You're sure about that?"

"Uh, yes. Positive. Why?"

"You didn't see him drunk in town walking toward you as though he wanted to talk to you about something?"

Mikey peeked through the crack again and saw the Reverend Johnson shake his head no.

"You didn't take him to the café that morning to drink some coffee? You know, to sober him up?"

He chuckled. "Why no. Seems to me someone's been telling you some stories. No. The last time I saw ol' Ed Stuckey was months ago."

Mikey looked away. *Why would he lie about that?* He thought. *Maybe he forgot?*

The detective smiled and put away his notepad into his jacket pocket.

"Why are you asking all these questions?" the Reverend asked.

"Well, it's a homicide, Reverend. That's my job. Just need to check up on a few things. Pretty cold outside for early November isn't it?" He stood to leave.

"Uh, yes. Looks like we'll be hit with a big storm soon." Reverend Johnson walked behind the detective as he headed for the door. "More snow."

"Oh geez." Mikey ran out from behind the door and hid around the side of the church. He hoped they didn't see him. He held his breath and listened.

"Well, thank you Reverend." Detective Williams handed him a card. "Here's my business card. If you suddenly think of anything that might help this investigation, don't hesitate to call me at my office. I'll be at the Sheriff's headquarters for a few days."

Reverend Johnson studied the card. "Yes, I sure will, detective. You have yourself a good day." He began to close church the door as the detective walked away, but before it closed, the detective turned around as if to say something else.

"Oh, one more thing, Reverend," the detective asked. "How long have you lived here in Sherman Oaks?"

"Oh only about four years. Almost five. Not that long," he said. "Well, so long."

"And where did you live before that?" the detective asked.

The Reverend exhaled loudly. Mikey could tell he was frustrated.

"In Raymond," he said. "It's just south of here."

Detective Williams nodded.

"Down south a bit," he said. "Nice calm winters there. What made you move up here with these harsh winters that last almost seven months long?"

The Reverend chuckled.

"Oh, what makes any man of God move around? I felt led to come here and shepherd God's people." He smiled a wide smile.

Mikey rolled his eyes when he heard that answer.

Detective Williams grinned. "Can't argue with that," he said. "And the Reverend who was before you? Where's he at?"

"Uh, you mean Reverend Ellis? Oh, he retired," the Reverend said. Mikey could feel the frustration in his voice. "He moved away."

"I see," the detective said. "Well, you have yourself a nice day."

Mikey peeked around the corner. He observed as the Reverend Johnson watched Detective Williams walk off before heading back to the house. The Reverend wiped his forehead and seemed surprised as though he hadn't noticed he was sweating. He took in a deep breath then exhaled slowly. Then, he put the detective's business card inside his pocket. He frowned.

"Those darn meddling kids." Mikey heard him say before closing the church doors.

Mikey carefully tip-toed away from the church making sure no one could hear him. He turned to head to the store, when he ran into Deputy Rogers.

"Whoa, hey, Mikey," he said. "What are you doing here?"

"Uh…um, nothing," Mikey said as he scooted by him. "Just walking by...on my way to the store."

"Oh, okay," Deputy Rogers said. "Need a ride?" He pointed to his patrol car parked on the side of the road.

"Uh, no thanks." Mikey scurried away before the Reverend came out of the church. "I can walk!"

Deputy Rogers waved. "Alright. Take it easy!"

CHAPTER 17

The Key

Finally, Mikey's dad said he had some news about the cloth the kids found at the pond. Mikey could barely contain himself as he waited for his dad to come back to the office. He was finishing up his patrol when Detective Williams called. Mikey sat in the waiting area of the Sheriff's office playing drums on the coffee table. He turned his head and noticed the candy machine. He dug into his jeans looking for a quarter. When he found one, he headed to the machine, but heard the office door swing open.

"Hey Mikey," he heard deputy Rogers say as he rounded the corner. "Waiting for your dad?"

"Uh, yeah."

"He should be along any minute." He smiled and placed some paperwork on the counter, then walked down the hall. "See ya!"

"Yeah, see ya." Mikey placed the quarter into the slot and pulled the lever that matched up with the chocolate bar.

"Hey Mikey," his dad said he walked into the office.

"Any news, Dad?" Mikey raced over to the couch in the waiting area.

"Yep. Have a seat," he said. He smiled as he watched his son take out a small pad of paper and a pencil from his pocket in order to take notes. "You look like a real reporter there, son."

Mikey nodded and wrote down the date and time.

"Now, I cannot discuss the details of an open case with you, but Detective Williams said I can tell you that the cloth you gave him tested positive for a man's jacket with silk lining. Apparently, it was like some jackets that are for sale right here in town."

Mikey's eyes grew wide and his mouth dropped open. He scribbled down the details.

"Wait a minute," he said. "You mean the killer is here in town?"

"Like I said, I can't talk about an open case, but I just wanted you to know. You and your friends go straight home from school. No stopping in town for anything. You got that?" he said.

Mikey understood as he wrote down more details, and then

bolted toward the door.

"Thanks Dad!" he shouted.

Mikey always thought he could run fast, but that day his feet barely touched the ground as he headed to Chad's house. He spotted Lexie outside with her mom and waved for her to follow him. Together they made it to Chad's house and banged on the door.

A few minutes later, all of them were huddled together outside.

"Wow," Donnie said. "So the children under the ice aren't murderers after all."

"Still doesn't explain all those disappearances over the years though," Destrey said. "My dad told me that people were seen walking by the pond and then never heard from again. That's why families were moving away. They said the pond is haunted!"

"That's just a legend, I guess. Well, we know the pond is haunted, but now we know the children aren't doing the killing, you know?" Mikey said. "Obviously the killer has been taking those people."

"So what do we do now?" Lexie asked him.

"I say we sneak out to the pond tonight and ask the ghosts for more help," he replied.

"I dunno, Mikey," Donnie whined. "There's a killer out there! Maybe we shouldn't be out at night anymore."

"Yeah, Mike. Even your dad said for us to go straight home." Chad chomped on some candy from his Halloween loot.

"Come on, guys," Mikey said. "We can't quit now! There's something going on and I need to help solve my uncle's murder. Together we can do this."

Lexie smiled at Mikey as though she liked his new attitude.

"I'm in," she said with determination in her voice.

Donnie and Destrey looked at each other. Then they agreed to meet that night too.

"Oh, alright," Chad said. "With no hockey practice, I've got nothing better to do."

"What about homework?" Lexie asked as she headed toward her house.

"Like I said," Chad repeated. *"I've got nothing better to do."*

§

The storm clouds had rolled in that night. Thunder was heard from far away and lightning lit up the sky. The wind was bitter cold, but the kids still managed to sneak out to the pond.

"My mom thinks I'm at your house," Lexie said to Anya. She had to shout to raise her voice above the wind.

"And our mother thinks we are at your house!" she answered. They laughed.

They all walked to the edge of the pond. And waited. Each wore a thick scarf around their necks and knit caps over their ears to keep warm, but it was no use. The icy wind went right through them. They huddled close together.

"If you fall into that cold water tonight, Mikey, you'll freeze to death for sure!" Destrey said as he moved back and forth trying desperately to stay warm.

"Yeah, be careful! I don't think we can risk you falling through the ice," Chad said.

Mikey nodded and slowly walked out onto the pond trying to balance himself against the wind and slick surface. The wind shuffled the dry snow across the surface like all the other nights. But this time, Mikey wasn't afraid.

"Hey!" he shouted. "We're here to help!"

No answer.

He also searched the trees for any sign of Kevin's ghost. They bent in the harsh wind sending more dead leaves all around.

"Are you there?" he shouted again. "We know you gave us a clue."

The ice beneath his feet cracked. He looked down then gave the "thumbs up" sign to the gang.

"He sees something out there," Destrey said craning his neck to see.

Mikey took a few more steps and stared at the ice. He saw some movement below and bent down to sweep away the snow with his gloved hands.

"Hey, we want to help you, but you gotta help us too," he said to the children below. There was no response. He looked back at his friends shivering in the cold. He waved them over. They slowly and cautiously stepped onto the ice.

"Oh boy," Donnie said. He nervously rocked back and forth with his arms wrapped around his middle. "I hate this part."

It took a few minutes, but they finally made it over to Mikey who was still talking to the ice like a crazy person.

"We know about the piece of cloth," he shouted above the wind. "It's part of a man's coat. We know it didn't belong to the victim. Did it belong to the killer?" He took a few steps away from the group.

"This is nuts," Stanny said. He wiped his runny nose with his glove. "We should go home. It is too cold out here."

"Shhh," Mikey said. "Listen."

When the wind paused, the gang strained to hear something.

"I don't hear anythi—" Donnie stopped mid-sentence. "What a second. Did you hear that?"

His eyes grew large with surprise and he shivered. "It sounds like a kid crying."

"Yeah!" Destrey said. "I hear it too."

They stood in amazement as they heard a child's cry in the distance.

"Look at the woods," Mikey said. "Do you see anything from here?"

The thick darkness made it almost impossible to see more than a few feet in front of their faces. The lightning lit up the sky once in a while, but not much could be seen in those few seconds.

"I can't see a darn thing," Donnie said. Yet in the distance they could still hear the child crying.

"This is giving me the chills," Lexie said. Her eyes welled up and she rubbed her arms up and down.

"Well keep looking!" Mikey shouted and he took a few more careful steps toward the trees. "It sounds like it's coming from over the—"

Before he could finish his sentence, an arm busted through the ice just a few feet away from him. Mikey jumped with fright, and when he did, the ice cracked underneath his feet. In seconds, the cracks grew. Mikey fell to his knees and frantically crawled away, but it was no use. The ice broke, and he fell through.

"No! Mike!" Chad yelled.

Lexie and the others screamed and jumped back. Donnie ran slipping and falling to the edge of the pond, and shouted from there to the others. “Get away from there!”

“Watch for Mikey!” Chad shouted. He swept away more snow dust from the surface to see if Mikey was below.

“Look!” Lexie pointed toward the arm the instant it went beneath the surface again. “The ghost’s arm is gone!”

In the water, Mikey felt the sting of the icy water soak his clothes again. He felt himself being yanked, so he opened his eyes. He could barely see who had a hold of him, but he knew it was Kevin. He stopped struggling.

Mikey gazed into the dark waters and saw several faces staring back at him. He saw the ghosts of more children. Then he looked at Kevin who opened his hand to reveal a shiny object in his palm. Mikey winced because his ears stung from the frigid water. He turned to Kevin who started to pull him to the surface, but Kevin stopped and opened his hand. The shiny object was missing. He jerked his head back and forth searching for it in the dark water, and then frantically swam toward the bottom of the pond. Mikey felt his lungs start to burn so he desperately tried to swim to the surface, but Kevin grabbed his arm and pointed to the pond grass swishing in the current.

Mikey turned to see what was at the bottom. All he saw was pond grass until, finally, a lightning strike lit up a shiny object. Mikey turned toward Kevin who nodded. He swam down and helped Kevin find what looked like a silver key. The instant Mikey grasped it, Kevin whisked him back to the surface again and shoved him up and out of the hole where his friends grabbed him and helped him out.

“What happened!” Lexie shouted at Mikey’s soaking wet face with ice already forming on his eyebrows.

Mikey coughed up water and spat on the ice. Without speaking, he opened his glove to reveal the silver key.

“What the heck?” Chad looked at Mikey who shivered uncontrollably.

§

Once all his clothes were hung by the furnace in the school boiler room, Mikey sat shivering under the janitor's blanket. It wasn't easy getting him there. Donnie, being the biggest, carried him over his shoulder, but they all helped get him through the window and down the stairs.

"I bet the janitor wonders who keeps messing with his blanket and stuff down here," Donnie said. He sat down on the bench across from Mikey. He took out a cherry flavored Tootsie-roll pop from his pocket and unwrapped it. Before he put it in his mouth, he offered it to Mikey who shook his head no.

"I don't know how we made it here." Lexie held up Mikey's clothes. She shook the excess water out of them, and then placed them one by one onto a metal shelf next to the furnace. "I'm surprised you didn't freeze to death."

Mikey nodded. His teeth chattered so fast, he couldn't talk. He jerked his head to the side to try and get the water out of his ear.

"So, what's with the key?" Chad asked

Mikey tried to answer, but he shivered too much to talk.

"I guess Kevin was going to give it to Mikey when the ice cracked," Lexie said. "I guess he saved your life, huh Mikey?"

But all Mikey could do was shiver.

Lexie inspected the key, turning it over and over while holding it to the light coming from the furnace.

"Looks like the key to a diary," Destrey said.

Donnie laughed. "How do you know? Do you keep a diary?" he teased.

Chad laughed, too.

"No!" Destrey said. "But my older sister had one and the key looked like that one."

"Sure," Donnie said.

"It is not a diary key," Anya said. She stood up to look at it.

"How do you know?" Destrey asked.

Anya reached under her jacket and pulled out a chain. At the end of the chain was a key. A diary key. "This is how I know," she said.

"Oh. Well, it could be a *different* kind of diary key," he said.

"I don't think so," Lexie said to Mikey. "Looks like a keepsake key to me."

"A what?" Donnie removed the lollipop from his mouth. His lips and tongue were already bright red. "What's that?"

"A keep sake box, you know. A special box people keep things in?" Lexie said.

Chad sat next to Mikey who seemed to be warming up. "Does your dad have any keep sake boxes around the house?"

Mikey shook his head.

"Hmm," Chad said. "Well, it's a clue. We asked the ghost for help and your uncle gave you this." He took the key from Lexie and held it up.

"At least, I *think* it's another clue," he said.

"It's a clue alright." Lexie took it and gave it back to Mikey.

All the kids agreed.

"Come on, we've got to get you home before you get sick and your dad gets angry. And before we all get in big trouble," Chad said.

Mikey opened his mouth and tried to say something.

"What is it Mike?" Chad asked.

"I ssssaw more ghosts." His teeth chattered. Chad looked at Lexie.

"What?" Lexie asked Mikey.

"I sssaw more children under the ice," he said.

"You mean ghosts other than the kids that were on the bus?" Chad asked.

Mike nodded.

"Who do you think they are?" Lexie asked.

"I think they are the ghosts of the mmmmissing kids that were taken." Mikey tried to stand. They all gathered around Mikey and helped him stand up. His clothes were almost dry. He did his best to dress under the blanket. Once he zipped up his jacket, they all headed to the window, eased out.

"Do you suppose they're trying to help us, too?" Lexie asked.

"Yep," Mikey said. "We've got to solve this crime."

They all headed home.

CHAPTER 18
Snow Storm

The snow storm blew hard for several more days dumping record levels of snow all over the state. The snow plows had to be called in from Saint Paul to help Sherman Oaks townsfolk get out of their driveways. Mikey enjoyed watching the plows in action outside on the streets. They piled the excess snow along the sidewalks where he and his friends could play in the six feet tall piles of snow on either side of the street. Snowmen appeared in every yard along with ample supplies of snowballs for the fights that were soon to occur.

All the shops closed down as did the church since no one could drive anywhere. The city streets resembled a ghost town. But all that Mikey and his friends cared about was that the mayor cancelled school for that entire week. That meant snowball fights, sledding, and plenty of hot chocolate. After a few days, the cold winds stopped and the sun shone brightly. Parents couldn't keep their kids inside. The kids knew they had better take good advantage of the snow before it all melted away.

One thing his friends did miss was hockey. The Sheriff had forbidden anyone from playing on the frozen pond until the murder of Dr. Stuckey was solved. Day after day, the kids would stand along the pond's edge dreaming of when they could get back to playing their favorite sport.

"It is not fair," Stanny said. He angrily shoved his hands deep into his jacket pockets. "We should be able to play on the ice during the day."

Mikey nudged him. "I know," he said. "But we'll be able to get back out there soon." He didn't have the heart to tell Stanny how glad he was not to play hockey, so inside he smiled.

"Still no ideas about the key?" Chad asked.

Mikey shook his head. "I've looked all through my dad's stuff and can't find anything like a keepsake box."

"Well, we've got to keep searching for clues. I think we should try interviewing people again now that the storm has passed," Lexie said.

After the ghosts showed Mikey the key, the kids took it upon themselves to ask around for more details about the accident. To their dismay, they discovered that so many people were new to the town and didn't know anything about the accident.

But they decided to keep trying.

"This stinks," Donnie whined. He kicked away small pile of snow.

"Hey, being an investigative reporter isn't easy'" Mikey walked along the sidewalk with Lexie, Donnie, Chad, and Destrey. He wrote down some notes onto his small notebook. "You just have to keep going even when there aren't many leads. It's like the storm. The snow blows in and interrupts everything for a few days, but eventually, things get back to normal.

"Wow, that's so optimistic of you, Mikey." Lexie smiled.

"Thanks." He smiled back. "We just have to keep on asking questions. Like Woodward and Bernstein, you keep asking questions."

"Like who?" Donnie asked.

"Woodward and Bernstein, you know," Mikey said, "The Washington Post reporters who investigated Watergate?"

Donnie had a blank stare on his face.

"Nevermind." Mikey sighed. "Just trust me. Investigative reporting isn't easy. It takes a lot of work and persistence."

"Yeah, Donnie," Destrey smirked.

"Oh yeah? What information have you uncovered lately?" Donnie asked him.

"I asked my folks some questions. That's something." Destrey took out a piece of bubble gum from his pocket, tore open the wrapper, and started chewing it. "It's more than what you've done."

"And what answers did you get from them?" Donnie turned and started walking backwards so he could face Destrey as he talked to him.

"Well…" Destrey chewed his gum. "Not much. Not anything new, anyway."

Donnie chortled. "Thought so."

"Come on, now," Lexie said as they walked past the park. "Just a few more houses. Someone's bound to know something."

"Terrific," Donnie sighed heavily then turned away.

"I was reading a history book about Sherman Oaks during lunch last week," Lexie said, "and discovered something interesting."

Mikey looked at her. "Really?"

She nodded. "I read that there's a sister city in Canada near Toronto."

"A *sister* city?" Chad asked.

"Mmm, hmm," Lexie replied. "A sister city is, well, sort of a twin of a city. So, there's this small town near Toronto that is a twin of Sherman Oaks."

Donnie and Destrey looked at each other, then at Lexie.

"And?" Destrey asked.

"And, so, the book said many people from the sister city moved here and after the accident, many people from Sherman Oaks moved back there over the years and I thought that maybe—"

"Maybe that's where the bus driver went to?" Mikey interrupted.

"Yeah!" Lexie lit up with excitement. "What do you think? I mean, my dad said a lot of criminals move to Canada to escape punishment."

Destrey grimaced and shook his head. "I don't know," he said. "I heard most criminals head down to Mexico."

Donnie shoved him. "Dummy, Canada is a heck of a lot closer than Mexico."

"Duh." Destrey shrugged his shoulders. "That makes it easier for cops to find them. Hello? Lexie, a 12 year old kid, figured it out by reading a book about how maybe criminals are hiding there. You don't think the cops checked out our sister city for the killer?"

Lexie frowned. "I suppose you're right."

Destrey's face softened as if he felt bad. "I didn't mean to, you know, ruin your story," he said.

Lexie smiled. "Don't worry. You didn't. I just thought it was interesting that we had a sister city in Canada and thought, for a moment, that maybe the killer went up there since it's a lot like our little city."

They all stopped at a picnic bench. Mikey held out the page from the phone book so everyone could see it.

"Okay, we tried all the A's, let's move on to the B's," he said.

"Who's next?" Lexie asked.

"Mr. and Mrs. Brandenburg," he said, "but they live too far away. They're pretty close to the edge of town that way." He pointed west.

"Maybe using the phone books isn't such a great idea," Destrey said. "Some people will be too far away to walk to."

Lexie sighed. "Well, I guess we could just go door to door and see what happens."

They trudged through the snow together like some band of misfit detectives. Cars passed and honked at them as they crossed the street and made their way up the driveway to the front door. Time and time again, they asked the people inside if they could answer a few questions, but time and time again they were met with slamming doors or rude comments. Until finally, someone wanted to talk.

§

"Sure, come on in," said the woman listed as Ms. Capetown.

The kids were thrilled to finally be out of the cold air that afternoon. They slipped out of their snow boots and left them in the mudroom along with their coats. They entered into the old lady's parlor and sat down on the antique furniture. Each one watched as Donnie sat. They hoped the small delicate sofa could hold his large frame.

He noticed them all staring. "What?" he asked with hands raised.

They each chuckled under their breath.

"Tell me, what can I do for you this afternoon?" Ms. Capetown said.

Mikey went on to explain how they were asking townsfolk about the accident that happened in 1961.

Ms. Capetown frowned. "Oh my," she muttered. She stood and walked to the window. They turned to see what she was looking at and, to their shock, they noticed her home faced the far side of the pond near the bridge.

"I remember that day well," she said softly.

Lexie nudged Mikey, but he ignored her.

"Um, ma'am," he said. "Did you live here at that time?"

She nodded and fiddled with her fingers as she continued to gaze out the window.

"Do you remember whatever happened to the bus driver?"

She remained silent long enough to make them all uncomfortable. Mikey started to think that maybe they ran into another dead end. He motioned to the others to go. They stood to leave, but then she began to speak.

"Yes," she said.

They all sat down.

"He escaped," she said. "You see…" she turned to reveal tear stained cheeks and eyes still shiny with tears. "My sister was one of the victims."

Lexie looked down.

"Oh, she was on the bus?" Mikey asked.

The woman shook her head.

"No, she was one of the women killed by *that man*…the bus driver."

Mikey cocked his head. He hadn't heard this one before. He looked at the others and they seemed just as confused.

"Excuse me?" he asked.

"She was one of the victims. There were several murders over the years. Young women abducted and killed. Their bodies dumped right out there." She pointed to the frozen pond.

Mikey stood and looked out the window.

"Oh yeah," he said. "I remember now…"

"What?" Lexie asked.

"My Uncle," he said to her. "He had a suspicion about the bus driver. My dad told me about how his brother and his friends thought the bus driver was a kid killer."

"Oh yeah!" Destrey bounced up.

"Yeah, remember how they said that's why the kids were out there that day. They thought the bus driver had something going on. So they followed him. Anyway, that's what was brought up in the law suit, but it was never investigated. The whole thing was ruled an accident and the murders went unsolved," Mikey said and turned and walked away from the window.

"But you think it was the bus driver?" he asked the woman.

She wiped her face with her hands and sat down.

"Oh dear, it was so many years ago," she said. "Late January,

1961. No one knew for certain. But I had a strong feeling it was him. My sister talked with him once or twice. She told me he had asked her out for a date and she refused. He was so much older than she was and, well, he was separated from his wife. She said he gave her the creeps or something like that. So she turned him down…and a few days later she disappeared."

The kids sat mesmerized.

"And then her body was…" She sniffled. "Her body was found a few days after that."

"What a horrible tragedy," Lexie said.

"This just keeps getting worse and worse." Donnie shook his head and nervously shuffled his feet.

Mikey felt it was time to go. He didn't want to make the woman cry anymore. He stood to leave.

"Well, thank you," he said. "Sorry. We didn't mean to make you…you know, cry and stuff."

The woman stood and wiped her face again.

"I'm sorry. I don't know why I get all weepy after so many years. You kids are so nice," she said. "I appreciate your kind words. What were you researching again? A school project?"

"Uh, yeah." Mikey put on his jacket. "A school research project."

"It was later that fall when the bus accident happened," she said.

"Yes," Mikey said.

"So tragic." The woman sighed and followed them to the door. "It was soon after that many families moved away."

"But you stayed?" Mikey said.

She smiled. "Yes. This was our home, my sister's and mine. I had to stay."

"Yeah, I see," Mikey said. He turned to say something to the others.

"So many people moved back to Kew Gardens near Toronto," she said softly. "You know, our sister city?"

Mikey stopped putting on his jacket. His mouth fell open as his eyes met Lexie's. She raised her eyebrows and mouthed the words *sister city*.

Mikey turned to Ms. Capetown. "Uh, excuse me?" he asked her. "Sister city?"

Ms. Capetown picked up Donnie's snow shoes and handed them

to him. “Uh, huh. Kew Gardens is a lovely little town. It’s our twin city. So many people here in Sherman Oaks came from there. After the accident, many decided to return there.”

“And you’ve been there?” Lexie asked.

“Sure, I’ve visited.” She held open the door.

“Well, thank you,” Mikey said as he walked past her, “for your time.”

They all departed the warm house and stood on the sidewalk. They faced the pond across the way.

“She knew about the sister city stuff,” Destrey whispered.

“I know.” Lexie took his arm and moved him further down the drive way. “I don’t want her to hear us.”

“What do you think, Mike?” Chad asked. Mikey wrote down more notes.

“I think we should look into this sister city,” he said.

“Creepier and creepier,” Destrey said. “This just gets creepier and creepier!”

“I know,” Lexie agreed. “Makes me not want to go on interviewing people.”

“Well, we’ve got to,” Mikey said. “Let’s think about what the woman said. She said the bus driver asked her sister out and was refused. And then her sister disappeared and ended up dead.”

“Yeah, so?” Destrey asked.

“So, that’s a motive,” Mikey replied as he scribbled more into his small notepad.

“Motive? What’s that?” Donnie asked. He turned to Destrey and shrugged.

“A motive is a possible reason why a person murders someone. So, we know that the killer murdered the woman because she rejected him,” Mikey answered. He jotted down some of the details. “Now let’s ask around about the murders. Let’s see what comes up.” The whole group shuffled off in the snow. They walked in silence for a few minutes as though deep in thought.

“Now that the storm’s passed, I hear old man Stuckey’s funeral is this Thursday night at the church.” Destrey broke the silence. “I think we should go and see if any of his old friends know anything.”

“Good idea,” Mikey said. “Come on, let’s go back and get something to eat.”

§

Mikey thought more and more about old man Stuckey as he walked home. *Maybe there's a connection between the key and the murder,* he thought. He took out the key from his pocket and studied it once again. *Maybe I should ask Dad.* But something inside him knew that was a bad idea.

He opened the front door only to see his dad home for lunch.

"Hey, where've you been?" his dad asked.

"Goofing around with the guys. Why?" Mikey took off his jacket and gloves and hung them on the peg by the front door. He sat down on the bench to take off his snow boots.

"I've got some good news." His dad walked over to him. "Looks like the murderer has been found."

Mikey looked up.

"Really?" he couldn't believe it.

The bus driver who eluded the police for years was finally caught. He couldn't wait to tell the others and the ghosts. Mikey stood up and smiled a wide smile.

"What happened?"

"Well, Detective Williams said they found out another bum in town killed old man Stuckey and dumped his body in the pond."

Mikey frowned.

"Oh, *that* murder," he said solemnly. He walked over to the couch.

"What do you mean *that* murder?" his father asked.

"Uh, never mind. I thought you were talking about something else," he said. "So a bum killed poor old man Stuckey?"

"Yeah. Seems the jacket can be traced to an old man who slept on the park benches in town. He went to the church for shelter during the storm and Reverend Johnson reported the torn jacket the bum was wearing to the Deputy Rogers. We gave the jacket to Detective Williams who ran some tests and, well, to make a long story short… it's a match."

"So, it was an old bum who did it, huh?" Mikey said.

"Yep. You seem a little disappointed," his dad said as he walked over to Mikey.

"No. Actually, I'm pretty glad because now it means we can hang out at…er, I mean we can *skate* on the pond again. Right?" he grinned.

His dad smirked. "Yes, I suppose you are right."

"Yes!" Mikey jumped up and was about to head out the door again when his dad stopped him.

"Lunch first." His dad grabbed Mikey's shoulders and turned him around toward the table where a sandwich sat on a plate. "Then you can go back out to play with your friends."

His dad watched him eat. "Hey, I wanted to run something past you," he said.

Mikey chomped through his sandwich. "Yeah?" he said with food in his mouth.

"Uh, I asked Miss Jennings out for dinner and I wanted to let you know," he said with some hesitancy in his voice.

Mikey looked up from his lunch with a big grin.

"Yeah? When?" he said.

"Wow! I wasn't expecting you to be so…happy about it," he said. "Friday night. You sure you're okay with that, bud?"

Mikey decided it might be best to act nonchalant about the whole thing. He shrugged and took another bite of his sandwich.

"Yeah, sure," he said as he chewed. "I suppose."

"Good." His dad chuckled as he shuffled through some mail. "You're a funny kid."

"Dad, the gang and I are going to old man Stuckey's funeral this Thursday, okay?"

His dad looked at him. "Hey that's a good idea. I think you and I will go together. You can meet your friends there."

"I like Miss Jennings," Mikey said as he finished his sandwich. His dad raised his eyebrows as though surprised.

"Oh yeah?" he said.

"Yeah. She's nice," Mikey stood and took his plate into the kitchen.

"I think so too," his dad said with a chuckle.

CHAPTER 19
Miss Jennings

The next day, Mikey and his gang of investigator friends continued to walk from house to house asking questions. Unfortunately, they were still met with slamming doors in their faces, but once in a while a person was willing to hear them out. Yet no one seemed to have any interesting information that would lead them to where the killer was.

They walked down each street wondering what to do next. Mikey would endure the whining from Donnie or the complaining from Stanny. All the while, he would take out the silver key from his pocket and study it hoping something familiar would come to mind.

But each time, he'd place it back in his pocket with no idea what it opened or why the ghosts had given it to him.

Finally, Mikey decided it was time to interview Miss Jennings. The kids stood outside the door, daring each other to knock first.

"You go," Destrey said to Mikey.

"No, you go," he said.

Donnie shoved Destrey. "You go," he said.

"No way!" Destrey moved out of the way. "You go."

And it went on and on until Lexie just couldn't take it anymore.

"For crying out loud," she exhaled as she stepped toward the door. "You're a bunch of babies."

She knocked hard on Miss Jennings' door. They heard some footsteps approaching and the wooden door opened. Miss Jennings smiled when she saw her visitors.

"Hey kids," she said. "What can I do for you? I bet you're glad school starts up again next week, huh?"

They all looked at each other.

"Um, yeah, I guess," Donnie shrugged.

Miss Jennings chuckled. She wore a long sleeve navy blue sweater, jeans, and had her hair down around her shoulders. As usual, she wore long silver dangling earrings that sparkled.

"Well, come on in," she opened the door wide and ushered in her guests. "I was just getting ready to make some lunch. It's so nice to have visitors. All this snow had me cooped up all day long everyday. I was going insane!"

They all wiped their shoes on the mat, took off their coats in the mud room, and then headed into the house. Miss Jennings showed them to the living room then disappeared into the kitchen.

"I love your earrings!" Lexie smiled.

Miss Jennings gently touched them. "Oh, thank you, Lexie."

Mikey noticed her house was the same floor plan as his, only much brighter. The walls were painted a sunny yellow and the sofa was in a different part of the living room. He sat down on a chair with a red floral print. It was oversized and soft. He sat back and instantly felt comfortable. On the coffee table were some magazines and more books.

I like this, he thought. He looked around and saw tastefully framed art on the walls, bookcases filled with books of all sorts, family photos on tables, and antiques all over the place. Lexie looked at each photograph while the guys ate from the candy dish. Mikey thought for a woman so young, Miss Jennings made her house feel like an older woman lived there. And he liked it.

This is definitely what we need at home, he thought. *A woman's touch.*

He pictured his own house so dark and dank with its pitiful table in the kitchen and old chair in the living room. There were no photographs on the walls and hardly any furniture throughout. His mother took most of it when she left and his dad never bothered to buy anything to replace what she took. Mikey liked how bright and cheery Miss Jennings's house was. He couldn't help but smile.

Out of the corner of his eye, he saw Lexie gesturing toward the upright piano near the staircase. He looked at it and shrugged. Lexie pointed frantically at what looked like a box…a *keepsake* box sitting on top of the piano.

Mikey's eyes widened. Lexie motioned for him to come over and look at it, but they heard Miss Jennings's footsteps approaching. She came out of the kitchen with some cups of hot chocolate, which amazed Mikey.

"Hot chocolate anyone?" she said in a sing song voice.

"Sure! You don't have to do all this for us, you know," Mikey said as he took a cup.

"Oh, it's no bother at all," she said. Once everyone had a cup and sat down, Miss Jennings joined them.

"So, to what do I owe this pleasure of having you all here to visit me?" She took a sip of her hot chocolate then adjusted her glasses on her nose. She seemed genuinely interested.

They all turned to Lexie who took out her notebook and pencil.

"Well, we wanted to ask you some questions," she began. Miss Jennings looked intrigued.

"Really? About what?" she said. Her eyes sparkled with excitement. She sipped her hot chocolate again.

"About that bus accident that happened a long time ago. Uh, 1961," Destrey said.

Miss Jennings swallowed hard as though shocked by what she'd heard.

"Oh, really," she said wiping her mouth. "I wasn't expecting that answer." She laughed a little. "You're still researching that incident?"

"Yes, we're still researching it," Mikey said. "—for that school project."

"Um, okay. What do you want to know?"

"You were in high school when it happened, correct?" Destrey took a formal tone. Mikey shot him a look. "What?" Destrey mouthed.

"Yes. I was in high school when it happened," she said.

"What do you remember about the bus driver for the middle school?" Mikey asked.

Miss Jennings looked up at the ceiling as though trying to remember something.

"The bus driver, huh?" she took some time to think. She moved some hair from her forehead and exhaled. "I never took the bus, so it's hard for me to remember him. I do know the kids were afraid of him. They thought he drowned stray cats and dogs or something creepy like that, even though no one ever saw him do anything, you know?"

They all nodded.

"Some kid says something and by the time the day is over the whole school thinks it's true. I never heard much about him, just that he was pretty strict." She took another sip.

"So, where were you when it happened?" Lexie asked.

"Oh, let me see…" She rubbed her forehead. "I was at a friend's house after school. It was early November wasn't it?"

Mikey nodded.

"Then we were probably getting ready for the homecoming dance. I think we were on the decorating committee or something. I remember we met at her house right after school. Then a couple of hours later, her dad came in to tell us there was an accident at the pond."

Lexie wrote everything down.

"Mikey, your dad lost his little brother that day, right?" She had a sad look on her face.

"Yes," Mikey said.

"So tragic. We couldn't believe what happened. I remember going to school the next day and it was shut down. All of us stood around talking and asking questions before the teachers came out and told us all to go home. They had tear-stained faces. It was so sad."

The kids sat quietly taking it all in.

"There were funerals for a few days. Then the investigation started." She took one last sip and placed her cup down on the tray.

"Investigation?" Mikey asked.

"Yes, of Principal Stuckey," she said.

The kids all looked at each other.

"So sad to think he's gone now too, huh?" She took off her glasses and cleaned them.

"What were they investigating him for?" Destrey asked.

"I guess some of the parents wanted to know why Dr. Stuckey hired the bus driver. They wanted to know if Dr. Stuckey knew the bus driver had a criminal record or not."

"Did he?" Mikey asked.

"I don't know what was discovered after the investigation. All I know is that Dr. Stuckey resigned. He was never the same again. His wife and kids left him. He shut himself in the house for years. And then he became the town drunk," she said. Her eyes became shiny with tears. "How tragic, huh? He was such a nice man and a good principal. Yet everyone blamed him for the accident."

Lexie wiped her eyes, and then continued taking notes.

"I guess they needed to blame someone. I'm glad they found his killer. Now everyone can feel safe again. Anyways, a few months later, families began to move away. We graduated from high school that next spring. And then I left for college. My family moved eventually, but I came back. I've always loved it here in Sherman Oaks. It's my home."

All the kids smiled at Miss Jennings.

"Any idea where the bus driver might be today?" Mikey asked.

"Today?" She gently adjusted her glasses. "Oh, he's probably dead by now I would think. He was old back then. I can't imagine he's still around." She stood and gathered the cups onto her tray then headed into the kitchen. "Anyone want a snack? I have graham crackers," she shouted from the kitchen.

As soon as Miss Jennings left the room, Lexie and Mikey jumped up and made their way to the piano. Mikey reached into his pocket and pulled out the key, but in his haste, he dropped it. Lexie saw it bounce under the piano.

"Oh no," she sighed as she closed her eyes. She bent down to find it, but they thought they heard Miss Jennings coming. "Distract her."

Mikey walked over to the kitchen.

"So, this is a nice kitchen…" The kids heard him make small talk with Miss Jennings.

"Help me find it," Lexie whispered to Donnie and Destrey who leapt off their chairs and crawled on the floor looking for the silver key.

"I noticed your house is the same floor plan as my house," Mikey said. He leaned over to see if Lexie had found the key. He frowned when he saw all his friends on the ground searching.

"Is that right?" Miss Jennings asked. She turned to place the crackers on a plate.

"Uh, yeah," Mikey said. "But we don't have as much furniture in our house."

"Here it is!" Destrey said.

"Shhh!" Lexie grabbed the key and was about to try it on the keepsake box when she heard Miss Jennings. The kids quickly ran to their chairs and sat down. Lexie noticed they were all sitting in the wrong seats!

"Move!" she said as she motioned for them to get back into the correct chairs. They accomplished this right as Miss Jennings and Mikey turned the corner.

She handed out several crackers to her guests then sat down.

"Now that the weather is clear, looks like his funeral will be this week. I'll be attending it this Thursday night. I don't think very many people from town will be there since they really never knew Dr. Stuckey. To them, he was always the town drunk," she said.

"Yeah, we're going too," Mikey said. He gazed over at Lexie who shook her head no. He rolled his eyes then turned to Miss Jennings. "Do you think people from the old school will be there?"

Miss Jennings thought about it. "I would think maybe some might return," she said. She picked up her cup of cocao and sipped it. "Probably his old secretary."

Mikey looked up. "His old secretary?"

"Well, his *former* secretary. They were very close. They almost married once years before, but things didn't work out, so he married someone else and so did she. I know she lives right outside of town. She'll probably show up," Miss Jennings said, rubbing the cup with her fingers.

The kids sat for a few moments more eating their crackers. He thought about asking her if she remembered the murders.

"So, did you ever hear of the murders that happened around the pond?" he asked.

She frowned. "Yeah, that was a horrible year."

"What happened?" Lexie asked.

"A couple of women ended up dead. Their bodies were discovered in or near the pond, I can't remember," she said. "It was so scary. People were afraid to come out at night. Especially, young women."

"When did these murders happen?" Mikey asked.

"Well, right before the bus accident," she said. She leaned over and placed her cup down on the tray. "One young woman disappeared for days. They thought she ran away, but she wasn't like that. She was a nice girl."

"One neighbor said the bus driver, Mr. Davis, asked her out for a date and she refused him, then she disappeared," Mikey said. "Then her body was found in the pond soon after that."

Miss Jennings shivered and rubbed her upper arms.

"I do remember that," she nodded. "My father wouldn't let me walk home from school at that time."

"Do you think the bus driver might have had something to do with the girl's murder?" Mikey asked.

Miss Jennings tapped her chin with her finger as she thought about it for a moment. "Wow. I suppose so. I guess it could have been him, but like I said, I never really knew him."

Mikey leaned over and noticed many black and white photographs along the hallway walls.

"We don't have many photographs in our house. What photos are those?" He pointed to the hallway.

"Huh? Oh, those are old family photos," she said.

"Can we see them?" Lexie asked.

"Uh, certainly, I guess," Miss Jennings led Donnie, Lexie, and Chad over to the hallway. Lexie was able to hand off the key to Mikey who only pretended to walk over, but then swiftly turned and headed toward the piano.

He picked up the box and tried to insert the key. It didn't fit. He sighed and put it back down.

"Oh, that's just an old antique keepsake box I found in Lexington," Miss Jennings said as she returned to the family room. Mikey quickly put the key in his pocket.

"I like all the old furniture you have." He turned his head. "It's really…uh, really nice."

"Antiques," Miss Jennings said.

"Huh?" Mikey asked.

"All the furniture, it's all antique," she corrected.

Mikey smiled an awkward smile. "Oh yeah, right," he said. "Sorry."

Miss Jennings laughed. "It's alright," she said.

The kids returned to their seats and patiently listened to Miss Jennings tell a few more stories about high school days. They told her a few jokes and enjoyed making her laugh.

"Why is the ocean water salty?" Donnie asked.

Miss Jennings thought about it for a second. "Why?"

"From all the sharks crying…from being so misunderstood," he said with a proud grin. Miss Jennings chuckled. "Cute," she said.

Mikey sat back in his chair. He relaxed as though he felt safe in the house. He was glad his father finally asked her out on a date.

Soon it was time to leave. Miss Jennings walked them all to the door and watched as they put on their coats.

"I am so grateful for this visit," she said while helping Destrey zip up his coat. "I hope to see you soon at the library. If there's anything else I can do for your research project, just let me know."

She waved goodbye as they walked down the sidewalk.

"I'll see you at the funeral," she said before closing the door.

CHAPTER 20
Mrs. Stevenson

Once outside Miss Jennings house, Lexie grabbed Mikey's arm.

"Well? Did the key fit in the box?"

He shook his head. "No, unfortunately."

"Crud. Okay, well, at least we got some good information from Miss Jennings," Destrey said. They all walked along the sidewalk. The snow glistened in the sunlight.

"Yeah, and hopefully, the secretary will be at the funeral, huh?" Lexie said.

"Hopefully," Mikey sighed. "So… who should we interview next? Reverend Johnson? Any more townsfolk you can think of?"

"Reverend Johnson won't know anything," Destrey said. "He didn't live here back then."

"Oh yeah," Mikey said. "I forgot."

"I don't know about Reverend Johnson," Lexie said. They all turned to her.

"What do you mean you don't know about him?" Donnie asked.

Lexie shrugged. "I guess there's just something about him that…that is unsettling."

Destrey looked at Donnie. "Uh, okay…"

"Can you, um, *elaborate* for us?" Donnie joked. He nudged Destrey and the two chortled.

"Go ahead and make fun of me, but I'm serious." Lexie walked a little faster. "There's something about him that gives me the creeps."

"Yeah, me too," Mikey said. Destrey and Donnie looked at him with raised eyebrows as though shocked.

"Really?" Donnie said.

"My parents stopped going to church because they said Reverend Johnson never really preaches, but just tells stories or holds meetings at the church," Lexie continued.

"Really?' Destrey said.

"Yeah, and sometimes he says strange things," she said.

"Like what?" Chad asked as they turned the corner and headed down the sidewalk behind the school. He kicked some snow off the sidewalk.

Lexie turned around and walked backwards so they could see her as she spoke. “Well, this one time, I was telling him how upset I was about getting a B on a math test and he started lecturing me about how I wasn’t a very good student and should spend less time talking with boys and more time studying. He called me a tease and a flirt!”

Donnie crinkled his brow. “Seriously?”

Mikey shook his head. “What a jerk.”

“Doesn’t sound like what a reverend would say, you know?” Destrey said.

“Yeah, it was so strange. I mean, he made me feel pretty bad.” She turned around and looked down at her feet as she walked.

“I know what you mean.” Mikey walked next to her. “There’s something about him.”

Mikey wanted to tell them how he caught the Reverend in a lie, but he wasn’t sure.

“And, the other day…” Mikey hesitated.

“What Mike?” Chad asked. But Mikey had second thoughts when he saw his house nearby.

“Nevermind,” he said. For some reason, he didn’t feel like telling them about what he heard at the church when the detective was there.

“Well, I guess we can talk to my dad,” Destrey said. “He and my mom might be able to add something.”

“Alright. After the funeral, we’ll interview Destrey’s folks. Okay?” Mikey said as he approached his house. “Now let’s go play.” He bent down, took some snow, and threw it in Chad’s face.

Lexie gasped and covered her mouth. Destrey and Donnie laughed as Chad wiped the snow off his face.

“You are so dead, man!” Chad shouted as he chased a laughing Mikey down the street. The others followed, each with fistfuls of snow.

§

The night was bitter cold. Mikey stood outside the church

rubbing his hands together. He pulled at his collar. He hated that his dad made him wear a tie. He tugged at it until he noticed Donnie, Destrey, and Chad walking toward him. They all were buttoned up to the neck too.

"I hate this," Destrey said. "I hate wearing a tie."

"I know," Mikey said. "I was just thinking the same thing."

"It's only for a couple of hours, fellas," Destrey's dad said. "Let's go inside. Mikey, where's your dad?"

Mikey looked over and saw his father talking to Miss Jennings as they approached the church door. She appeared to be laughing at something his father said. She reached up and smoothed her hair with her hand. When his dad saw Mikey, he motioned for him to come over. Destrey's dad looked over at Mikey, winked, and grinned.

Once inside, the Reverend stood next to an enlarged photograph of Dr. Stuckey taken when he was the school principal. Mikey recognized the photo as the one in the newspapers they saw on microfilm.

Once the guests quieted down, the Reverend spoke of how kind Dr. Stuckey was to all who encountered him and couldn't understand how anyone could do this man any harm.

"Who could do such a thing?" he asked. His voice cracked. "I've been here for almost 5 years now, and Ed was always so kind to me. I just cannot imagine why someone would hurt him," he said. Some women in the pews wept quietly.

Mikey looked around at those in the pews. He knew most of them, but saw a few unfamiliar faces. He had never been to a funeral before. He wasn't sure what to expect. He thought for sure there would be a coffin.

"So where's Dr. Stuckey?" he asked his dad. He pointed to the nave of the church.

"He was cremated. See that urn on the table next to the photograph?" his dad pointed out.

Mikey nodded. He had never seen an urn before. Cremation to him seemed like something out of a movie.

They burned his body, he thought. *It's now a pile of ashes? Cool.*

The Reverend finished talking and asked if anyone would like to come to the podium and speak about Dr. Stuckey, but only one person made it to the front: Mrs. Stevenson.

"That's his former secretary," Mikey's dad whispered. Mikey sat up and craned his neck in order to get a good look at her. He searched for Lexie and the others. When he found them in the pews, he noticed they stared at Mrs. Stevenson, too. She was old and a little plump, with silver hair teased up into a pile on top of her head. She wore a floral print dress, pearl earrings, and dark red lipstick. In her white gloved hands was a handkerchief which she used to dab her eyes now and again.

"I knew Dr. Stuckey for many years." She sniffled as she spoke. "He was the most wonderful boss a person could have. He cared deeply for the students and all his teachers. He was a brilliant educator who never deserved the ill treatment he received after the accident."

Mikey sat back. He felt bad for the woman. Then, he felt guilty for having thought bad of old man Stuckey. He only ever knew the man as a drunk asleep on the park bench all summer long.

I guess you never really know about a person, he thought. His eyes found Reverend Johnson's staring at him. He quickly looked away.

He looked around and noticed the people weren't as emotional about Dr. Stuckey as Mrs. Stevenson was. She continued to talk about her time at the school and how thoughtful Dr. Stuckey was to the students.

"He made sure he knew when their birthdays were so he could enter the classroom and wish them a happy birthday," she sniffled.

"Is that true, Dad?" Mikey asked. His dad nodded.

"And he fought hard to get all of his teachers raises because he knew what diligent workers they were," she continued.

The man next to Mikey exhaled loudly as though bored. Mikey gazed all around the church.

"Because that's the kind of man he was," Mrs. Stevenson said.

The Reverend walked up and escorted her down the steps to the pew where she sat down, still sniffling and dabbing her cheeks with the handkerchief.

When he returned to the chancel, he said, "Anyone else?"

Mikey noticed no hands went up and no one stood to speak.

"It's so empty in here," he whispered to his dad. "I thought there'd be more people."

"Yeah, the old man had no family nearby. No one came to claim his body, so it was cremated," his dad explained.

"What about his ex-wife and kids? Don't they care?" Mikey asked.

"Apparently not," his dad sighed.

The thought of having no family around to claim him made Mikey depressed. He sat and wondered about his own life. At least he had a dad who was there.

"There will be a small reception at the parsonage behind the church. Please feel free to join us for some refreshments and fellowship." The Reverend motioned with his hands for everyone to get up and head over to his house.

§

When the service was over, some people meandered over to the Reverend's house for snacks and coffee, while others decided to leave and go home. All the kids went with their parents to the house. As soon as he entered, Mikey eagerly sought out Mrs. Stevenson to ask her a few questions. Lexie and the others caught up to him.

"Do you see her?" he asked them. Together the gang searched the house until finally they found her in a corner of the dining room talking to some people.

"What should we do?" Lexie asked.

"I'll walk up to her," Mikey said. With that, he took a deep breath and forced his way through the people standing around chatting and drinking coffee.

"Excuse me, excuse me," he said as he used his elbows to maneuver his way through the people. Once they stepped aside, Mikey found himself standing in front of Mrs. Stevenson.

"Why hello young man," she said with a kind smile. Mikey instantly noticed her soft skin and sparkling eyes. She seemed like the woman you'd want for a grandmother; the kind of sweet old lady who baked cookies and sewed quilts.

"Um, Mrs. Stevenson?" he said. "My name is Mike Thompson."

He held out his hand and she politely shook it.

"My, what a firm handshake you have!" She giggled. "Nice to meet you, Mike. Mike *Thompson* did you say?"

He nodded. He could see in her eyes that she was remembering his last name.

"Thompson....Thompson. That sounds familiar. Oh, your father is Douglas Thompson?" She pointed over to Mikey's father who stood at the other end of the room talking to Miss Jennings.

"Yes, my dad is the Sheriff," Mikey said.

"And your uncle was little Kevin Thompson?" The smile left her face.

Mikey slowly nodded again. Mrs. Stevenson leaned over and wrapped her fleshy arms around his shoulders. The hug caught him off guard and he almost fell over.

"Poor boy," she said. "That poor, poor boy. You look so much like him, that poor sweet boy." She squeezed him harder with each syllable.

When she pulled away, he noticed she had tears in her eyes. Mikey felt bad. He didn't want to make her remember such a tragic event in the midst of a funeral, but he just had to ask her some questions.

"Well, I wanted to ask you a few questions about that day," he said.

"Me?" she said. "I don't know if I remember that day, frankly. It was so long ago," She looked around. Mikey got the impression she was nervous about something. She surprised him when she took his arm and gently led him through the kitchen and into the laundry area. She looked left then right and over Mikey's head to make sure they were alone.

"Why are you asking about that day?" she said with a more serious tone in her voice. Her eyes focused completely on Mikey. He nervously took a step back.

"Uh, well, I'm researching the accident because I think it was a murder and also because it's an open case. No one ever found the bus driver. So, I feel strongly about helping catch him," Mikey said. "You know, because of my uncle...and my dad."

Mikey hoped she would understand his reasons because he couldn't mention his uncle's ghost was pretty much asking them to solve the mystery.

"I see." She looked behind him again to see if anyone was watching them. Her eyes darted all around in a nervous manner. "Well, I've been investigating the crime myself for years."

Mikey's eyebrows went up.

"Really?" he asked. "You have? Why?"

"Dr. Ed Stuckey was a wonderful man." She sniffled. "What they did to him was reprehensible. He didn't deserve to be blamed for what happened. The bus driver and the bus driver alone killed those precious children. Ed had nothing to do with it and yet he suffered the wrath of all those parents." She dabbed her eyes with the handkerchief again.

"I understand," Mikey said. He turned his head to locate Lexie and the others so he could wave them over to listen to her story, but they were all eating cookies and talking to one another in the entrance to the dining room.

"No, you *don't* understand." She took Mikey's face in her hands and turned it to face hers. "That man, the bus driver, was a sick, sick man."

Mikey noticed a certain fierceness in her eyes. He nodded. She let go of his face once she saw she had his complete attention.

"So, I have been out to prove Dr. Stuckey's innocence and find the bus driver to bring him to justice," she said as she adjusted the white gloves on her hands. "And I have uncovered some truths that will make the police have to start the investigation again."

Mikey gasped and stood with his mouth open.

"What have you discovered?" Mikey leaned in close to her face. *Maybe she knows about the ghosts,* he thought. But she shook her head, no.

"No, not here," she said. "Too many people around. Too many people with secrets they want to protect." Her eyes narrowed and she nodded toward someone. But when Mikey turned to see who it was, the Reverend Johnson blocked his view.

"Why hello you two," he said as he walked up. "What are you whispering about? Why don't you come out and enjoy some refreshments?"

"Oh, hello Reverend," Mikey said. "No thank you. Uh, we'll be out in a few minutes."

The Reverend smiled and nodded at Mrs. Stevenson. "Good of you to come tonight, Delores." He said.

"*Reverend*," she said rather curtly.

Mikey noticed the sweetness had left her voice and she smiled a forced smile. When the Reverend walked away, she reached into her purse and pulled out a business card and pen. On the back she wrote her address, fumbling with the pen as though nervous.

"Here, take this. I've got to go now." She handed Mikey the card and dropped the pen into her purse. "Come see me next week after school and I'll show you everything I know."

She turned to leave. "Come see me Monday, after school."

Mikey took the small card and read the front. "Delores' Quilts" it read and it had the phone number of her shop outside of town. Mikey knew exactly where it was. He knew they could all get there by riding their bikes after school.

"Okay, my friends and I will come by Monday," he said.

Before she walked off, she turned around, reached out, and wrapped her jiggly arms around him yet again. He could barely breathe.

"Such a sweet boy," she said. She cupped his face in her soft gloved hands one more time. "Such a sweet, sweet boy." Then, she walked away.

"Wow, this is great" he studied the business card in his hand. "I'm sure glad I came tonight. I wonder what she's discovered…"

"Everything okay, Mike?"

The voice startled Mikey who turned his head to see the Reverend standing over him reading the business card.

"Uh, yeah, everything's fine," he said then placed the card in his pocket and walked toward the dining room.

"I don't know, you seem upset about something," Reverend Johnson said as he followed.

Mikey stopped and sighed. "Yeah, you know Reverend." He turned around. "So many strange things have happened lately. It's hard to take it all in."

The Reverend put his hand on Mikey's shoulder and led him through the kitchen. "You can tell me, Mike."

Mikey swallowed. *Should I tell him?* He thought. *I mean, he is a reverend. Maybe he knows something.*

And then Mikey took a deep breath and was about to tell the Reverend about what Mrs. Stevenson had told him, but something stopped him. The Reverend waited.

"Well?" he said.

"Do you believe in ghosts, Reverend?" Mikey asked with a sorrowful look on his face. "I'm starting to feel like I'm going crazy. I mean, do you think ghosts exist?"

"Ghosts?" the Reverend cocked his head.

"Yeah," Mikey continued. "Do you think that a ghost could help solve a crime?"

The Reverend squinted his eyes. "Are you kidding around?"

Mikey shook his head. "No, I'm serious. At least, I think I am. There are times when I don't know what I'm thinking. You see, I thought I saw a ghost…out there in the pond. And now this ghost is asking me to help solve a murder."

The Reverend nodded.

"I know." Mikey looked down. "It's nuts, isn't it?"

"Now, Mike, you and your family have been through a lot with your mother leaving you and your father's…*drinking*," the Reverend said. Mikey cringed when he heard those words. He gently turned Mikey around and led him back to the dining room. "That sort of thing is hard for any boy to take. Why, most boys would blame themselves for such a thing as their mother abandoning them, you know? Like it was all their fault. As if she walked out because of something they did, you know? It's no wonder you're so upset and thinking up strange things like ghost stories and such. A father's heavy drinking would make any son feel insecure about himself. I don't think you're crazy for thinking such things and wanting to make a difference…wanting to prove something to yourself. Not at all."

But Mikey didn't believe him. He felt the Reverend *did* think he was crazy for wanting to solve an old murder mystery. So, he simply shrugged and took a couple of steps away. He wasn't sure if telling the Reverend was the right thing to do. After all, it didn't make him feel any better. In fact, he felt worse. He did blame himself for his mother leaving and thought it strange that the Reverend would bring it up. He did feel awful about his father's drinking and wondered why the Reverend would remind him of it. It didn't make any sense. Mrs. Stevenson told him not to say anything to anyone. But surely it was okay to tell the Reverend, wasn't it? He wouldn't try to stop them, would he?

"Thanks, Reverend Johnson." Mikey reached out to shake his

hand. "I appreciate it."

"No problem. Take care, Mike," the Reverend said as Mikey walked off.

CHAPTER 21

The Shadow

That next night was the big night for Mikey's dad. He stood in front of the hall mirror combing through his brown hair while Mikey stared at him with a wide grin.

"Well? How do I look?" He put his comb in his back pocket.

Mikey shrugged. "Okay, I guess," he said.

"Just okay?" his dad said and he reached over and tickled Mikey. "Just okay? Whaddya mean *okay*?"

Mikey laughed as he tried to get away from his dad, but his dad was too strong.

"I look better than okay, I think." His dad inspected himself in the hall mirror again rubbing his smoothly shaved chin. He turned to the side and rubbed his belly. It started to protrude over his belt. His dad sighed. "I guess I need to start exercising again."

Mikey chuckled and continued to watch his dad stress over his looks.

His dad turned his head to the side and frowned. "Some grey hairs, but not too many."

"You look great, Dad," Mikey said. "She's one lucky woman. And Dad? Make sure you tell her you like her earrings. Girls like that."

His dad looked over at him. "They do, huh?"

Mikey grinned.

Together they strode down the stairs toward the door that led to the garage. His dad finished tucking in his dress shirt while he went over the rules for the night.

"No one comes over, got it?" he said. "And I want you to stay here."

"But Dad!" Mikey said. "We were heading out to the pond tonight to…"

"Mikey, it's melting. The ice is way too thin for skating. You'll have to wait until next month. More snow is coming, you know that," his dad said as he put on his jacket.

"But what if we just hung out by the pond?"

His dad cocked his head. “Why? What’s so great about standing around the pond?”

Mikey had to think of something quick. “Uh, um…a bon fire. Yeah! We can make a small fire and roast marshmallows, sing songs,” he said.

“Sing songs? Donnie and Chad singing songs?” his dad said. “You’ll have to do better than that.” He chuckled as he put on his felt cowboy hat then took it off again.

“Come on, Dad,” Mikey whined. “I can’t stay locked up inside all night. I’ve got to do something.”

His dad closed his eyes and sighed heavily. “I hope I don’t regret this, but alright. You can go make a bonfire by the pond with your friends. Come home no later than ten. Got it?” He said. He rubbed his son’s head and messed up his hair. “And be careful. Stay away from the ice.” He opened the door to the garage.

“Do you think it’s haunted?” Mikey asked. He was half serious.

His dad looked at him with a furrowed brow.

“Huh?” he asked.

“You know, the pond. Do you think it’s haunted?”

“Mikey…”

“You know, like the legend goes. Some people say at night you can hear a child’s cry near the pond,” Mikey said. “And some still say that people have disappeared near the pond.”

His dad shook his head. “Mikey, really?” he said. “Old wives’ tales.”

His dad chuckled and walked toward his truck.

“No cowboy hat, Dad?” Mikey asked.

His dad swiped his hand through his thick hair. “Nah, not tonight. And you’ve got to stop listening to those tales, son,” his dad said as the garage door rose. “Soon you all will be able to practice on the ice again and, hopefully, get into the tournament. So, stop thinking about all those stories, okay?”

Mikey smirked and shrugged his shoulders. His dad slammed the door of his pick-up truck shut and started the engine. Mikey ran to the front door and watched his dad pull out of the driveway and head down the street. He hoped deep inside that his dad and Miss Jennings would hit it off.

§

Almost an hour later, all the kids gathered together outside his house to head out to the pond.

"Do you think she knows who the killer is?" Destrey asked Mikey about the conversation he had with Mrs. Stevenson.

"I believe so," Mikey said. "She knows something. But she seemed…afraid."

"Yeah, she didn't want to tell you anything specific there that night, right?" Lexie said "Makes me wonder if the killer was there in the room."

The kids thought about that for a moment. Donnie took out a sucker from his pocket and started to unwrap it.

"Hello kids!" came a voice behind them that made them all jump about a foot off the ground.

"Ahhh!" Donnie screamed and dropped the sucker. He turned to see Reverend Johnson standing behind them.

"Wholly smokes, Reverend. You scared the cra—I mean, beejeepers out of me!" Donnie clutched his chest.

"I'm sorry," the Reverend said as he bent over to pick up the sucker from the snowy ground. He handed it to Donnie. "I just wanted to thank Mikey for consoling Mrs. Stevenson at the funeral. She's had a rough time through all this."

"Yeah, she seems like a real nice lady," Mikey said avoiding eye contact.

"Oh, yes, she is, she is," he said. "She and Ed Stuckey were once engaged to be married a long time ago."

"Really?" Lexie asked. Her eyebrows rose.

"Oh yes. It's quite a romantic story, but it just wasn't meant to be. He married someone else and so did she. Too bad it all ended with that tragic accident so long ago." His face frowned. "That's why I am so glad you were able to talk to her, Mikey. She seemed much happier thanks to you."

Lexie turned her head and smiled at Mikey who was looking away.

"Well, I appreciated your kindness." Reverend Johnson placed his hand on Mikey's shoulder.

Mikey pulled away. "We're off to go play in the snow now,

Reverend," he said. "See ya."

"Really? This late? Well, be careful out there. Yes, see you all Sunday morning!" The Reverend watched the kids walk off toward the pond as the sun barely peeked through the tall pine trees.

He turned and walked toward the church with the snow crunching beneath his boots.

§

They all made it to the open snowy field together as the sun set behind the tall trees surrounding the area. A few sparrows fluttered off into the deep violet sky and a hush of cold wind swept over the pond.

"So, Monday it is," Mikey said to his friends as they threw wood into the pit they dug. Donnie sprayed some lighter fluid on the pile and Destrey threw in a match. The pile of wood was soon engulfed in flames that reached at least six feet high. Lexie, Anya, and Stanny sat in their lawn chairs watching the flames get higher and higher into the starlit sky.

"Yep, Monday right after school," Lexie said. "We'll all ride our bikes to Mrs. Stevenson's house and see what information she has."

"This is pretty exciting," Destrey said. "So, she made it seem like she knows who the bus driver is and where he is?"

"Yep. She seemed pretty confident." Mikey took off his gloves and warmed his hands by the fire.

"I dunno," Donnie whined.

"What now?" Chad said with frustration.

"I don't have a good feeling about this," Donnie said.

"You never have a good feeling about anything," Chad said. "Except *food*."

Lexie giggled.

"About what?" Destrey asked. He tore open a box of graham crackers and began to hand them out to everyone. "What's the big deal? We're only going over there because she wants us to."

"I know. It's just that..." Donnie was about to complete his thought when a flock of ravens flew out of the bushes and into the night. All the kids watched them fly off. "What was that?"

Donnie stood and looked out over the pond. There was no moonlight, so it was pitch black away from the fire.

"Yeah, what was that?" Mikey said.

"I didn't hear anything." Lexie handed out some chocolate bars and marshmallows to Anya and Stanny. "It was just some birds flying—"

Lexie stood up. She heard the noise too.

They stood completely still.

"Sounded like a car door closing," she said.

Mikey grabbed a long thin piece of firewood and set the tip on fire. They began to walk toward the far side of the pond.

"Where you going?" Donnie asked. "Oh great, he's going toward the noise."

"Come on." Destrey grabbed Donnie's arm and dragged him along. "You're comin' too."

"Ah man." Donnie closed his eyes and whined. "I just wanna eat some marshmallows and sit by the fire like we said we were going to do, remember?"

Together they entered the thick trees surrounding the pond and quietly made their way to the far side. They could hear some rustling of leaves ahead of them. They stopped. Mikey threw down the torch into the snow. The fire went out.

"And now we're off looking for ghosts again," Donnie murmured to himself.

"See anything yet?" Destrey whispered to Mikey.

Mikey shook his head. He motioned for them all to stop and be quiet.

"I've gotta go to the bathroom," Donnie whispered.

"What?" Destrey turned his head and shot him a look of disbelief. "Now? Right now? Right when we're about to catch a killer in the act?"

"Stop dramatizing everything." Donnie ran to the side and disappeared behind a tree. "There's nothing out there, but birds." A few seconds later, they all heard the sound of a zipper unzipping.

"Eww." Lexie covered her eyes and shook her head. "Boys." She sighed.

"Look!" Mikey said.

They all froze. A few feet ahead they heard footsteps. Lexie looked nervously at Mikey whose eyes were wide open now.

"Up ahead," he whispered. "I saw something move."

They each hid behind a tree trunk for few seconds hoping no one saw them.

The sound of approaching footsteps was getting closer and closer.

Mikey took a deep breath, and then peeked around the tree toward the sound. He didn't see anything. He exhaled with relief. Then he turned around to tell the others it was safe.

When he did, he saw the shadow of a very tall man standing only a few feet away from him.

"Run!" Mikey shouted.

"Ahhhh!" Donnie screamed as he took off out of the forest.

Mikey ran as fast as he could. All he could hear were the screams of his friends echoing all throughout the area. He felt bad that he took off without them.

"Mikey!" He heard Lexie's voice. He kept running.

"Mikey wait!" she yelled again. This time he stopped and turned to see her running toward him. They had made it out of the wooded area and into the neighborhood.

"The others," she huffed. "They're behind us."

Just then, Destrey, Chad, and Donnie appeared with Stanny coming up behind. They all bent over trying to catch their breath.

"Who was it?" Destrey asked. "Did you see a face?"

"No," Mikey said between breaths. "I only saw… a shadow of someone. Someone pretty tall."

"Oh man." Donnie cringed and grabbed his chest. "My heart…my chest…it can't take much more of this."

"I wonder who it was," Chad asked. He stood and looked back at the woods.

They all heard the sound of a car engine starting. Then, they saw headlights shine between the trees.

"Quick!" Mikey shouted. "Hide!"

They each jumped behind some shrubs in Mrs. Konves' yard. They peeked through the bushes and saw a car tear out of the woods sending mud and snow flying behind it. The driver was in a bug hurry. As it drove by, they strained to see who was driving, but it was too dark.

When the car was gone and the coast was clear, they came out of the bushes.

"It was him," Destrey said.

"Who?" Lexie asked.

"The killer, that's who," Destrey said in an ominous voice.

"Whoever it was," Mikey said. "He sure was in a big hurry to get out of here."

"Yep," Donnie said. "Now can we go and eat some s'mores or something?"

Chad groaned. "That's all you ever think about is food."

"Anya!" Lexie ran off toward the pond. "We left her there!"

When they all caught up, they saw Anya roasting marshmallows by the fire looking calm and relaxed as though nothing happened.

"Did you see anyone?" Lexie asked her. Anya winced and looked at Lexie with confusion.

"No, why?" Anya asked.

Donnie picked up some marshmallows and stuffed them into his large mouth. "No reason."

Lexie sighed and sat down on the lawn chair.

"Never mind," she said.

CHAPTER 22
The Quilt Shop

The wind began to pick up again that next Monday morning and the smell of snow was in the air. With Thanksgiving around the corner, almost every house was decorated with pumpkins and fall wreaths. Mikey looked out the window while finishing his breakfast cereal. When he finished it, he tossed the bowl and spoon in the sink.

"Put it in the dishwasher, please," his dad shouted from the other room.

Mikey obeyed and as he closed the dishwasher door, he thought about asking his dad about the date with Miss Jennings. He had avoided the subject all weekend.

"So, how was your date with Miss Jennings?" he said.

His dad adjusted his gun halter and looked up at his son.

"Why do you want to know?"

Mikey shrugged.

"Don't know. I was just wondering, that's all," he said.

"Get your books, we're running late." His dad opened the door to the garage.

Mikey pulled on his coat and grabbed his books. He wasn't sure if he should press the issue or not since his dad didn't seem eager to talk about it. But his curiosity got the best of him.

"I like Miss Jennings," Mikey said. "She's a nice lady, uh, librarian."

He hopped in the cab of the truck.

"Don't you think so?"

His dad looked at him with a stern, fatherly look. Mikey frowned.

"Mike, I know what you're trying to do," his dad said. He started the truck and roared the engine. "But it's just not gonna work out."

Mikey sighed.

"What do you mean? After only one date you already know this?"

His dad shifted the truck into reverse then truck backed out of the garage.

"Grown-ups know these things," his dad said. He put the truck into gear and stepped on the gas.

"What do you mean?"

"I mean, she's ready for something I'm not ready for," he said.

"But Dad—"

"Enough, Son." His dad raised his hand. He reached over and turned on the radio.

Inside his head, Mikey tried to think about what could have happened on the date that was so bad. *All they did was go out for some coffee.* He rubbed his eyes. *I don't get it. I don't get adults.* They didn't make sense to him. Nothing, lately, made any sense to him.

§

After school, the kids rode their bikes out of town along the old road toward Mrs. Stevenson's house. Dried leaves scattered everywhere as they rode by.

"What do you call a man with no arms and no legs in the swimming pool?" Donnie said as he pedaled his single-speed bike.

"What?" Chad asked.

"Bob." Donnie grinned and Destrey bursted out laughing.

"I don't get it." Lexie shook her head as she rode alongside them on her bright pink bike with a white banana seat.

"Okay, why do sharks swim in saltwater?" Donnie said.

"Why?" Destrey answered.

"Because pepperwater makes them sneeze!" Donnie laughed so loud, he startled Lexie.

Donnie and Destrey laughed so much, they could barely contain themselves as they pedaled.

"Okay, I've got one." Destrey cleared his throat. "What did one lawyer say to the other lawyer?"

Donnie thought for a second. "I dunno, what?"

"We're both lawyers," Destrey said and then laughed out loud. Donnie rode up next to him and shoved him while they laughed.

Lexie smirked and looked at both of them. "Alright, enough," she said.

"One more. Why did the chicken cross the road?" Donnie rode up next to Lexie.

"Why?" Destrey shouted.

"Because it was stupid. It got hit by a car!" Donnie threw his head back and laughed.

"You're stupid!" Lexie said.

"No, you're stupid!" Donnie said.

"No, *you're* stupid!"

"No, you are!"

"No, *you* are!"

"Alright, enough with the jokes," Mikey said as he rode between the two of them. "You're giving me a headache."

Lexie looked at Donnie. She stuck her tongue out at him and pedaled off.

They all stopped at the cross walk to cross the railroad tracks. Across the tracks was the little one-road town where Mrs. Stevenson lived. The Main Street was lined with several businesses. A liquor store stood next to the hardware store and beside that was a small coffee shop. Across the street was Delores's Quilts next to a dry cleaner which stood next to a vacuum cleaner repair shop. After the local businesses, were some quaint homes lining the street all the way down to the last stop sign before leaving town.

"What a cute little town," Lexie smiled.

"Looks sorta creepy to me." Donnie smirked. "There's no people around. Where's all the people?"

"It's called a *quiet* town." Lexie shook her head and said in a snooty tone. "Don't you know anything about life?"

The kids looked both ways, rode their bikes across the railroad tracks, and then proceeded along the old road. It was lined with old fashioned lampposts. A slight breeze caused the trees to sway, sending their dry leaves along the ground.

"I don't know about this investigating a murder and stuff," Donnie said as they rode their bikes. "That was pretty scary what happened the other night."

"Yeah, well, what don't you get?" Chad said. "That guy out there in the woods must have known we were going to be out there."

"So?" Donnie asked with frustration. He stopped his bike and leaned on the handle bars trying to catch his breath. His large body was too big for the boy's bike he rode. He tugged on his jeans.

"Doesn't that bother you? Doesn't it seem like maybe the killer knows we're on to him?" Chad said as he stopped riding.

"Yeah, so what are we doing out here alone then?" Donnie said.

"Or maybe that was the bus driver," Destrey said. He raised his eyebrows and laughed in a spooky voice. "He's come back to get us!"

Donnie shot him a harsh look. "Shut up," he said as he peddled on.

"Hey, I'm serious!" Destrey shouted after him.

Mikey stopped his bike and looked around.

"Which way do we go, Mike?" Destrey asked.

Mikey turned to the left and recognized the name of the street.

"That's it, just off of Libby Street. Come on," he said.

They all dutifully followed behind him, taking in the frigid air. As they approached the small shops that lined the road, they spotted the signpost that read "Delores' Quilts" in large red letters. A fall wreath hung on the sign post. Even though it was late afternoon, the sun was already low in the sky.

The kids skidded their bikes to a stop, stood them up with their kickstands, and hopped off. Mikey saw the "Open for Business" sign on the door.

"Well, this is it," he said. He patted his pocket and felt his notebook.

Lexie took out her notebook and stood on the front stoop. The others followed and stood next to her.

"Just remember, ask good solid questions. Keep it short and to the point," Mikey said. He was speaking more to himself than to the others. "That's what a good journalist does."

"Do you really think she knows who and where the killer is?" Destrey asked.

Mikey shrugged. "I sure hope so. That's what it seemed like." Then he reached out to turn the brass door knob.

It was locked.

He looked at Lexie who squinted as though confused.

"That's strange." She looked at her Princess watch. "It's only four o'clock. It's too early to close shop."

"The sign says the shop closes at seven," Donnie said pointing to the sign.

Mikey frowned. "I told her we were coming today."

He tried to turn the door knob again.

"Maybe she forgot?" Lexie said.

"No way. She knew this was important. You should have seen her face when she talked about it. There's no way she'd forget," Mikey said.

"Hello!" he shouted and knocked on the glass part of the door. "Anyone there?"

All the kids walked over to the large picture window that faced the street and peered inside. The shop was dark. They noticed dozens of elaborately designed quilts hanging along the walls. A few antiques decorated the store front. The counter was near the back of the store and had some sewing supplies lined up next to the cash register. There was no sign of anyone in the store.

"Hello!" Mikey shouted again. He observed a light on in a room at the back of the store. "Someone there?"

Still, no answer came from the store.

He banged on the door one more time. Lexie hopped off the stoop and wandered around the back of the store. She noticed Mrs. Stevenson's house in the back.

"Hey guys," she shouted. "Over here!"

They ran around to the back of the store and found Lexie already on the front stoop knocking on the front door of the little white house with a flowerbox garden by the door.

"Are you sure this is Mrs. Stevenson's house?" Mikey asked.

"Look." Lexie motioned toward the mailbox a few feet away. "Stevenson."

"Hello," Mikey knocked on the wooden door. "Anyone home?"

No answer.

"This is so strange," Lexie said. "You told her we'd come by right after school?"

"Yep," Mikey nodded.

Lexie peeked around the corner and saw a powder blue 1957 Thunderbird parked in the driveway. "Wow!" she said. "What a fancy old car."

Mikey whistled. "Now that is a nice car for an old lady to drive," he said as he ran his hand along the shape of the car.

"Not too shabby," Destrey said as he walked up.

Lexie walked on the gravel driveway. She removed her mitten and touched the car hood. She heard a few clicking noises coming from the engine underneath. "The hood is warm."

Mikey touched it. "Yeah," he said. "She must have just pulled up."

"Okay, so now what do we do?" Donnie asked. "I'm getting hungry and tonight my mom made macaroni and cheese for dinner." He rubbed his large belly with his gloved hands. He turned to see a small coffee shop across the street.

"Hello?" Mikey shouted out. "Anyone home?"

"Hey, let's go over there to that coffee shop so I can get a milkshake!" he began walking over to it even before anyone answered.

"That's all you do is think about your stomach," Mikey said. He bent over and peeked into the car passenger side window. Nothing was on the front seat.

"Oh yeah? That's because I got a mom at home to cook for me." Donnie turned to walk off. "And all you've got is your old man."

"Hey," Chad shouted angrily after Donnie. "Knock it off."

Mikey reached out and stopped Chad. "It's alright."

Chad shook his head and looked angrily at Donnie.

Mikey knew Donnie was right, but he also thought it might be a good idea to maybe ask the coffee shop manager if he knew where Mrs. Stevenson was.

"Yeah, come on. Let's go to the coffee shop and ask them some questions," he said.

They ambled across the street, opened the glass door of the coffee shop, and heard a bell ring. It dangled off the door handle by a red satin ribbon.

The coffee shop was warm and smelled of fresh brewed coffee and pancake syrup even though it was late afternoon. A few customers lined the front counter drinking coffee or eating dinner while a juke box played some old songs from the nineteen fifties. A few movie posters from the 1950's hung on the walls. One was of a Marilyn Monroe movie and another was a John Wayne movie. An American flag stood in the corner. The cook behind the back counter looked up from his work, noticed the kids, and then returned to his cooking. The sound of sizzling could be heard coming from the kitchen. Just then, a waitress dressed in a yellow uniform walked out from the kitchen with some plates full of food. She placed them in front of the customers sitting at the counter.

"Something smells good." Donnie sauntered over to the counter and ordered his milkshake with a big smile.

The others stood around waiting to ask the manager a question. He soon approached them. He was a short thin man with greying hair. He wore a white dress shirt with the sleeves rolled up and some black trousers. When he approached, he adjusted the thin black tie around his neck. Then, he pulled out some menus from the podium near the door.

"What can I do for you kids? Here to order something?" he asked with a wide tooth smile.

Mikey cleared his throat.

"Uh, no sir. We were wondering if you know where Mrs. Stevenson is?" He motioned across the street.

The manager looked across the way at the little quilt shop.

"Mrs. Stevenson? Why? She's not over there?" he asked.

"No sir. We were just there knocking on the door," Mikey said. "And no one answered."

The manager squinted as though confused.

"Well that's odd," he said. He looked past Mikey to the counter where the customers, including Donnie, sat. "Hey Mabel!"

A woman in her forties came out from behind the kitchen area. She, too, was dressed in a yellow waitress outfit and had her red hair piled on top of her head. She grabbed a towel.

"Yeah boss," she said without looking up from wiping the counter.

"Did Mrs. Stevenson come by for her sandwich today at lunch?" he asked. The kids turned to see her response.

"Nope. Not today," the waitress said as she chewed her gum.

"Huh," the manager said. "That's strange. She usually comes here every day at noon for her lunch order."

He reached for his coat. "You kids said you tried her at the house?"

Mikey nodded. "Yes sir. No answer."

The manager opened the door. "Heading over to the quilt shop. Be right back," he shouted to the waitress who continued to wipe the counter.

"Yeah, boss," she shouted in return without looking up.

Donnie gulped down the last of his milkshake. Plopped down two quarters on the counter then hopped off the stool.

"Keep the change," he said with a matter-of-fact tone.

The waitress looked at the coins then looked at Donnie.

"Gee, thanks big spender," she said with a dull look in her eyes.

They all exited the coffee shop and stood facing the line of shops across the street. The manager buttoned up his coat, looked both ways for traffic, and then led the kids to the other side of the street. The wind had picked up as the sun set. A few flurries of snow floated down. Lexie caught one in her mitten and admired it. She looked up and saw the quilt shop.

"Hello?" The manager knocked rather loudly on the front door. He peeked in through the glass panes. "Anybody there?"

No answer.

"It's freezin' out here," Donnie stated the obvious.

"No duh, Sherlock," Chad said. He walked around toward the back of the house.

He stopped in his tracks.

"Mikey!" he shouted. The others made their way to the back of the shop.

"Whoa," Mikey uttered.

The manager came up from behind them. He looked around but saw nothing in particular that would alarm him. He studied the faces of each kid and raised his eyebrows when he saw the looks of shock on each of them.

"What is it?" he asked. "What's the matter?"

Mikey and Chad pointed to the empty driveway.

"Her car," Mikey said. "It was here just a few minutes ago."

"Yeah, we all saw it right here," Chad said.

"The hood was warm as if the engine was just turned off," Lexie said. "It was right here! Now it's gone!"

The manager put his hands on his hips and walked over to the front door of Mrs. Stevenson's house.

He banged on the door.

"Hello?" he shouted.

"I guess she's gone," Mikey said.

"But that was fast. I mean, we were just here a few minutes ago. Did anyone else know we were coming over here?" Lexie asked.

"No," Mikey said. "Well, except the Reverend. He asked me, so

I told him. I doubt he told anyone."

The manager turned around. His brow was furrowed as though he was confused.

"But why would she lock up shop so early? That's not like her at all." He scratched his head. "Well, sorry kids. I have no idea what to tell you. Come by and see her tomorrow. If I see her, I'll let her know you stopped by."

The kids watched him walk away toward the street. "This is so strange," he mumbled as he walked away.

"Yeah, thanks," Mikey said with a frown. He turned to the empty drive-way. "Her car was here just a few minutes ago. Didn't she hear us knocking? Why wouldn't she answer the door?"

Lexie walked up beside him. "The only thing I can think of is that she didn't hear us."

"But she knew we were coming over, right?" Destrey asked.

Mikey nodded. "Come on, guys, we'd better get home. It's getting late."

Donnie chortled. "Yeah, well, I'm sick of this," he said as he picked up his bike.

"Sick of what?" Mikey asked.

"Sick of this wild goose chase," Donnie said. "I mean, I could've been home finishing my homework. Instead, I'm out here wasting time chasing nothing."

"Hey, I thought she was gonna be here." Mikey stood his bike up and straddled it. "She said to come by. It's not my fault she isn't here."

Donnie smirked then yanked his bike around in anger.

"Whatever," he mumbled.

"Come on, let's get outta here," Chad said.

"Yeah, we'll come by again tomorrow," Destrey said.

"No way!" Donnie shouted. "You can come back. I'm through with all of this."

He pedaled away with Mikey following him.

"You saw what happened on the ice, Donnie!" he shouted.

"Yeah so?"

"So you know I'm not making this up!"

Donnie stopped his bike in the road and turned his body toward Mikey.

"This is all bogus!" he shouted. "You've got us knocking on

doors, walking in the woods late at night, now we're in another town…it's nuts!"

Lexie pulled up on her bike.

"Come on, Donnie," she said. "You've got to admit. It's pretty exciting!"

Donnie mocked her high-pitched voice. "No, I don't gotta admit nothing."

Destrey and Chad stopped next to the boys.

"We all saw the ghost's arm coming out of that ice," Destrey said. "We know they're trying to tell us something."

"Yeah, we can't quit now," Chad said.

But Mikey was angry at Donnie. He could feel the anger building in his chest.

"No, forget it!" he shouted. "If he wants out, then he's out!"

"Hey, Mikey, come on," Chad said.

"No! If he wants to be a baby about it, then let him go," Mikey pedaled off a few feet.

"Fine!" Donnie shouted. He saw a car approaching and pedaled off the road. "I'm outta here!"

"Donnie!" Lexie shouted after him. "Wait for us!"

She could see the headlights approaching. She pedaled off too.

"Wait for us!" she shouted to Mikey, but he was already down the street.

"Oh drats," she said as she looked all around the ground.

"What is it?" Destrey asked.

"My Princess watch. It fell off my wrist," she frowned. "Do you see it anywhere?"

Destrey inspected the ground. "No, I don't see anyth—"

Just then, they heard tires squealing and the smell of gasoline mixed with exhaust. Lexie turned around in time to see Chad and Destrey jump for their lives as a large car sped toward them.

"Destrey!" she shouted.

Mikey stopped so abruptly when he heard the scream that he almost fell off his bike. He turned in time to see his friend, Destrey, fly off his bike and land on the side of the road.

CHAPTER 23
Blackest Moment

"No!" Mikey heard the scream come from his own mouth, but his eyes followed the car as it sped by. Then he dropped his bike and ran back to where Lexie and Chad leaned over Destrey's limp body.

"Destrey!" Mikey skidded down onto his knees before his injured friend.

Destrey groaned from the pain. Lexie held his hand.

"What happened?" Mikey screamed.

"That car! It came straight at us!" Chad yelled.

"Destrey," Lexie consoled him. "Hang in there."

"Donnie! Go get the coffee shop manager. Tell him to call an ambulance!" Mikey ordered.

Donnie took off on foot toward the shop. Meanwhile, many townspeople were already running out to see what happened.

Mikey stood and turned around to where the car was.

He froze.

The car that hit his friend hadn't sped off after all. It stopped down the road. It was a white car with two doors and a chrome rear bumper. Mikey could see the brake lights in the twilight. He walked toward the stopped car.

As he walked toward it, he tried to see who the driver was, but it was too dark inside the car.

"Mike, what are you doing?" Lexie asked. "Come back here!"

But he ignored her.

He could hear the low rumble of the engine as it idled. A few snow flurries floated down in the glow of its headlights. He could smell the exhaust. Down near his feet on the asphalt were the skid marks.

The driver slowly rolled down the window and an arm covered in a dark sleeved coat reached out and adjusted the side mirror.

Mikey stopped walking.

The arm rested on the door. The car remained idle for a moment as though the driver was waiting for Mikey. Waiting for *something* to happen. But what?

But Mikey stood there, watching. And the driver did, too. It was some sort of a standoff.

Then, the engine revved one time. The brake lights stopped glowing as the white car sped off.

That's when Mikey knew.

"Coward!" he shouted as loud as he could, but his voice was lost in the roar of the car's engine. It disappeared down the hill in a cloud of exhaust.

For a moment, Mikey thought his heart would burst through his chest. He could taste the anger in his mouth. He'd never felt this way before. But now he knew for certain.

He knew the killer was in that car. And, for the first time, Mikey knew he had to be the one to stop this once and for all.

§

Inside the hospital waiting room, it was warm and decorated for Thanksgiving. Donnie sat nearby on the couch eating candy corns from a bowl set out for visitors. His eyes seemed distant. Mikey looked over and saw Lexie crying with her mother. Her shoulders heaved as she wept and her long blonde hair fell around her face. Her mother tried to calm her down. Chad talked with his parents. Even Donnie's father stood nearby talking to a nurse.

But Mikey sat alone.

He looked down at his muddied shoes. He studied them for a moment. He remembered when his dad had bought them. They went to the shoe store together. It was a Buster Brown shoe store off Main Street. He had outgrown the shoes his mom had bought him, so they had to buy new ones. He still had the old shoes in his closet. He didn't want to throw them away because, well, *she* had bought them for him. His mother. He could see her face.

"It'll be okay, Mikey," she said as she leaned in close to his face. "I'll see you soon."

"Take me with you," Mikey cried.

His mom looked behind him. He knew she was looking at his father sitting at the kitchen table.

"I'll come back for you real soon, okay?" Her eyes returned to

Mikey's and she looked deep into her son's large brown eyes shiny with tears.

"Promise?" Mikey said. He could feel the warm tears on his cheeks.

"I promise," she said. She leaned in and gave him one last hug. He breathed in her smell: A mixture of hair spray and drugstore perfume. He knew he'd never forget that smell.

She released him, stood back, and then turned around. She picked up her bag and car keys, but then put the keys back down on the small table by the door. "I guess I won't be needing these anymore," she whispered. Then, she approached the door and grabbed the door knob.

"Mommy," Mikey said, hoping she would turn around. She hesitated only for a second, and then turned the door knob.

He watched his mother walk out the front door.

"Mommy!" he shouted as the door closed. But he could hear the waiting taxi drive off.

"Mikey!" his dad said. "You okay, son?"

Mikey awoke from his memory to find his frightened dad standing over him in the hospital waiting room.

Mikey nodded and rubbed his face. He knew he'd been crying.

"Yeah, can we go see him, Dad? Can we go see Destrey now?"

"Not now, son," he said. "Come on, let's go home."

Mikey stood.

"But I want to see him." He walked past his dad. "I need to see him."

"No visitors, son," his dad said. "Come on, let's go."

"Hey, Sheriff, what were these kids doing out there anyway?" Donnie's dad asked.

Mikey cringed.

"Uh, well, I'm not exactly sure, but…" his dad replied.

"Yeah, well, my son tells me that your kid led them out there to talk to some old woman. Is this true?" He pointed at Mikey.

Mikey's dad looked over at him.

"Uh, yeah, well, that's part of it…" Mikey mumbled.

"Look, those kids could have been killed out there!" Donnie's dad shouted. "I don't want my son hanging around your kid anymore. Got that?"

"Yeah, sure," Mikey's dad said in a defeated tone.

"Late night jaunts in the forest, goofing around on the thin ice at night, and now this!" Donnie's dad gathered up his coat. "No more! Understand?"

He and his son huffed past Mikey and the Sheriff and stomped out the door into the parking lot. They could still hear the man shouting outside.

At least Donnie didn't tell his dad about the ghosts, Mikey thought. Then he sat completely still. He feared any movement. He crossed his arms over his chest and waited. Then, he felt it. The heaviness of his father's hand on his shoulder.

"Let's go home, son," he said in that low ominous voice Mikey knew all too well.

§

The silence was so thick on the drive home; Mikey thought for certain he'd drown in it. He looked out the window and as the pond passed by, he thought about hopping out of the truck, running onto the ice hoping it would crack open and freeze him up forever.

But the truck made its way down their street. No such luck.

"When we get inside, I want you to explain to me just what the heck happened, understand?" his father said.

But Mikey was too disgusted to answer. He was too disgusted with himself, with his father, and with…*everything*. When the truck stopped, he quickly swung open the door and ran inside the house. He could hear his father shouting after him.

Mikey ran upstairs, threw off his coat and gloves then slammed his bedroom door closed. "All you have is your old man," he could hear Donnie's voice in his head. "All *you* have is your old man."

He swallowed the tears back for as long as he could, but they won the battle. He wiped them off his face so his father wouldn't see.

He sat on the bed and waited.

Then, he heard the thumping of his father's footsteps on the stairs. He could see his father's shadow darken the sliver of light coming from underneath his bedroom door.

"You wanna talk now or in the morning?" his father asked.

Mikey thought about it. He honestly didn't know how to answer. So, he remained silent in the dark room.

His father waited patiently for an answer. When none came, he exhaled loudly.

"In the morning, then," he said. "Get some sleep."

Mikey watched his father's shadow disappear and the hall light shut off. He reached over and flipped on the lamp next to his bed. He looked around his room with its dark paneled walls. The hockey posters stared down at him as did the movie posters. He reached up and yanked. A piece of one hockey poster came off. Then, he yanked again, and again, and again until he tore each of his hockey posters to pieces and threw the scraps on the floor.

He raced over to his dresser and pulled open the drawer. He reached in and took out the framed photo of the family he admired.

He looked at it and gently slid his hand across the frame. Then, he saw a hint of his reflection in the glass.

"No!" he shouted and threw the photograph across the room. It hit the wall and the glass shattered.

"Are you alright?" he heard his dad yell.

"Just leave me alone!" Mikey ran to his bed, fell on top of the covers, and cried himself to sleep.

CHAPTER 24

The Truth

"Well, I guess it's over, huh?" Chad asked. "The investigation?"

He and Lexie stood outside Mikey's house that next morning waiting to see if he would go to school or not. Mikey peeked down from his bedroom window carefully so they wouldn't see him. He could hear them talking from upstairs.

"I guess so," Lexie sighed. Mikey sensed the sadness in her voice. She wasn't her usual chipper self and he knew why.

"Well, we'd better go." Lexie looked at her new watch. "The bell's going to ring soon."

"Hey, where's your Princess watch?" Chad asked.

Lexie frowned. "I lost it at the side of the road where Destrey was— nevermind."

Together, she and Chad walked off. Mikey craned his neck, watching them until they were out of sight.

§

He had made his bed, brushed his teeth, and got dressed all in a fog of confusion and regret. He knew he wasn't going to school that day, and he was glad. He sat on his bed picturing how the students would react to his presence. Heck, even the lunch ladies would probably shake their heads and snap their gum in disapproval. *Who needs that?* He thought.

He heard a light rap on his bedroom door.

"Breakfast is ready," his father said.

Mikey sighed, picked up his coat, and then headed downstairs.

He was met by his father who sat at the small kitchen table. Mikey sat down opposite his worried father.

They faced each other.

"So, you ready to tell me what happened out there?" his dad asked. His large hands folded in front of him. The metal table squeaked.

Mikey took in a deep breath, and then slowly exhaled his fear.

"Dad," he said. "I don't want to play hockey."

His dad cocked his head as though confused. "Huh?"

"Like, ever," Mikey said.

"What?" his dad said. "…But I thought you liked hockey?"

"Dad, *you* like hockey. You like me playing hockey," he said. "But I never liked hockey. I suck at it. I hate it, everything about it. I'm not any good at sports."

Good job, Mikey thought. *You did it. Now keep going.*

His dad sat back in his chair and ran his hands along the table top.

"I only played it because you wanted me to. You want me to be this sports *hero* that you never were." Mikey crossed his arms tightly.

His dad reached up and rubbed the nape of his neck trying to figure out what his son was talking about. "Huh, well," he said. "I'm glad you told me this, son. I think."

"I don't like any sports," he said. "I only pretended to because you do."

"Well, what *do* you like?"

Mikey thought for a moment. His mind went blank for some reason.

"Is this why you've been acting so strange lately?" His dad leaned forward.

Mikey frowned.

"Sneaking out at night, going to the pond, riding your bike to the next town without permission…Mikey, I'm confused by all this strange behavior," his dad said. "Is this why you're doing all this? To get back at me for making you play hockey?"

"No! Trust me, Dad. It's complicated. You wouldn't understand." Mikey shook his head defiantly.

"Try me."

"I did!" Mikey heard himself shout. "I tried to tell you, but you didn't believe me. No one believes me."

"When did you try to tell me—"

"At the hospital!" Mikey stood and jabbed his finger at his father. "I told you and you didn't believe me!"

He quickly ran to the door and put on his coat while his father tried to remember what his son was talking about.

"No one ever believes me," Mikey muttered.

"You mean about the *ghosts*?" his dad said, "Of the kids under the ice?"

"Yes!" Mikey zipped up his coat and made his way to the mud room.

"Son…"

"I told you what I saw and you didn't believe me." He slid on his snow boots.

"What does this have to do with what happened to Destrey?"

Mikey groaned from frustration. He looked up and shook his hands. "You see? I knew you wouldn't understand. No one does!"

He opened the front door and a clap of thunder startled him. A few drops of rain splattered along the sidewalk leading up to the house. Mikey stood in the doorway for a moment summoning up more courage to tell his father how he felt. He turned toward his dad.

"I can't talk to you, Dad," he said. "That's just the way it is. I can't talk to you about what happened because you don't listen! You don't know me. You don't know what I want. You want me to be like you, well, I don't want to be like you! I don't want to be alone drinking myself to sleep every night."

He could see the hurt in his father's eyes.

I didn't mean that, Mikey thought.

"See, it's all linked together. What happened to me in the ice, old man Stuckey, Mrs. Stevenson, Destrey…it's all linked together. But you wouldn't understand. You just don't get it!"

"Mikey," his exasperated dad said. "Sit back down. I'm not through talking to you yet."

"No Dad." Mikey clenched his fists. "Don't you see? I can't talk to you because you just don't understand. You don't listen. You never listen. *And that's why mom left!*"

His eyes burned with tears. He watched his dad's face change from concern to plain confusion. The rain outside was pouring down now soaking everything in sight.

"She left because you just don't get it! You don't listen to us! You never do!" Mikey shouted and wiped his tears. He reached for the front door. "And then there's Miss Jennings. With her, you have the chance to be with someone nice and sweet and beautiful, but you go and you blow it. Miss Jennings is about the nicest person around, but you blew it. You want to be alone. Well, I don't! I want a family again. I don't want to end up alone. That's why you called it off with Miss Jennings! *You want to be alone.* Well, fine then. Be alone!"

He slammed the door behind him and ran down the street through the pouring rain. He headed away from the school and toward the library with his dad's hurt and confused face still in his mind.

§

Well, that's it, Mikey thought as he ran. The raindrops stung his face. *I really did it this time. There's no going back now.* He stopped running and sat on a park bench across from the library downtown. He panted, trying to stop crying. With wet hair was matted to his face, he wiped the water away from his eyes, but it was no use. The rain kept falling, blurring his vision. As he calmed down, he wiped his nose with his gloves. *The old man won't let this one go. You dork. You said some stuff you can't ever take back. What were you thinking, anyways?*

"Hello Mikey," a voice startled him.

He looked up to see Reverend Johnson standing over him with a large umbrella momentarily blocking the rain. He wore a bright orange rain slicker over his clothes.

"Oh, hi Reverend," Mikey mumbled, shivering in the cold. He looked down at his soaked shoes. He just couldn't look the Reverend in the eye, not after yelling at his dad like that. He felt too guilty.

"What seems to be the problem?" The Reverend sat down next to Mikey.

"What makes you think there's a problem?"

The Reverend chuckled.

"Well, it's almost nine in the morning and you're out here sitting on a park bench in the rain, and you're not in school," he said. "Plus, you don't seem too happy at the moment and you act pretty happy most days. You're one of *those* kinds of persons. So, I figured something must be wrong."

Mikey nodded his head. *Those kinds of persons?* He thought.

What does he mean by that?

"I know what happened to your friend, little Destrey." The Reverend put his arm around Mikey's shoulder. "Don't worry about him. He's going to be okay. Kids are resilient that way."

Mikey looked up at him with blinking eyes, trying to keep the rain out of them.

"Really?"

"Yes. I saw him this morning." The Reverend smiled. "He only has a broken leg and a few scrapes. Other than that he is just fine. So I don't see what the big deal is."

Mikey sighed with relief.

"Oh, thank you Reverend." He turned to face him. "Thanks so much for letting me know."

"His parents are making more out of it that they should," the Reverend said flatly while looking off. He turned his head. "It could've been a lot worse. I've seen worse."

"Do you think they'll let me see him?" Mikey asked.

"Oh, I don't see why not," the Reverend said. "Probably a little later on. I'm sure he'd be glad to see you."

"Good," Mikey stood.

"Where you headed now?"

"To the library," he motioned.

"Still researching?"

Mikey felt his smile disappear when he thought about the whole mess. "Yeah, well," he said. "I guess so." He put his hands in his pockets and looked down at the puddles forming on the sidewalk. More thunder echoed in the distance.

"Researching the past can be difficult sometimes." The Reverend stood to leave. "I firmly believe you shouldn't meddle with the past. What's done is *done*." He made a chopping motion with his hand. "One thing I have learned over the years, Mikey, is to let the past go. You can't go back and change things anyway. Live in the present, you know? I fix what I can in the here and now, and then I never look back. You know what I'm saying?"

"Yeah, I know."

"No use looking back." He patted Mikey on the shoulder. "Look forward to the future!" The Reverend headed down the street toward the church. "Never look back, Mikey! Never look back."

Mikey watched the Reverend walk off for a moment or two.

Ain't that the truth, Mikey thought. *I should just leave things be. Who am I to try and solve this murder mystery? I'm just a kid. I never should have started this stupid investigation in the first place. I should just forget the whole thing. The Reverend is right. It's not like I can change things or make a difference anyway. What's done is done.*

Then, as soon as that thought came to him, he saw Kevin's face in his mind along with all the other ghosts. Their faces haunted his mind. *But I can't forget about it*, he thought. He rubbed the rain off his face with his gloved hands as though trying to rub the image of Kevin out. *I've got to try and do something.*

Then he turned and ambled over to the library, hoping to see Miss Jennings there.

CHAPTER 25

History Lesson

As usual, the library was warm and inviting to Mikey, but most importantly, it was dry that rainy day. He took off his coat, shook off the excess water, and glanced up at a sliver of sunlight streaming through the large windows. The rain had stopped and the sun tried hard to peek through the clouds. He walked over to the spacious counter and waited. An elderly woman came out to greet him.

"Hello, how can I—" She stopped. "Hey, aren't you supposed to be in school, young man?" She reached below the counter and pulled out a small towel. She handed it to Mikey with a frown. "You can catch pneumonia being out there, you know."

"Yeah, I know. Is Miss Jennings here?" Mikey took the small towel and wiped his face.

The old woman smirked then pointed to the aisles of books. "She's stacking books over there."

Mikey turned his head and saw Miss Jennings. He handed the towel back. "Thanks."

Mikey made his way past the tables and peered down a few aisles before he spotted Miss Jennings stacking books. She wore her usual long sleeved black turtle neck sweater, a long denim skirt, and boots. She looked up and smiled when she saw Mikey approaching. The usual sparkle in her eyes was missing and he knew why.

"Hey there," she said softly as to not disturb nearby readers. "How are you?"

She gave him a gentle hug.

"Okay, I guess," Mikey said.

She felt his wet hair. "Still raining outside?"

Mikey shook his head no. "Can I use the microfilm again?"

"Sure. Come on." Together they walked down the aisles, but this time Miss Jennings led him away from the stairs leading to the basement.

"But first, I want to show you something. Sit here for a minute," she said as she pulled out a chair. Mikey watched her disappear down an aisle. Curious, he sat down and waited for her. He thought about the first time he met Miss Jennings. It was fourth grade and he sat alone near these same tables after school one day reading a book about the United States Marine Corps. She came over and picked up his jacket that had fallen off the back of his chair. She took it and placed it near him as a mother would do for her son. She smiled at him then walked off. Mikey never forgot that moment. And he spent many a time revisiting that image over the years just for comfort. He supposed that's why he kept coming back to the library since then.

A few minutes later, Miss Jennings returned with a couple of books in her hands. She gently placed them on the table in front of Mikey. Then, she began to thumb through one of them.

"I know the last couple of days have been hard for you," she said softly. "And I know you want to give up on everything. But I don't think you should, Mikey."

He looked at her with raised eyebrows as though shocked by what he'd heard.

"Yeah, well, investigative reporting isn't what I thought it would be," he sighed. "Sometimes things are better left uncovered, you know?"

"Mikey, Lexie came to see me yesterday. She told me what happened and why you all were looking for Mrs. Stevenson at her shop that day."

"What? What do you mean?" he asked.

Mikey looked away with embarrassment. *Oh great*, he thought. *Now even Miss Jennings thinks I'm nuts.*

Miss Jennings tapped his arm and he looked into her warm eyes.

"And, no, I do not think you're crazy," she said. "Mikey, I believe you," she said.

He stared hard at her and sat up straight.

"Wait, what?" he said. "You do?"

She nodded and smiled that familiar smile.

"*I believe you.* It makes sense that the bus driver would be the killer of those girls and the one who would kill those school children," she said. "I looked up some of the articles and I think your uncle Kevin knew something about the bus driver. And that's why he and his friends were killed. They knew too much."

Mikey felt his face become warm.

"I think the ghost of Kevin Thompson *is* trying to tell you something. I think he wants you to help solve the crime. It makes sense. He's your dad's uncle. No wonder he would reach out to you for help."

"Really? You think he's reaching out to me?" he said with a wide smile.

But the smile quickly left his face as he thought more about it.

"Yeah, but I'm all alone now. My friends can't help me anymore. I have to do this all by myself." He rested his chin on his palm. "What can I do? I'm just a 12 year old little kid. I'm barely over five feet, five inches tall. I can't play hockey, or football, or—

Miss Jennings nudged him as she opened the books she had brought to the table. "And that's why I want to show you a few things," she said.

She flipped through a few pages then pointed to a photograph of Audie Murphy, the famous World War II hero.

"You know, Mikey," she said. "Audie Murphy, the most decorated soldier from World War II, was a little guy." She pointed to another photograph of the hero.

"He was only five feet five inches tall yet look at all he accomplished!"

Mikey listened as Miss Jennings read a list of the medals awarded to the American soldier.

"Medal of Honor, Medal of Conduct, Purple Heart, Bronze Star, Distinguished Service Cross and the list goes on and on…" Mikey was intrigued with the story. He leaned in and looked at the many bright colorful photographs of the famous soldier. "He was even a movie star."

"Wow," Mikey mumbled.

Then, she pulled out another book and showed him a photograph of another American hero.

"This is Lewis "Chesty" Puller," she said. "He is a highly decorated and respected Marine in the United States Marine Corps."

Mikey studied the photograph of the tough looking man with a chest full of military ribbons. "Yeah, I've heard of him," he said.

"He was known for being a warrior on the battlefield and guess what?" she asked.

"What?"

"He was a little guy too. He was only five feet seven inches tall." She grinned and closed the book. "You see, Mikey. How tall or how big you are doesn't matter when it comes to doing the right thing. Yeah you may be a little kid, but you can still do heroic things."

She opened another book and flipped to a page with the famous painting of George Washington on it.

"Mikey, when our first President was 12 years old, he was already doing geometry and trigonometry at home."

"Really?" Mikey studied the photograph of the painting.

She nodded and pointed to another painting of the president. "And at age fifteen, he started his own business as a land surveyor." She flipped to another page.

"His own business?" Mikey asked incredulously, "as a teenager?"

She nodded again and pointed to another photograph. "And this is Alexander Hamilton." Mikey looked at the photograph of a painting of a very distinguished man with silver hair and a dark suit.

"Who's he?" he asked.

"He was our first Secretary of the Treasury and when he was only 12 years old, he was helping his mother run a business in the West Indies…in *two* languages." She held up two fingers. "He was an avid reader and read both Greek and Roman classics."

"Cool," he said. "I had no idea…"

She closed the book. "History is a wonderful thing, Mikey. We can look to the past and see that many came before us to lead the way so that we might be able to do great things, too."

Mikey ran his fingers over the book.

"At *any* age," she said.

Mikey took in all she had said.

"Yes, you are only 12 years old and a little kid." She put her hand on his shoulder. "But you can still do great things…" She slid the books over to him, "…Just like these great men did. I know you can do this. You have it in you. I can see it. And I think Kevin sees it too."

She smiled. "So, promise me that you won't give up."

He looked up into her kind face.

"I promise," he said. He carefully stacked the books on top of each other and thought about what the Reverend said about the past and forgetting about it. He compared it to what Miss Jennings showed him in the books. Then, he stood to leave. "I will. I'll do the right thing."

"Good. That's the spirit," she said.

"By the way, how did your date with my dad go the other night?" he asked.

She stood and nervously adjusted her glasses while fumbling with the chair.

"Oh, well, it was…uh, it was… pleasant, I guess you could say that. Yes that's the word. *Pleasant*, I guess," she said with a look of embarrassment. "Thank you for, uh, asking. Your father is a very nice man. A true gentleman." She picked up the history books and hugged them close to her body like a shield for protection.

"Pleasant?" Mikey said. "*That's all*?" He knew his voice sounded disappointed even though he didn't mean it to. He had high hopes for the two of them hitting it off.

"Um, well, you know. It's always hard for two people to hit it off right away." She played with her earrings.

"Yeah, but you two have known each other for a long time, and…"

"We knew of each other a long time *ago* back in high school, if you can even call it that." She turned her head. "Mikey, your dad, well, he said he's not ready."

Mikey cocked his head.

"Huh?" he asked. "No ready. Not ready for what?"

She nudged her glasses up the bridge of her nose and cleared her throat.

"You see, he said he's just not ready for a, um…a relationship at this time in his life," her voice filled with emotion and Mikey could see tears form in her eyes. "and so, well, uh, let's just leave it at that."

Mikey felt his blood boil. He couldn't believe his father said that to Miss Jennings. *Isn't ready?* He thought. *Who's he kidding? It's been over three years now since the divorce. Why is he doing this? How could he hurt Miss Jennings the nicest most kindest of all people?*

Mikey exhaled and rubbed his forehead in frustration.

"I'm sorry," Mikey said. "I'll talk to him."

"No, Mikey. Please don't tell him what I told you." She raised her palm to him. She seemed nervous.

"Oh, okay, I won't," he sighed. "But please don't give up on him yet."

"Thanks, and well, I hope he and I do see each other again soon." She turned to head back to her books. "Thanks for coming, Mikey. I hope you feel better. Let me know how Destrey is doing, okay?"

He could hear the disappointment in her voice and see it in the way she walked off with her shoulders hunched over and her head down.

"I will," he said as she walked off. "And thanks for, you know…everything."

She turned, smiled, and waved.

"Of course. Anytime," she said.

And she means it, he thought as he pushed in his chair and turned to leave. *She would be there anytime to help me…or anyone, for that matter. I can't believe he could be mean to such a nice lady. What was he thinking? He wasn't thinking, that's the problem. At least he wasn't thinking about what we need.*

§

A couple of days later, Mikey sat in his room on his bed for a few minutes that Thanksgiving morning. He wore his black dress shoes, black slacks, and a fuzzy sweater his grandmother sent him. She always expected everyone to dress up for Thanksgiving at her house. All that remained on his bedroom walls were the articles from the school newspaper that he had written and a JAWS movie poster above his bed. Mikey walked over and stood in front of the mirror that hung on the back of his door. He hated the sweater and the way he looked in it. He thought about his dad again.

Why does my dad do this stuff? He thought. *He had a chance for a real nice relationship and he blows it. What's he afraid of? Doesn't he know she isn't coming back anytime soon?*

Mikey looked intently at himself in the mirror. "She isn't

coming back anytime soon," he said out loud to no one there. "Ever."

Who are you to judge him? He thought. *You're just as afraid as he is. You're a big fat chicken. You're afraid of everything...*

He put his hand inside his pocket and pulled out the silver key. He had almost forgotten it, but decided to keep it with him at all times hoping it might trigger a memory or something. Now he just wanted to throw it away and forget about the whole thing.

You're afraid to investigate any further. You're afraid to do it alone, he thought. *You're afraid of what you might find.*

He inspected the key again. It had no markings on it to make it special, but he had a feeling the box it belonged to had special meaning to Kevin, his uncle.

"Mikey, let's go!" his dad shouted from downstairs breaking his concentration. He put the key down on his dresser and opened the bedroom door. Then, he hesitated for a second. He turned and picked up the key, gripping it in his palm again. He thought, for a moment, about throwing it away. But something inside told him not to. He put it back in his pocket.

In the truck, the two sat in silence as they drove passed rows and rows of trees lining the highway. The sun shone, but piles of snow were seen alongside the road. Each night for several days the snow fell and Mikey knew the pond was frozen solid again. He also knew his friends were back to practicing on it for the hockey tournament coming up in January. He leaned his head on the window glass and sighed. He knew nothing would ever be the same again. He wished he'd given Chad that hockey stick after all.

His dad reached over and fiddled with the radio until settling on some station that played a song by George Jones. Mikey listened to the music for a few seconds. Then another song came on. This time it was by Olivia Newton-John. He remembered her from his mother's record albums. He leaned forward and turned down the radio.

"Dad," his voice was barely above a whisper.

"Yeah son," his dad answered in a flat voice. He tapped his hand on the steering wheel to the rhythm of the song.

"I'm, uh, sorry... about the other day," Mikey mumbled.

"Don't worry about it," his dad said.

Mikey looked over at him. His dad looked alert as he drove. His face was clean shaven. He wore a dress jacket over a sweater and his usual jeans with boots. In his mouth was a toothpick. Mikey felt pangs of guilt as they drove. He suddenly felt sorry for his dad now that he knew his grandparents blamed him for the death of Kevin. He realized how hard it must be for his dad to appear at their house year after year as though nothing ever happened.

The truck pulled up into the long driveway of his grandparents' house. They came out and waved. Before Mikey opened the truck door, his dad touched his arm.

"Thanks for apologizing, Mike," his dad said. "Means a lot."

"Sure," Mikey said.

"And…" his dad inhaled, "You're right."

Mikey cocked his head. "Huh?"

"You're right. She…your mom…um, she left because of *me* not because of anything you did. Understand?"

Mikey sat there looking into his father's eyes and he slowly nodded.

"Hey, do you believe me?" his dad asked.

Mikey looked away and shook his head no.

"Hey, Mike," his dad said. "Look at me."

Mikey reluctantly looked at his dad again.

"She left because of *me*, not you."

His dad reached over and gave Mikey a big hug. Mikey could smell the Old Spice cologne on his dad's cheek. It made him feel safe. He hugged his dad back realizing that was the first time since the accident on the ice that they had really hugged.

"Now let's go eat some turkey." His dad got out of the truck and walked toward his waiting parents.

§

The Thanksgiving feast at grandma's house was the same every year: a twenty-pound turkey stuffed with grandma's famous cornbread and pecan stuffing with rosemary seasoning. Rows of every sort of vegetable lined the center of the table making a colorful display. Homemade baked dinner rolls, homemade cranberry sauce, her famous gravy in an antique gravy boat, and grandma's finest silver all adorned the long mahogany table. Mikey sat in his usual spot watching grandpa carve the turkey. Everything smelled amazing. They said grace first and then everyone dug in. His grandparent's neighbors joined in the feast along with some of Mikey's younger cousins visiting from Omaha. He remained quiet as he ate more and more food that was passed to him by arms reaching over his plate from every direction.

I guess they think I need to eat or something, he thought as he scooped more mashed potatoes onto his plate. Before he knew it, everyone had slowed down, leaned back, and began to drink coffee as the homemade pumpkin pie was passed around. Mikey declined any dessert and excused himself from the table. He decided to leave the adults there to talk sports and politics.

As they talked, Mikey meandered through the living room and, for the first time, noticed the décor. It was similar to Miss Jennings's home. Grandma had many antiques in her home mixed in with newer furniture. He leaned in and inspected all the nicely framed photographs of his father. There were school photos and some family photos mixed in with grandpa's retirement photos and a vacation picture of his grandparents in Hawaii. They looked happy in the photograph.

Oddly, there were no photographs anywhere in the room of his dad with Kevin. So, Mikey decided to see what lined the hallway. He flipped on the hall light and gazed into each photograph that hung on either side of the hallway. These photos were old black and white photos of his grandparents when they were young. Mikey didn't care much for those. So, he was about to leave the hallway when he noticed he was by a door to a bedroom. He reached out and twisted the door knob. The door was unlocked. He began to push open the door, but paused and looked down the hall to see if anyone spied him. He knew his cousins were outside playing touch football on the lawn and the adults were still talking. Satisfied that he wasn't being watched, Mikey opened the door and entered the room.

CHAPTER 26

The Keepsake Box

As Mikey looked around the room, he noticed a few things that seemed familiar to him. He noticed a pennant from his school on the wall, but it was older and slightly faded. A few books on the bookshelf were similar to the books he had in his own room at home. And the bookcase on the opposite wall matched his bed at home. That's when he realized he was in his dad's former bedroom. Mikey quietly looked around the room and walked over to the closet doors. When he opened them, he saw that no clothes hung on the hangers, but a few old suitcases were stacked on the top shelf. It reeked of moth balls. On the bottom in the back of the closet were some boxes. He reached in and pulled one out then opened it up. He winced when he saw the contents. Old trophies.

"Huh?" Mikey said as he reached in and pulled a trophy out. It was a hockey trophy. He looked in and saw more hockey trophies inside. One was for football and all had his father's name engraved on them. *I don't get it,* he thought. Mikey put the trophies back into the box and he slid it into the back of closet. He closed the closet door and turned around.

Mikey saw another door across the bedroom. He approached it and opened the door only to discover the bathroom. A few old cologne bottles sat atop the counter, all the towels matched, and it looked impeccably clean. But it was the door across the way that intrigued Mikey. He knew the bathroom connected with another bedroom.

He slowly opened the connecting door and found himself inside his Uncle Kevin's former bedroom. The room had a musty smell to it like dust mixed with rain. Mikey looked around at the old western themed posters on the walls. The lamp by the bed was made from a cowboy boot. The lamp shade had horses on it and so did the curtains. One wall was covered with cowboy themed wall paper. Mikey walked over to the small twin bed and sat on it. The mattress was stiff. He wasn't surprised since no one had slept on it for probably many years. He sat in his uncle's room for a moment and gazed around. He liked it. Everything felt comfortable as though a kid his age lived there. A thought came to his mind.

A keepsake box, he thought. He stood and began looking around the room for anything resembling a keepsake box, but he didn't find anything. He took out the silver key from his pocket and fingered it, still curious about why Kevin showed it to him. He went to put back inside his pocket, but it slipped. Then the sound of the silver key hitting the wooden floor startled him. He watched it bounce under the bed.

Mikey bent down and started to look for it, but was interrupted when he heard some loud laughter coming from the family room. He hurried over to the door and opened it enough to peek out. He could hear more laughter and smelled some vanilla scented pipe smoke. He knew the adults were probably playing cards now and his grandpa was smoking his pipe.

Mikey closed the door and quickly looked under the bed for the silver key. He couldn't see it lying nearby, so he used his hand to feel around the dusty floor under the bed for it. He couldn't feel anything, so he lay down and peered under the bed. He reached for it again and grabbed the key, but when he did his whole body froze up.

He couldn't believe his eyes. Right there under the bed was a keepsake box. Mikey quickly grabbed it along with the key. He sat down on the bed with the box on his lap. *A keepsake box*, he thought. *Could it be the one?*

It was made of wood stained dark and varnished to a shine. It was covered in dust, so Mikey wiped it clean with the sleeve of his sweater. He picked it up and turned it around inspecting it for any clues. There was no engraving or any marks that made it unique at all. Then he took out the key and put it into the lock.

It fit.

Should I open it? He thought. His hands quivered. He closed his eyes and slowly twisted the key. He heard the lid pop open. Mikey opened his eyes and carefully lifted the lid. Inside the box, he saw only a small piece of paper and a one dollar bill. He picked up the paper. "Happy birthday!" was all it read. He picked up the dollar bill. It was dated 1961.

He probably got it for his birthday that year, Mikey thought. He put everything back in the box and closed it, locked it, then put the key back in his pocket. *That's it? That's all that's in there? That's the clue I was supposed to find? What the heck does it all mean?*

He set the keepsake box down on the bed and stared at it for a few minutes thinking about what to do next. *Maybe I should show it to Miss Jennings. Maybe she'll know what to do.* He thought heard someone coming, so, he quickly took off his sweater and wrapped the box in it. Then he headed back to his dad's bedroom and waited. When he heard no one in the hallway, he peeked out the bedroom door and quietly walked to the front door. The television was on, blaring the football game. The Dallas Cowboys were playing the St. Louis Cardinals. No one paid attention to Mikey sneaking by.

"Where ya headed Mikey?" he heard his grandpa ask from the other room.

"Uh, out to the truck for a minute," he said as he walked out the door with only his undershirt and pants on.

"You should put that sweater on. It's still pretty cold out," his grandpa shouted after him.

"Um, okay, grandpa. I will," Mikey said as he closed the front door and headed for the truck. He opened the truck door and placed the box wrapped in his sweater on the floor of the truck under the passenger side hoping his dad wouldn't see it there.

"I'll deal with the box later," he mumbled to himself. And he slammed the truck door closed.

§

The drive home was quiet. Mikey was glad his dad never said anything about the fact that his son wasn't wearing a sweater that cold evening. Mikey stared out the window as they drove along the highway. The sun peeked through the trees as they passed by the window. The snow piled up on the side of the road had a bluish glow to it. He sat and tried to figure out what he would do next to solve this mystery. Of course, he'd have to do it alone now that no one was allowed to help him.

"Did you get enough to eat?" his dad asked. "Because grandma packed up some leftovers and—"

"Yep. I'm stuffed, thanks Dad!" After the truck pulled into the driveway, Mikey grabbed his sweater off the floor of the cab and headed upstairs before his dad could say anything else. He closed his bedroom door shut and waited for his dad's footsteps. Instead, he heard the television turn on and the sounds of a football game playing. He knew his dad would crack open a beer and fall asleep on the couch as usual.

Mikey placed the keepsake box on his dresser, sat on his bed, and stared at the box across the room. He crossed his legs and rested his elbows on his thighs in deep thought trying desperately to figure out why a ghost would want him to see a dollar bill inside a keepsake box.

What do I do now? He thought. *I guess I could continue interviewing people. But who's gonna want to talk to me now? I'm the kid that almost got Destrey killed. I'm the kid who believes in ghosts. I'm the kid who thinks there's a killer out there. No one's gonna want to talk to me.*

When the room turned dark, he reached over and turned on the lamp. He continued to stare at the box on the dresser across the room. *Talk to me*, he thought. *Tell me something. I need to know more from you.* In some way, he hoped Kevin could hear him. He slid over to his pillow, propped it up, and then lay back on his bed. He folded his hands on his chest thinking more about the ghosts.

What does it all mean? He thought. *A dollar bill and a happy birthday note? It doesn't make any sense, yet the ghosts wanted me to find it. Kevin wanted me in that room.*

The phone rang interrupting his thoughts. He could hear his father walk to the phone and answer it. The voice was garbled. The receiver went down hard.

"Mikey!" his father shouted.

Mikey ran to the door and headed downstairs. He found his father strapping on his gun holster.

"I just got a call. They pulled another body out of the pond," he said. His face looked worried.

"Oh, okay," Mikey couldn't believe it. *Another* dead body?

His dad put on his heavy coat and walked over to Mikey.

"Son, it's...well," his dad sighed heavily. "Son, it looks like it's the body of Mrs. Stevenson."

Mikey's eyes widened and his mouth dropped open.

"Isn't she that older lady you and your friends went to visit the other—"

"Yes," Mikey interrupted him. He covered his mouth with his hand. His stomach turned. "I…I can't believe it. I just talked with her at the funeral." He sat down on the step still gripping the banister as though he needed it for balance.

"Sorry, son," his dad said. He put on his cowboy hat and opened the door that lead to the garage. "You stay here. Don't head out to the pond or anything. I'll probably be late. Call grandma if you need anything. Okay?"

Mikey felt himself nod his head, but he was still stuck in fog of confusion. Mrs. Stevenson's face came into his mind.

"Mikey," his dad said.

Mikey looked at him.

"You okay?"

"Uh, yeah, dad. I'm okay. Just shocked, I guess."

His dad squeezed his shoulder then headed out the door.

Mikey sat by himself listening to the garage open and the truck engine start. And then he heard it back away out of the garage. *She's dead*, he thought. *How'd this happen? I just spoke to her the other*— He quickly pulled on his boots and coat then headed out the door.

§

"Mikey, I'm not supposed to talk to you," Lexie said in the doorway of her home.

"I know, but I've got something important to tell you," he whispered so her parents wouldn't hear him. "Please come out for a minute. Tell them it's Chad or something."

She sighed then carefully closed the door.

Mikey paced back and forth in the driveway for a few minutes. Many houses already had Christmas lights blinking in the night.

Finally, she came out through the side door of the garage. She wore a pink knit cap with matching pink mittens. He thought she looked like ice cream.

"Thanks." He motioned for her to come across the street.

"Mikey, what is it?"

"Mrs. Stevenson," he said.

"Yeah?"

"She's dead."

Lexie gasped and cupped her mitten covered hands over her mouth. She reacted exactly like he knew she would.

"What? When?" she asked. "*How?*"

"I don't know, but my dad just got the call." Mikey started walking toward Chad's house. "They pulled her body out of the pond."

"The usual dumping ground…" she whispered with a faraway look in her eyes.

"Yep. And I think the killer was in the car that hit Destrey that night," he said. "Remember?"

"What? Really? How do you know, though? Did you see him? Did you get a good look at his face?" She walked a few steps then stopped.

"No, but I have a feeling," he said.

"Mikey, I can't go any further. I'll get in trouble." She looked back in the direction of her house.

Mikey frowned, revealing his disappointment.

"Yeah, okay," he murmured. "I guess I messed up big time, huh?"

She gently touched his arm.

"No, we all went with you on our own. No one forced us to go with you. That car hit Destrey. There was nothing you could do about it. And now if you know it was the killer inside that car, well then that explains why he came after us. Mikey, he was probably going to hurt all of us," Lexie said.

"Yeah, well, the parents don't see it that way," he said. He walked off. "Night."

Lexie watched him walk away with hunched shoulders.

"Night." Then she headed back home.

"Hey, loser!" Came a shout from in front of Mikey. He recognized the angry voice of Donnie. Chad and Stan were walking with him with their hockey sticks in hand and skates slung over their shoulders by the laces.

"Shut up, Donnie." Chad nudged him then turned to Mike. "Hey, Mike. How've you been?"

"Hey," Mikey said without making eye contact.

"What are you doing out here? There's no way you're gonna play hockey with us," Donnie said.

"Donnie, *shut up!*" Chad said. "Man, keep walking. I'll meet you guys there."

"If you're heading toward the pond, you won't be able skate on it tonight," Mikey said.

"Oh yeah? Why not?" Donnie said.

"Because they found another dead body," Mikey answered. He began to walk away toward the pond leaving the boys behind.

"What? Who is it?" Chad asked.

"Mrs. Stevenson," Mikey said as he walked off. He could hear them discussing what they'd just heard.

"Hey, Mikey, wait up!" Chad shouted.

CHAPTER 27
The Letter

Mikey carefully made his way through the thick tree branches with the headlights of the many patrol cars ahead guiding his way. Chad, Donnie, and Stan followed closely behind navigating over logs and rocks.

"Shhh!" Mikey said. "You're making too much noise.

Then, they stopped right at the edge of the forest spying on the investigation of the latest murder. They spotted Detective Williams and Mikey's dad talking while Deputy Rogers placed the usual yellow caution tape once again around the edge of the pond.

"Well, Sheriff, this probably wasn't committed by an old bum," Detective Williams said.

"Nope," Mikey's dad said. They both stood over a dead body covered with a white sheet. The detective bent down and lifted up part of the sheet.

"Looks like a bashed in skull," he said.

Donnie cringed. "Ewww, gross," he whispered.

"Shh!" Chad said.

"Yes, and a slit throat," the Sheriff said.

"I think I'm gonna puke." Donnie covered his mouth.

"Shhh!" Mikey said.

"I took plenty of photos of the scene and the medical examiner is ready to take the body," Mikey's dad said. "A tragic ending for such a nice lady."

"I sent a patrol car over to her house," the detective said. "He radioed back that they found a lot of blood in the back of the quilt shop, forced entry in the back, and her car is stolen. No fingerprints."

"The killer probably wore gloves." Mikey's dad scratched his head underneath his cowboy hat.

"Was it a robbery?" Deputy Rogers asked as he approached them.

"Nope. All the money was still in the register and her business checkbook was still there under the front counter." The detective wrote down a few notes.

"I still don't get it." Mikey's dad shook his head. "Why would someone want to hurt her like this?"

Mikey couldn't believe what he heard.

"She must have been dead when we went to see her," he said. "That's why she didn't answer the door and that's why her car was gone."

They watched as the coroner and his assistant lifted the body bag onto the gurney and wheeled her off to the waiting van.

"She was such a nice lady," Deputy Rogers said to Mikey's dad.

"Yes. Yes she was," Mikey heard his dad say as he headed toward the patrol car.

Mikey felt his eyes sting with tears.

"I can't believe this is happening," he said. He turned to leave. The others followed him. "Dang, she knew who the killer was, too."

"Oh, here we go again," Donnie said. He stormed passed Mikey and out of the forest.

"What's that supposed to mean?" Mikey asked.

Donnie turned around revealing anger in his eyes.

"You're crazy!" He pointed at Mikey. "You probably still believe in that stupid ghost story, huh?"

"It isn't stupid!"

Donnie waved off Mikey and stormed off.

"Like I said, you're crazy," he muttered.

"You saw the ghost too, same as I did!" Mikey shouted after him.

"Will you two knock it off?" Chad said.

"No, I won't knock it off. He saw the ghost that night!" Mikey said.

Donnie came stomping back.

"I don't know what I saw. All I know is that you led us on some wild goose chase, Destrey was almost killed, and now this old lady ends up dead," he shoved his finger into Mikey's chest. "You know what I think? I think you're bad luck!"

Mikey pushed his finger away. "Who cares what you think!"

But Donnie persisted. "Yeah, I think you're bad luck and anyone who hangs around with you ends up hurt or dead!"

"Guys, knock it off!" Chad stepped between them, but Donnie's large body overwhelmed him. He shoved Chad aside then he turned to Mikey and shoved him hard.

"You're a freak!" Donnie screamed. "It's no wonder your mom left you!"

And that's all Mikey needed to hear. The next thing he knew, he was moving his arms so fast he couldn't see them anymore. He tasted blood in his mouth and felt pain in his chest, but other than that, he didn't know what was happening until he felt the ground under his back and Chad lying on top of him trying to hold him down.

"Mikey, stop!" Chad shouted. Mikey looked at his friend's face pale with fright and worry.

"Leave me alone," Mikey said. He pushed Chad off his chest, rolled over, and got to his feet. He saw Donnie sitting on the ground with Stanny hovering over him. Blood dripped from Donnie's mouth and he was crying.

Mikey spit blood onto the muddy snow and wiped his mouth. Chad stood next to him.

"You hit him good, Mike," Chad said. "He won't bother you anymore, that's for sure."

"Doesn't matter," Mikey said. "Nothing matters anymore."

He turned and took off running toward his house as fast as he could.

§

That next Monday, Mikey sat at the kitchen table working on his homework. School had been almost unbearable that day. Not only was everyone talking about him, but most were angry with him thanks to Donnie's lies. Heck, even the lunch ladies looked at him funny, so he decided to eat lunch alone in the hall. To make things worse, his homeroom teacher hung up a large poster board for everyone to sign and take to Destrey who was home from the hospital. Every time Mikey looked at that poster, he felt ill. Christmas was coming, and so was the end of 1976. Mikey was beginning to think it would end up as the worst year of his life. With Christmastime, came decorations. After school, each classroom began to decorate for the Christmas decorating contest they had every year. Lexie and the other girls made paper chains out of red and green construction paper and hung them from the ceiling. Chad, Donnie and the other boys cut out snowflakes from white paper and taped them to the windows while music played in the background. His teacher asked him to stay and help, but Mikey's heart just wasn't into it. So, he walked home alone.

Now he sat at home, alone, trying to finish a writing assignment, but nothing was coming to his mind except images of Mrs. Stevenson, Destrey lying on the ground in pain, and the keepsake box.

For the first time in a long time, he wasn't excited for Christmas. Most of the houses were decorated and the shops down town already had lights up with big Christmas trees in their windows. But all he could think about was how Mrs. Stevenson was killed and how he lost all his friends.

Mikey turned his head and looked at the blank wall at the other end of the family room. That's where his mom usually put the Christmas tree. He and his dad would go pick one out at the lot at the edge of town and bring it home while his mom played Christmas music on the hi fi system. He loved decorating the tree with the scent of baking cookies coming from the kitchen. Those were happier times. Mikey closed his eyes and regretted how he never truly appreciated those times like he does now. But it's too late. Everything was lost.

He sighed and scribbled something onto the blank piece of wide ruled paper in front of him. He heard the garage door open and his dad's truck pull in. Moments later, his dad walked in.

"Hey son," he said. "How was school…or should I not ask?"

"Don't ask." Mikey leaned his head on his hand. He could hear his dad shuffling through the mail.

"Oh, I completely forgot." His dad walked over and tossed an unopened letter onto the table. "You got some mail last week, but with the holiday and, well, everything…I forgot to give it to you."

Mikey looked at the letter. It was addressed to him, but there was no address showing who had sent it. Intrigued, Mikey picked it up and tore it open.

"Dear Michael," it read in a woman's cursive handwriting. "I'm writing this to you in case something happens to me."

He scanned down to the end of the letter where it was signed:

Mrs. Stevenson.

"Holy cow!" he shouted.

"What is it?" his dad asked from the kitchen.

"Uh, nothing," Mikey said and grabbed his notebook and the letter. He headed upstairs. "It's just a letter…stating that I won…a writing contest."

"Hey that's terrific!" his dad said.

"Yeah, well, I'm going upstairs." Mikey rushed up the stairs, entered his bedroom, and then sat down on the bed with his letter. It was post-marked the day she was killed. *She must have mailed it that morning*, he thought.

"*I hope I am wrong, but I don't think I am,*" she wrote. "*You see, I have discovered that the killer of those precious children is: The Reverend Johnson.*"

Mikey gasped and read that line over again. "Holy cow," he murmured. Then, he continued reading.

"It took some researching, but I did it! The Reverend is Mr. Davis, the very same bus driver from Sherman Oaks. Michael, he is a very dangerous man. He has disguised himself as a layman reverend, but he is not. Please tell your father the news and ask him to do some digging on the Reverend. And Michael, please keep away from the Reverend. Let your father handle things."

"Mikey," his dad shouted from downstairs. Mikey jumped.

"Uh, yeah?"

"I have to head to a town meeting at the church," he said.

Mikey furrowed his brow. "Why?" he opened the door and asked.

"The townspeople want to talk about the recent murder. Seems there are some fears and concerns," he said and peeked up the stairs. "You stay here, okay? Remember, you're grounded; so stay here."

"Uh, sure, Dad," Mikey said. He hated being grounded for fighting with Donnie, but that's how it had to be. *Should I tell him about the letter now?* He thought. *But I haven't read it all yet. I'd better wait until he gets back.*

"Okay. I'll be back in about an hour." His dad picked up his keys.

"Hey Dad," Mikey shouted down the stairs.

"Yeah?"

"Will Reverend Johnson be there?" Mikey asked.

"I believe so. Why?"

"Um…just wondering. Thanks!" Mikey closed his door. He could hear his dad's truck pull out and head down the street. Mikey picked up the letter and continued reading.

"Michael, I wrote this letter and sent it off today because I know he will come for me. And if you are reading this letter, my deepest fears have come true. But I wanted you to know the story.

Years ago, when I worked at the school, Mr. Davis found out his wife was having an affair with Dr. Ed Stuckey. That's why he killed her. I believe your uncle Kevin discovered this and that's why he and his little friends were drowned on that school bus. So many people suspected that the bus driver escaped to Canada. Years later, on a trip to see my cousins in Toronto, I went to the records office on hunch that maybe, just maybe Mr. Davis had escaped to Canada after the murders. Well, after much research, I discovered that a man who looked exactly like Mr. Davis did live in a small town near Toronto. The town is our sister town, Kew Gardens. I went there and found out the man was working there as a school janitor. But before I could question him, I discovered that he left that school and came back to Minnesota. I drove down to some smaller towns around Sherman Oaks and asked around and showed them a photo of Mr. Davis. Soon, I discovered that a man resembling him worked for another small town school as the janitor. So, I went to the school and hid across the street so I could spot him. That's when I saw him! I saw Mr. Davis. I knew it was him.

I told the police, but they did not believe me without more proof. Michael, that was about ten years ago. I had to return to Sherman Oaks. I couldn't follow this man forever. But I would go and visit that small town every chance I could and each time, there he was working at that school.

Inevitably, it happened, as I feared it would. One day Mr. Davis wasn't there when I visited the town. I asked the school and they said the janitor left suddenly. I returned to Sherman Oaks defeated. I felt I had let your Uncle Kevin and principal Stuckey down. I didn't know what else to do.

It was around that time that our Reverend Ellis decided to retire. He introduced us to his replacement, Reverend Johnson, a layman preacher from a small town down south. I thought he looked familiar, but I dismissed my feelings right away. The Reverend had white hair and a beard and he talked differently. He even carried himself differently. So, I put my suspicions aside.

Yet, something about the Reverend always bothered me. He didn't know much about the Bible and He didn't seem to have much time for his parishioners. When I talked to him about this, he would become irate. Still, I guess he was a decent man. No one else seemed bothered.

One day, I saw Ed Stuckey talking to Reverend Johnson near the church. I could tell they were arguing. I hid around the back of the church and listened in. That's when I heard Ed Stuckey say that he knew the Reverend was really Mr. Davis! Frankly, I feel Mr. Davis returned to get even with Dr. Stuckey.

They argued and the Reverend threatened Ed with some harsh words, so I decided to investigate even further. That was as recent as three years ago. Unfortunately, Ed Stuckey began to drink more and more. I knew the likelihood of anyone believing his story about the Reverend was slim at best. When Reverend Johnson saw Ed had become a drunk and a disgrace, I suppose he decided not to kill him as long as he kept quiet. I knew it was up to me to investigate and prove that Ed Stuckey was right. I was a fool. I should have just gone to the police. Now look at all that's happened. It's too late for me.

Michael, I have proof that Reverend Johnson is Mr. Davis, the murderer that haunted Sherman Oaks for years, and he is the same man who drove that school bus into the pond. I wanted to show you my proof, but if you are reading this letter, well, it never happened.

It's up to you now! I know you will do the right thing. Take this letter to your father and ask him to investigate further. Ask him to go to Kew Gardens and talk to the police about any suspicious disappearances there. You can do it, Michael! I have also sent letters to the police at Kew Gardens and to the police in the city explaining to them the evidence I uncovered. I have included photographs of Mr. Davis and the Reverend for you and your father to compare.

Please be careful! Mr. Davis has killed many times before. He will not hesitate to hurt you once he finds out you have this letter. And if something has happened to me, please know that you had nothing to do with it. You are a good boy! I am proud of you."

"*Sincerely*," Mikey read out loud. *"Mrs. Stevenson."*

He covered his eyes with his hands felt them fill with tears as he remembered her soft grandmotherly hug. *It's too late for me*, he heard her voice inside his head.

"I'm so sorry, Mrs. Stevenson," he sobbed. "I'm so sorry that he killed you! I should have gotten there sooner. I should have been there to help you."

Mikey stood then grabbed a book off his desk and threw it across the room. "I hate this!"

He looked at the letter lying on the bed. "I hate letting people down all the time. I've got to do something about this."

He picked up the letter then ran downstairs, put on his coat, and headed to the church.

§

Mikey slowly approached the church doors which were pried open. People passed by him as they entered the foyer. They were discussing the recent murders as they walked by and removed their coats. Mikey gulped. They seemed a lot angrier than he expected. *You can do this,* he thought. *You can tell these people the truth. Who cares if they scream at you and call you crazy.* He sighed.

As he stepped inside the church, he saw his father in the foyer talking to the Reverend.

"That's a nice jacket," his dad said to the Reverend. He fingered a winter coat that hung on a nearby chair.

"What? Oh that's an old coat of mine," the Reverend said.

"I see here it has a tear in it. Seems a piece of the fabric has been torn off," Mikey's dad said as he held up the coat.

"Like I said." The Reverend seemed nervous. "It's an old coat." He quickly picked up the coat and took it with him into the sanctuary. Mikey could see the Reverend was anxious to get away from his dad, the Sheriff. Mikey saw his father join several townspeople in the pews. They were murmuring and gesturing with their hands as though in a heated discussion. Mikey swallowed hard. He could see Destrey's father there along with Donnie's father. He saw Chad sitting with his parents and Lexie sitting by her parents.

Oh great, he thought. *Everyone's here.* He hesitated briefly, and then fingered the letter inside his pocket. *No, you cannot back down. You've got to do this. You've got to do this for Mrs. Stevenson....and for Kevin...and for Destrey.*

He walked into the sanctuary and immediately, his eyes found Miss Jennings sitting in the back. She grinned at him, but then her brow crinkled as though concerned. Mikey guessed that his face showed his fear. He was glad she was there, but he shivered because he was scared to death. He turned his head and looked up the center aisle. That's where he saw the Reverend sitting in the front. Mikey squinted his eyes and stared him down.

"Now, look Sheriff, we want answers!" Donnie's dad stood and shouted.

"Yeah, what's going on around here?" a woman asked.

Mikey's dad stood to speak. "We're still investigating. I cannot discuss an open case," he said.

"Ah come on," said one man. "Quit beating around the bush and tell us what we need to know!"

"Yes! Tell us what's going on?" a woman shouted.

"I know what's going on!" Mikey interrupted. Immediately, all the people turned their heads to look at him. He felt a rush of blood reach his head and dizziness come over him.

"What are you talking about?" Donnie's father asked. He looked very angry. "Sheriff, get a hold of your crazy kid."

Mikey's dad studied his son's face. "What is it, son?"

Mikey held up the letter. "This!" he shouted. The peopled looked at the letter in his hand. "This is a letter from the late Mrs. Stevenson!"

A woman gasped. Mikey's father furrowed his brow as though bewildered.

"Yes, it's true!" Mikey shouted.

The Reverend shot him a venomous look. But Mikey stood firm and stared back.

"That's right, a letter from the victim stating who her killer was," Mikey continued.

A woman stood to leave.

"No one's going anywhere," Mikey said. The woman looked at him then slowly sat back down. "Listen to me. I read this letter today. In it, she reveals the killer of Dr. Ed Stuckey…and the killer of those two young women murdered long ago..." he looked at Ms. Capetown who nodded and blinked away tears. "And this letter reveals the killer of my uncle Kevin Thompson and all the children who drowned on that school bus!"

More women gasped and all the people began to turn to one another and murmur.

"What nonsense is this?" Donnie's father said.

But Reverend Johnson remained seated and surprisingly calm.

"Let me see that letter," Donnie's father asked.

"Who is it, son?" Mikey's dad asked.

"What?" Donnie's father said. "You believe this nonsense, Sheriff?"

The Sheriff shot him a look that made him sit down. "I believe my son."

When Mikey heard that, he couldn't help but smile. He felt a surge of courage run through his body.

"The letter states that the killer is…" Mikey hesitated. "The Reverend Johnson!" Mikey felt the tears in his eyes.

Everyone turned their heads toward the Reverend who covered his forehead with his hand and shook his head as though deeply disappointed.

"What?" Donnie's father said. He chuckled and pointed to the Reverend. "He wasn't even living here at the time."

Some of the townspeople murmured while others laughed a little. Mikey looked at Lexie. She had a look of determination on her face. He knew she believed him. She nodded as though remembering things the Reverend had said. But Chad had a look of disbelief on his face.

"The Reverend Johnson is really *Mr. Davis* the old bus driver!" Mikey jabbed his finger at the Reverend. Mikey's dad turned to look at the man still sitting there shaking his head disapprovingly.

"What?" a man in the back shouted. "What proof did she state in that letter?"

"She said she heard Reverend Johnson arguing with Ed Stuckey because Ed Stuckey recognized him!" Mikey said.

"That old town drunk?" said one woman. "He didn't know what he was talking about half the time."

More people chuckled. Mikey started to feel frightened.

"That old drunk didn't even know what day it was most of the time," Donnie's father said. "And now she wants us to trust his word?"

Everyone was laughing now.

"Yes!" Mikey said. "Where's old man Stuckey now?"

They laughed over him.

"He's dead remember?" Mikey continued, but it was no use. "How convenient is that for the killer?" The people ignored him. Everyone ignored him, except his father who was nodding in agreement.

"She said Mr. Davis escaped to Canada. He went to Kew Gardens!" he shouted above the talking. "It's all here in the letter!"

Mikey started to hand the Sheriff the letter, but he was interrupted.

"This is ridiculous!" One woman stood. "Can we please get on with this meeting? I want to know what's being done about these gruesome murders!"

More people agreed with her and some motioned for Mikey to stop talking.

"But it's true!" Mikey shouted. "It's the Reverend!"

"Sit down!" Donnie shouted to Mikey. "See? I told you he was nuts." He nudged his dad who agreed.

"Listen to me!" Mikey tried shouting above the talking, but they ignored him. "He's the killer! It all makes sense. I'm telling you! She overheard him. She gave me photographs of Mr. Davis and the Reverend. It's him!"

Mikey saw the Reverend step off the chancel and walk toward him. He knew what that meant. "No!" Mikey shouted and turned to run.

"Mike." His dad walked toward him too. "Wait!"

"No!" Mikey turned around. "You can't stop me! It's all right here in the letter."

His eyes caught Miss Jennings.

"I believe you, Mikey," she said.

"Come on, Mike," the Reverend said. "Don't run off."

"No!" Mikey felt a man's grip on his arm. He shook it loose and ran through the foyer. The letter dropped to the ground.

"Sheriff! We want answers!" Mikey could hear the people shouting at his dad.

"Mikey wait!" He heard his father shout after him as he ran out the church and down the front steps into the cold night.

On the ground lay Mrs. Stevenson's letter.

CHAPTER 28
The Vision

While the townspeople in the church continued to argue, Mikey took off through the forest toward the far side of the woods as fast as he could until the glow of the streetlights in town and Christmas lights in the neighborhood could no longer be seen. He ran into tree limbs, deeper and deeper into their black tangled mess of branches and twigs.

"You're a freak! No wonder your mom left you!" he heard Donnie's words echo in his head. "All you have is your old man."

Donnie's right, Mikey thought. *It's all my fault.*

"What is this nonsense?" He could hear the loud voice of Donnie's father inside his head.

It is nonsense, he thought. *What was I thinking? Believing in ghosts? Asking a ghost to help me solve a murder? I'm such an idiot to think anyone in this town would believe me.*

He ran until the forest became so thick, he couldn't move anymore. That's when he turned and realized his jacket had become entangled in some branches. As tried to tear it free, he heard some footsteps nearby.

Probably a fox or raccoon, he thought. He continued to pull at his jacket while hot tears streamed down his face and his nose became stuffed up. He cried and pulled and wiped his nose all at once. And yet the sound of footsteps became louder.

He stopped moving.

The footsteps stopped.

"Who's there?" he asked. He wiped his cheeks and sniffled. *Maybe it's one of my dad's deputies searching the area,* he thought. *Maybe it's a ghost?*

Finally, he freed his jacket and took a few steps back. He looked in all directions, but the blackness revealed nothing but more branches. He turned and began walking out of the forest pushing twigs and branches out of his way. A few scraped and cut his face, but he didn't care.

Suddenly, he felt that strange feeling of being watched…watched by someone unfriendly.

The footsteps started again. He could sense someone was

behind him. He moved faster stepping over dead logs and large rocks trying not to fall. The feeling inside was so powerful, Mikey just had to look. He had to see what was behind him. So he turned.

And then he froze.

Standing only a few feet away from him was the silhouette of the tall man he'd seen in the forest that one night with his friends. The man held a branch away then slowly let it go. Eerily, at that exact moment, Mikey heard a voice coming from right next to him. It wasn't a loud voice or even a man's voice. It sounded like a child's voice.

"Run," it said.

But Mikey couldn't move his body.

The shadowy figure took a step toward him.

"Run," said the child's voice again.

Mikey had a million thoughts go through his mind all of them ending with his dead body being pulled from the frozen pond surrounded by yellow caution tape.

"*Run!*" the voice shouted waking Mikey from his trance.

He obeyed and took off as fast as he could away from the shadowy figure. But he could hear the footsteps following close behind.

The branches before him made it hard to escape and he knew the man was catching up to him. The end of the forest was nowhere in sight.

Why did I run in here? He thought. *No one saw me so no one knows where I am.*

His instincts told him to keep moving as fast as he could.

But it was too late. He felt the strong arm of the man grab his shoulder and push him to the ground. Mikey crawled away until a large metal object came crashing down inches away from his head. He turned to see it was a sledge hammer.

"No!" he shouted.

The man jerked Mikey's body over and raised the sledge hammer high above him. It was so dark, Mikey couldn't see the man's face. Yet he did see another figure shove the man so hard, he fell over to the side and got stuck in some branches. The sledge hammer went flying. The figure was of a child. *Kevin?* Mikey thought.

"Now, *get up and run*!" the voice demanded again.

Mikey leapt to his feet and ran out of the forest. He noticed he was near the old rickety bridge. He stopped. He had to stop and breathe for a moment because his chest and side ached. His warm breath appeared before him in misty puffs as he bent over trying to breathe.

He trotted away under the bridge out of sight of the man. In the darkness there under the bridge, he felt safe. Yet, he didn't feel alone.

"Thank you," he said to no one there. Deep down, though, he knew who it was that had helped him. "Thank you for helping me."

He reached up and wiped his forehead then peeked out of the darkness of the shadows that hid him from sight. That's when he saw the man hop out of the forest. Mikey leaned back into the shadows so he couldn't be seen. He watched the man carefully slide across the frozen pond to a parked car. He made his way around it and got into the *passenger* side of the car. Mikey cocked his head to the side as though confused. Then, the head-lights came on, so Mikey leaned back as far as he could to stay out of the glow of the lights. The engine revved and the car turned around, and then sped off. He couldn't see the type of car, but he had a feeling he knew who was in it.

The Reverend Johnson.

But who was driving? When it felt safe to come out of the shadows, Mikey stepped out from under the bridge.

But a hand stopped him. He looked at his arm and saw a boy's hand touching him. He followed the arm with his eyes and saw it led to a boy's face. He cautiously looked into the boy's face.

It was Kevin Thompson.

Mikey felt sick to his stomach as though he was on a fast roller coaster at the amusement park.

He pulled his arm away, but the ghost came toward him. Mikey knew his own face must have gone pale with fright because the ghost motioned for him to remain calm.

"What do you want with me?" Mikey asked. "Haven't I done enough?"

"Help me," the ghost said in a soft childlike voice.

"I'm trying," Mikey said. His voice cracked as he thought back over the last few weeks. "Can't you see that I'm trying to help you?"

He felt the warm tears roll down his cheeks again. He hastily wiped them away because he was tired of crying about the whole mess.

"I've lost all my friends," Mikey sniffled. "Good people have died because of me. Now the whole town hates me!"

"*Help* me," was all that the ghost said.

"What? I don't know what else to do for you," Mikey cried out. His eyes stung from the tears. "I don't know what else to do."

Just then, the ghost reached out and touched Mikey's arm.

And in that instant, Mikey saw a vision. It moved so fast across his mind, that he could barely keep up.

Instantly, he was in his uncle Kevin's bedroom in 1961 looking down at the keepsake box. His uncle placed a few items into a hidden compartment inside the box then closed it and locked it with the silver key. He placed the key in the front pocket of his jeans.

Next, Mikey was at the school walking across the front lawn with his uncle Kevin. They spotted the bus driver, Mr. Davis, near the school bus talking to a young woman. Mikey could see that Mr. Davis and the Reverend Johnson were clearly the same person. Immediately, Mikey and Kevin were transported to inside a classroom where many kids were making fun of Kevin, pointing at him and laughing.

"No one believes you and your stupid story!" One kid pointed and shouted at him. Kevin lowered his eyes. Mikey saw how hurt and embarrassed his uncle Kevin was.

Then, he was in the forest walking with Kevin and a few kids.

"Where are we going?" one kid asked.

They stopped when they saw the bus driver carrying something suspicious…

He nervously glanced behind him. "Don't look back, you fool," Mr. Davis mumbled to himself. "You know better than that."

The arms of the victim he carried dangled lifelessly while he walked.

Mr. Davis dropped the body into the small boat on the shore, adjusted his jacket, and then started to push the boat out into the water. He hopped in.

"Is that…is that a *dead* body he just put into that boat?" Gus asked. He covered his mouth. "I think I'm gonna be sick."

"Shhh," Kevin said when the other boys crept up.

"That's him," Shorty said as he nudged Kevin. "That's Mr. Davis alright."

"See? I told you so," Kevin pointed. "He killed his wife."

Mr. Davis paddled the boat out to the middle of the pond and paused. Then, he took Mrs. Davis' body and dropped her into the murky water.

Mikey stood there with his mouth open as he watched the scene.

"What the heck are you kids doing here?" Mr. Davis shouted at them with such anger, the veins in his throat bulged and spit flew from his mouth. He sprinted toward them and caught Kevin.

Mikey began to run away, the vision was that real.

Mr. Davis looked up at the boys staring at him with mouths gaping and he grinned. Then he rudely turned Kevin Thompson around to face the other boys. The boys looked at their friend, Kevin, shaking in the killer's arms. His large brown eyes watered.

Before he knew it, Mikey was on the school bus that fateful evening…

Once inside, the boys sat shivering in nervous silence as the bus began to move. Kevin looked at Mikey with saddened eyes.

Mr. Davis turned the bus around and started onto the bridge that went over the railroad tracks near the far side of the pond where they all played hockey in the wintertime.

The bus made its way down the other side of the rickety old bridge, but instead of driving forward toward the neighborhood, the bus made a sharp turn left, so sharp that the kids fell out of their seats.

"Hey, what are you doing?" Kevin shouted.

"Sorry, kid," Davis said. "Can't take any chances."

Kevin yelled for him to stop and tried to rush to the front of the bus, but it was no use. The bus sped out of control. Kevin watched as they headed toward the pond. Before Kevin or the others could do anything, the bus slammed into the water and immediately submerged almost up to the windows. The kids were thrown to the floor.

Kevin got up and tried to pry his window open, but he remembered how the old bus windows never slid open. He caught a glimpse of Davis scurrying out his driver side window as the waters rose around them. Kevin quickly ran to the window and tried to follow Mr. Davis , but the force of the water rushing in was too strong for him. He turned to the door and tried to open it with the lever. As he did, the frigid water rushing in pushed him back and shocked his body. He struggled to breathe. Some of the kids wadded back to the emergency door exit, but it was jammed.

"I can't swim!" Shorty shouted. The water was almost up to his waist.

"Help!" Kevin heard his friends scream over and over.

Kevin looked out the window and watched the bus driver swim to the shore and run away, never looking back. He banged on the windows trying to get his attention, anyone's attention. "Hey!" Kevin screamed after him. "Come back! Help us!"

But it was no use. The water inside the bus rose higher and higher.

"Help us!" Kevin shouted and banged on the window hoping someone in the houses nearby could hear them. He turned to Mikey. "Nobody could hear us! Nobody could help us!"

The last thing Kevin Thompson saw before the bus disappeared forever into the murky water of Sherman Oaks Pond was the bus driver, Mr. Davis, scurrying away.

"You can't just leave us here! Come back!" Kevin cried as he banged on the window. He turned to Mikey. "He never looked back. He never even looked back at us!"

§

The vision ended.

"He never even tried to help us," the ghost of Kevin said. "He never even looked back. *He never looked back*."

Mikey remembered those words. He remembered what Reverend Johnson had told him.

"I never look back, Mikey," the Reverend had said. "What's done is done. I never look back..."

Mikey blinked his eyes and immediately found himself right back under the bridge, but he was sitting on the ground trying to catch his breath. The ghost of Kevin stared over him.

"*Help me*," he said one more time with intensity in his eyes. It was as if he was asking Mikey not to quit.

Mikey nodded and stood.
"I will," he said. "I will help you."
Then, he ran off toward his neighborhood as fast as he could.

CHAPTER 29
The Trophy Case

When Mikey ran through the neighborhood, he ran so fast, he didn't even notice Chad, Donnie, and Stanny following him. When he reached the school, he climbed into the window and ran down the stairs to the boiler room. The others caught up to him.

Without a word, Mikey pulled a bench over to the lockers, climbed up, and reached on top of the locker like he was searching for something.

"What are you doing?" Donnie asked.

"Mikey, you okay?" Chad asked. Mikey could see genuine concern on his friend's face. "Look, stupid here didn't mean what he said."

Chad hit Donnie on the chest.

"Right, *stupid*?" Chad motioned for Donnie to apologize.

Donnie hesitated. "Yeah, right. I didn't mean it," he shoved his hands deep into his pockets.

Mikey wasn't even listening as he sat down on the bench with the keepsake box on his lap. He had hidden it in the boiler room because he didn't want his father to accidentally find it and return it to Grandma's house.

"Mike, your dad is looking for you," Chad said. "The Reverend ran out of the church and they're looking for him to question him."

Chad nudged Donnie.

"Uh, yeah, Mikey," Donnie said. "Um, it looks like your dad believes you and wants to check out the information in the letter."

Mikey ignored them as he dug deep into his pocket for the key to the keepsake box.

"Come on, Mike," Chad said. "The cops are coming to help out. It's over. You did it."

But Mikey continued with the key and began to insert it into the box.

"Hey that is the special box for keepsakes, huh?" Stanny asked in his thick Russian accent. "Where did you find it? What are you going to do with it?"

Just then, Lexie came through the door.

"What are you doing here?" Chad asked her.

"I saw Mikey running this way and knew something was up," she said as she removed her knit cap. "I told my parents. Did you tell Mikey about the cops coming?"

Chad nodded.

She immediately saw the wooden keepsake box on Mikey's lap and sat down next to him.

"What's going on?" she asked him. "Where did you find that keepsake box?"

Mikey ignored her too. He turned the key and then opened the box.

Lexie peered in.

Then, Mikey pushed down on one corner of the bottom just as his uncle Kevin did in the vision. The opposite corner popped up revealing a secret compartment underneath. Mikey carefully lifted the partition.

"Wow." Lexie peered inside the box with her wide eyes.

"What is it?" Chad slid over and sat on the other side of Mikey. Donnie came over with Stanny. They all peered into the little box.

"Newspaper clippings," Mikey said. He pulled out one and slowly unfolded the yellowed paper. He silently read it for a couple of seconds. "It's about…it's about *my dad*."

"Huh?" Chad said.

Mikey showed it to him. Then, he pulled out another newspaper clipping and another.

"This one's about my dad, too," he said. He shuffled through the other papers. "They all are."

"Wow, Mikey, your dad was a hockey star at this school," Chad said as he read through the clipping. "Looks like he was also a star football player. He was *the* star quarterback from freshman year all the way to his senior year!"

Donnie grabbed one and read it.

"They went to state and won the championship!" he said. "You never told us that!"

Mikey winced.

"Because I never knew," he said in a soft voice.

Lexie read one clipping.

"Says here he was awarded a hockey scholarship, but turned it down so he could stay with his mom and dad," she said. "He told the reporter that his parents were pretty distraught after his brother's death."

"But, how?" Mikey wondered. "How could Kevin have saved that article? He was already dead by that time."

"I don't know," Lexie said. "Maybe he haunted their house…maybe he's still there when he isn't in the pond."

Mikey looked at her and thought about it. He remembered how when he was at his grandmother's house, he felt he was guided to his uncle's room, and then to the box under the bed. "I think you're right. I did feel a presence there in his bedroom."

As they read through the clippings, Mikey saw one last piece of paper in the box. He picked it up, unfolded it, and then read it.

"It's a letter from my uncle Kevin…to my dad," he said.

"The ghost wrote a letter?" Donnie asked. "What's it say?"

"It's dated November 1961," Mikey said. "That's the month he died."

Mikey looked at Lexie whose eyes shone with tears.

"What did he write?" she asked and wiped her eyes.

"Dear Dougie, I wanted you to know that you are the best brother in the world. You are my hero," Mikey read. "And I am doing this because of you. I know no one believes me, but I have to try otherwise a killer will go free. I know that you would do this if you were in my position because you are big and strong and tough. But I am small and not so tough."

Lexie sniffled.

"But I have to try. So, if anything happens to me, I just wanted you to know that I love you because you are my big brother and you are my hero," Mikey tried to choke back tears. "Love, Kevin."

Mikey stared at the young boy's handwriting on the letter for a moment in silence with only the humming of the furnaces in the background. No one moved.

Finally, Lexie sniffled again.

"That is so sweet," she said.

"That goofy kid," Mikey said.

"I wonder what happened that day before the bus accident," Chad said.

"I know what happened." Mikey turned to Chad. He stood and paced the boiler room. "I saw the whole thing."

"What? You saw the whole thing? What do you mean? How?" Donnie asked.

"I'll tell you, but I don't want any commentary, got that?" Mikey shouted and pointed at Donnie. "I don't care if you don't believe me or if you think I'm crazy, understand?"

Donnie nodded. He still had the evidence of the black eye Mikey had given him.

"I saw the ghost of Kevin tonight," he said.

Lexie gasped and covered her mouth. "What? Where?"

"When I ran off into the woods," Mikey said. "I was alone, trapped in the trees and that's when I heard some footsteps behind me."

Donnie grabbed Chad's arm. "Oh, man. I hate this scary stuff."

Chad grimaced and pulled away. "Geez!"

"I turned and saw that it was a tall man following me," Mikey continued. "I couldn't see his face, but I had a feeling it was—"

"The Reverend Johnson!" Lexie interrupted.

Mikey nodded. "He raised the sledgehammer and tried to kill me with it. That's when I heard the voice."

"What voice?" Chad asked.

Mikey hesitated and looked at Donnie who stared with wide eyes and mouth agape.

"I heard…" he said. "I heard the ghost's voice."

Lexie stood up. "He was there? Kevin's ghost was there?"

"Yes," Mikey said. "He told me to run. So I did."

"Far out!" Chad said. "The ghost helped you."

"I ran and hid under the bridge until the Reverend was gone. And that's when Kevin's ghost showed me what happened," Mikey explained.

"So…what happened?" Donnie asked.

"He showed me what happened in a vision of some sort. You see, he had a feeling something was up with the bus driver, Mr. Davis, and he told his friends about it, but they only laughed at him." He looked at Donnie and Chad then Stan. "I know the feeling."

His friends frowned and looked down in shame.

"So, I guess he wanted to prove to them that the Mr. Davis was the murderer of those missing women."

They all leaned in closer.

"Go on," Lexie said.

"So, he led his friends to the forest that day after school because he had a feeling the bus driver would be there on the far side of the pond," Mikey looked at the letter. "And he was right!"

"Wow," Chad said.

"He and his friends caught Mr. Davis in the act as he was dumping a woman's body into the pond!"

"No wonder," Lexie said with a faraway look in her eyes. "No wonder they were killed."

"Yeah, that's right," Mikey said. "The bus driver killed them that day because he was sloppy. He needed to get rid of eye-witnesses."

Mikey put the letter in his pocket.

"So tragic," Lexie said.

"So, you were right, Mike," Chad said. "The killer is Reverend Johnson."

"I knew it!" Lexie stood and began pacing. "I've always had an eerie feeling about that man. I never trusted him!" She jabbed the air with her finger for emphasis.

"Wow," Donnie said. "He's Mr. Davis, the bus driver."

Donnie cocked his head and looked confused.

"What is it?" Chad asked him.

"I'm confused," Donnie said.

"What else is new?" Chad crossed his arms.

"Shut up," Donnie shoved him hard.

"What are you confused about?" Lexie asked.

"Well, why did he return to Sherman Oaks? Didn't he know he could get caught?" Donnie asked.

"Well, maybe…" Mikey said, "The old saying is true. The killer always returns to the scene of the crime."

Donnie nodded. "I guess so."

"Mikey, he ran out of the church after you left," Chad said.

"Really?' Mikey said.

"Yeah. Your dad ran after you, and that's when we saw the Reverend head out the back door," Chad said. "Your dad has the letter, too."

"He does?" Mikey's eyes grew wide. He exhaled. "Oh good. I

thought it was lost forever."

§

But Mikey didn't say anything after that. Instead, he ran to the boiler room door, headed up the stairs, and toward the door leading to the hall. He stopped in front of it for a moment and turned to the window leading out of the school. This time, he didn't climb out the broken window like usual.

Mikey picked up a chair and used it to break the door knob of the door that led to the school hallway. The others followed him.

"Dude, what are you doing?" Chad yelled.

The door opened and Mikey ran down the darkened hall with his friends running after him.

"I've never been in the school after dark like this before," Lexie giggled. "Except for parent-teacher conferences."

The halls were dark except for the light from the street lamps streaming in through the windows. Mikey turned a corner and headed toward the high school portion of the building. He ran toward the gymnasium. They all skidded across the tile floor after him.

"Mikey, where are we going?" Chad shouted. Donnie huffed and puffed behind them grabbing his chest.

"I'm gonna have a heart attack," he said. He patted his pockets. "Dang it!"

"What is it now?" Chad asked him.

"Dang! Why did I forget to bring a grape lollipop?" he patted his pants pockets. "Oh wait, here's one!"

"Not now, man!" Chad said as he ran past him.

Finally, Mikey skidded to a stop in front of the large trophy case at the gymnasium entrance the high school kids used. He stared at it when the others caught up to him. It was filled with plaques, trophies, banners, and framed photos. A single light from inside the case shone down on all its contents.

"Why…are we here?" Chad huffed.

Mikey motioned toward the case. Chad, Donnie, Stanny, and Lexie peeked through the glass. There, behind the numerous trophies and plaques were a few framed black and white photographs hanging in the back.

"They are old photographs," Stanny said.

"I've walked by this case a hundred times since I've been at this school and not once did I ever notice these photos before," Mikey said.

The others studied the photos as he spoke.

"Yeah," Chad said. "Me neither."

"Wow, Mikey," Donnie said. "Your dad *was* a hockey and football star."

In the photographs, Mikey saw his young father smiling and shaking hands with the governor of the state as the team was presented with the state championship trophy. Another photograph was of his father throwing the ball during the winning game. A third photograph was of his father standing with the championship hockey team. Mikey's mind raced as he tried to figure out everything. *I had no idea*, he thought. He remembered Kevin's letter. *I guess you wanted me to know more about my dad.*

"I never knew your dad was such a great athlete, Mikey," Chad said.

"Neither did I." Mikey felt that familiar sting of tears in his eyes. "I always thought he was a…just another loser. Like me."

Lexie cringed when she heard those words.

"And I guess I always thought I took after him," Mikey said.

"You're not a loser, Mikey," Lexie said. "You've helped solve a mystery."

"Yeah, you discovered the Reverend is the killer," Donnie said. "That's huge, Mikey. Not even the cops figured that one out."

Mikey felt rage rise up within him as he thought of his uncle on the bus with all those kids and the killer, Reverend Johnson, getting away with it for so many years. He turned to face his friends. Lexie's eyes grew large when she saw the anger in Mikey's face.

"Yeah," he said, "now we know for certain that the Reverend is the—"

Just then, he shoved his friends out of the way of a large object hurtling toward them. It crashed through the glass of the trophy case sending shards of glass and trophies flying. Mikey jumped out of the way right as he heard his friends scream.

“I knew I’d find you pesky kids here!” the Reverend shouted. He walked over and picked up his sledge hammer from the trophy case.

“Run!” Mikey shouted to his friends. They took off down the hall with the killer following after them.

CHAPTER 30
Confessions of a Killer

The Reverend Johnson slid the sledge hammer along the tiled floor at the kids, tripping Donnie and Lexie. They fell to the ground, turned over, and frantically scooted on the tile floor away from the killer. Mikey, Stanny, and Chad stopped and turned to see the Reverend standing over his friends, cackling.

"No!" Mikey shouted. He ran over to them, but the Reverend grabbed his sledge hammer and pointed it at Lexie, threatening her.

"You brats!" he shouted. "For almost five years I lived in peace in this town until you starting snooping around!"

"Why'd you come back here?" Mikey shouted. He cautiously approached.

"Peace and quiet, yes, that's what I had. Peace and quiet until you brats started up with your questions." The Reverend ignored Mikey's question. Lexie and Donnie started to crawl away, but the Reverend slammed down the sledge hammer near their feet, cracking the tile. Lexie screamed again. "Mikey!"

Mikey inched closer.

"Did you want to kill more women, is that why you came back?" he shouted.

The Reverend turned his head and looked at him with vitriol in his weary eyes.

"What do you know about it?" he said, stabbing a finger at Mikey. "You kids don't know anything about it. And once I get rid of you, I can go back to peace and quiet here again."

"Why'd you kill those women?" Mikey asked again. While he distracted the Reverend, he motioned for Chad to get Lexie out of there. Chad grabbed her arms and dragged her away. The Reverend picked up the heavy sledge hammer again and turned toward Mikey.

"I'm gonna enjoy killing you." He jerked the hammer at Mikey. "You're the trouble maker just like that old woman."

Donnie skidded out of sight into a corridor nearby while Lexie scurried behind some lockers in the hall. She peeked around them and watched the scene. Chad and Stanny ran and hid next to Donnie.

"What do we do now?" Donnie whispered.

"Shhh! Don't move," Chad answered.

"You leave her out of this!" Mikey shouted. Mrs. Stevenson's body being loaded onto the coroner's car came to his mind.

"I heard you two talking that night." The Reverend chuckled. "I heard what she said. She was on to me, so I had to get to her first."

"You make me sick." Mikey felt his face become hot. "How could you hurt such a sweet lady?"

"You're the kid causing all the ruckus around here," the Reverend hissed as he stepped toward Mikey. "So now I've come for you."

"Oh yeah? Come and get me," Mikey challenged.

"Your uncle was just like you," the Reverend said. "He was a pest too. Always following me. Always asking me questions. He had no friends. The kids laughed at him and his silly stories all the time. Yep, he was just like you. A real *loser*!"

Mikey was so angry, he tasted bile in his mouth.

"Yeah, that's right! That's why your mother left you and your father." Spittle dripped down Mr. Davis' chin. "She knew a couple of losers when she saw them!"

"Why'd you do it?" Mikey shouted. "Why'd you kill all those women!"

"Because they were tramps!" The Reverend slammed down the head of the hammer and cracked more tile. "They ran around with boys from college." He gestured wildly as he talked. "…but when I'd ask them out on a date, they'd turn me down. Tramps!" Spit flew from his mouth as he shouted. He came closer to Mikey.

"Weren't you married back then?" Mikey asked. "What about your wife?"

"Never you mind that! That's none of your business!" The Reverend shook his fist.

"Didn't you kill *your own wife?*"

The Reverend screamed. "You shut your mouth!"

"…And dump her body in the pond, too?" Mikey squinted his eyes at the mad-man before him.

"You little brat! You shut up!" The Reverend raised the sledge hammer and slammed it down a couple of feet away from Mikey. He leapt out of the way just in time. "I'm gonna enjoy killing all you kids!"

"You'll never get away with it!" Mikey took a step back.

"Oh yeah? Who are they gonna believe? Huh? Me? A man of the cloth? A *Reverend*? Or a bunch of loser, good-for-nothing kids like you?" he laughed.

"You're evil hiding behind that title of Reverend," Mikey shouted. "The town trusted you!"

"That's their fault!"

"And you tricked them!"

"They wanted to be tricked." The Reverend lifted the sledge hammer up again.

"Why'd you kill your wife? Did she find out about you?" Mikey asked. He spied the fire extinguisher to his left. "Is that why you got rid of her?"

"You shut your mouth boy." The Reverend hissed and pointed his long bony finger at Mikey.

"Yeah, that's it isn't it? She found out about you and you got rid of her," Mikey said. He inched his way toward the fire extinguisher.

"She was a tramp, too!" he shouted. Mikey could see tears form in the Reverend's eyes. "She was no good. I found out she and that principal were messing around behind my back!"

Mikey cocked his head. He didn't expect that answer.

"Yeah that's right. Can you believe it?" the Reverend continued. "She and that old drunk were messing around behind my back! Making a fool of me! The whole town knew. They all laughed at me!"

"You didn't have to kill her," Mikey said.

"I got rid of her and made sure the principal was ruined!" The Reverend laughed heartily. Then, his eyes narrowed as he approached Mikey. "And he *was* ruined! He was a pathetic drunk when I returned. My plan succeeded. Everyone blamed him for the bus accident."

"That wasn't an accident!" Mikey cried. "You murdered those little kids. You murdered my uncle!"

"And now I'm gonna kill all you kids and pin it on your drunk of a dad."

Mikey pursed his lips and made two fists with his hands. "What…did…you say?"

"I know all about your father." He chortled. "I know he's a

drunk, too. Drinks every night to make his problems disappear. He came to talk to me about it once. Said he blamed himself for his little brother's death. He was whining and crying about it. Pathetic."

"Shut up! Don't talk about my father that way!" Mikey screamed and jabbed his finger at the Reverend.

"He's just another pathetic fool. This whole town's full of 'em."

Mikey breathed in deeply, trying to muster up the courage to move.

"So now I can easily tell people how I tried to stop the drunken Sheriff from breaking into the school, breaking the trophy case because he was angry he couldn't relive the glory days. He was upset about his loser son embarrassing him in front of the whole town! Heh," the Reverend wiped the spit from his chin. "But I was too late. He came upon you kids snooping around. He killed you all because you knew too much. He killed you to cover his crimes. I'll tell everyone how he confessed to me about killing all those people.Tragic, really."

Lexie looked over at Chad, Stanny, and Donnie with frightened eyes.

"I'll make sure everyone in town knows he's the real killer of those women and old man Stuckey." He smirked.

"No!" Mikey shouted.

"And they'll believe me, because I'm the Reverend." He placed his hand over his heart. "Oh yes, all the townsfolk will believe me because they trust me."

Mikey despised how the Reverend's voice returned to the usual kind gentle manner he heard all the time.

"No they won't!" Mikey said. "They won't believe you."

"Yes, they will," he said. "They always do! Like when I killed old man Stuckey. They believed me when I told them an old bum did it."

"You're sick!"

"And they believed me tonight when I told them you were having a nervous breakdown. I told them not to hold it against you what with the pressure you've been under," he said in that gentle voice.

Then his face became twisted and contorted with evil again. "And they'll believe me when I tell them your father killed Miss

Jennings, too." He chuckled under his breath. "Oh yes."

Mikey's eyes grew wide. "No you won't!" he yelled. "You stay away from her!"

The Reverend cackled. "Yes, I think I'll be paying her a visit next," the Reverend patted the sledgehammer with his bony hand, "and I'll enjoy it, too."

"I'll never let you hurt her!" The very thought of the Reverend hurting Miss Jennings was all Mikey could take.

In that instant, he reached over and grabbed the fire extinguisher off the wall, popped the pin out, and sprayed the foam all over the Reverend as he cackled.

"Run!" Mikey shouted to his friends. They all scurried out of the corridor and down the adjacent hallway with Donnie screaming the loudest as they ran. They made it to a door, but it was locked.

"No!" Donnie shouted. "Now what do we do?"

"This way!" Mikey led them toward the cafeteria, but they were cut off by the Reverend.

"Caught ya!" he said. His jacket and pants were covered in foam. "You won't get away from me, this time."

Donnie took out a lollipop from his pocket and threw it at the Reverend hitting his right eye.

"Hey!" The Reverend looked at Donnie. "Why you little—"

"Sorry," Donnie forced a smile.

Mikey noticed the sledge hammer wasn't in the Reverend's grip. No, this time the Reverend reached into his jacket pocket and pulled out a hunting knife. He pointed it at Mikey.

"You brats won't get away from me this time," the Reverend said. "I killed a bunch of kids once, I can do it again."

"Mikey, watch out!" Chad yelled.

Mikey closed his eyes and waited for the knife.

But it never came.

"Hey!" Donnie shouted.

Mikey opened his eyes in time to see his dad come up from behind the Reverend and grab his arms. He jerked the Reverend and the knife fell to the ground as the two men struggled.

Lexie screamed. "Be careful!"

"Mikey, get outta there!" his dad shouted. The Reverend reached around and punched the Sheriff on the jaw sending him backwards. The Reverend reached down for the knife.

"No!" Mikey shouted and ran toward the knife and kicked it away just in time. Then, he punched the Reverend in the face with his fist. Mikey felt a couple of bones in his hand crunch. He yelped from the pain and fell down grabbing his hand.

His father rebounded and grabbed the stunned Reverend lying on the floor moaning with pain. This time, the Sheriff quickly handcuffed the Reverend's wrists and dug his knee in the middle of the Reverend's back as he lay face down on the floor.

"No!" The Reverend struggled to get free. "It was those kids! They did it!"

Mikey scooted back from the scene still writhing with pain. Lexie ran up to him.

"It was those kids!" The Reverend cried. "I tell you!"

"Yeah, yeah, yeah," the Sheriff said. "Tell it to the Judge. I heard the whole confession."

"Mikey, you okay?" she asked.

Mikey looked at her.

"Yeah, I'm okay," then he ran to his father. "Dad!"

He hugged his father's neck.

"Mikey," his dad said. "Are you alright? Are you hurt anywhere?" He inspected his son for any injuries. Other than cuts and scrapes and a swollen hand, Mikey was just fine.

"How? How did you know we were here in the school?" Mikey asked. His father stood and yanked the Reverend to a sitting position against the wall.

"When you weren't home, I asked the neighbors. Some said they saw you and the others running this way. My friends and I used to hide in the boiler room too, so I thought I'd take a chance and see if you all were messing around in there," His dad said. "That's when I heard the screams."

Mikey hugged his dad again.

CHAPTER 31
Kevin's Letter

The Sheriff made sure all the kids were safe, inspecting each one for injuries. They were shaken up, but physically okay. In the background, the sound of approaching sirens was heard. From the noise, Mikey could tell many patrol cars were on their way. He watched as his father talked on the walkie-talkie to his deputies.

"Boy, Mikey, that was scary!" Donnie said. "You were right. You were right all along. The killer was here in town." He bent down and picked up the grape lollipop.

"Yeah," Mikey said as he stared down the Reverend. "I knew no one would have ever believed me if I told them it was the Reverend, but I had to try. For Mrs. Stevenson, I had to try."

"This is so tragic," Lexie said. "And he was going to perform a wedding next week, too. How sick is that?"

She looked down at the Reverend. "You're sick, you know that? Sick!"

He tried to wriggle free and Lexie leapt back away from him.

"So what made you come in here and open the keepsake box?" Donnie asked.

Mikey took out the silver key from his pocket.

"Kevin, my uncle." He lifted the key up. "With the vision, I guess you could say tonight he gave me the final clue."

"There! Over there!" The kids heard someone shouting.

Down the hallway came Destrey using crutches and dragging his cast along the floor. Behind him was his father, the deputy.

"Hey guys!" Destrey shouted as he slowly made his way over to the group.

"Destrey!" Mikey ran over to him and hugged him nearly knocking him down. "What are you doing here?"

"I told my dad! I told him you all would be here. He said no one could find you all and parents were worried. So he asked me where you might be," Destrey said. His eyes sparkled with enthusiasm. "I told him I wouldn't tell him unless I could go along, too. So, he brought me with him."

Lexie hugged Destrey too. "You goof!"

"So what happened? What did I miss?" he asked.

Mikey showed him the Reverend, handcuffed, fuming, and leaning against the wall.

"There he is." Mikey pointed to the disheveled and broken man. "That's the killer. He killed all those women then tried to cover his crimes by killing the children under the ice."

"Wow," Destrey said. "Reverend Johnson *is* Mr. Davis the long lost bus driver. It was him all along?"

"Yep," Mikey said. "He killed old man Stuckey and Mrs. Stevenson because they were on to him. Now it all makes sense. He knew we were heading to Mrs. Stevenson's house that day. He said he overheard us talking in the house."

"Poor Mrs. Stevenson," Destrey said. "I heard they found her body in the pond."

Mikey hung his head low. He remembered her soft hug she gave him at the funeral and how nice she was. He sighed and blinked back tears.

"Yeah," he whispered. "I feel bad about it…I feel bad about a lot of things."

"Hey, don't feel bad." Destrey put his hand on Mikey's shoulder. Chad, Donnie, Stanny, and Lexie came up to him. "You helped solve a crime, Mike."

Mikey shrugged.

"You're the best investigative reporter I know!" Destrey said.

"Yeah, we're the ones who feel bad," Chad said. "We didn't believe you at first and we should have."

"We're the ones who failed," Donnie said. "And a killer almost got away with murder…*again*."

"Yeah, but you got your leg broken," Mikey said to Destrey. "You were almost killed because of me and—"

Destrey shrugged. "So? You know what? It's not so bad," he said. "I get to eat pizza and hot dogs and ice cream and watch cartoons all day long!"

They laughed at Destrey.

That's when the kids heard footsteps and the jingling of keys coming down the hallway. They turned and spotted Deputy Rogers running toward the scene with several deputies following him. The deputies hovered around the Reverend and one helped him stand. They led him down the hall and out the front doors to the waiting patrol car outside in the snowy night. As the Reverend walked past

Mikey, he sneered at him and growled through his yellow teeth.

"You enjoy prison," Mikey said to him and made a fake salute with his left hand.

"I won't forget this!" The Reverend turned his head and shouted. "I'll be back to get you! All you kids! You mark my words. I'll be back!"

"Yeah, yeah, yeah. Shut up, old man, and keep walking," one deputy ordered as he jerked the Reverend back around and forced him to walk through the doors.

Mikey's dad walked up to him and the other kids. He was listening to someone talk on the walkie talkie. He spoke for a few minutes then headed over to Mikey.

"Well, Mikey, after reading what Mrs. Stevenson's wrote in her letter, looks like she was correct in her hunch. Detective Williams had already checked on Kew Gardens last week. Seems they have had some mysterious disappearances around the time Mrs. Stevenson claims she saw Mr. Davis working up there."

"Really?" Mikey looked at his friends. "Whoa."

"That's scary." Lexie wrung her hands together.

"Yep. He spoke with the police and showed them a photo of Mr. Davis. They recognized him. So, it seems our Mrs. Stevenson was a fine detective in her own right. Detective Williams will head back up there tomorrow morning to check things out," Mikey's dad said. "One thing I didn't have the chance to tell you was that we found a piece of cloth in Mrs. Stevenson's hand when we pulled her out of the pond. I examined the piece of cloth and thought it looked like it came from a winter coat."

Mikey turned and looked at his friends. "Sounds familiar."

"At the townhall meeting, I saw the Reverend's coat in the foyer. I noticed it had a large section torn from it. But he took it away before I could inspect it more closely," the Sheriff said.

"Oh wow," Lexie said. "The ghosts gave us another clue!"

"So you were suspecting the Reverend, too?" Mikey asked.

His dad shrugged. "It was just a hunch."

"A good hunch," Destrey said.

"Come on now, kids, let's get you home." He motioned for a couple of deputies to come over. "These kids need a ride home, deputies. See to it that they arrive safely."

"Sure thing, Sheriff," Deputy Rogers said. But first, he pulled something out of his pocket. It was a pink Princess watch. He handed it to Lexie. "By the way, does this belong to you?"

Lexie shrieked. "Yes! That's my watch. Where did you find it?" she took it and inspected it.

"I found it on the street that night when Destrey here was hit by that car. I meant to give it to you earlier, but, well, things got a bit hectic," he said.

"Wow!" She put the watch on her wrist. "I don't remember seeing you there that night. Thanks so much! Hey, I didn't think I'd ever see this again."

"No problem." He turned to the boys. "Well, let's go guys."

Lexie hugged Mikey around the neck one more time and gave him a peck on the cheek. "I'm so proud of you," she said. "You did it, Mikey. You solved the crime."

"Nah, we all did this together," Mikey said as he looked at his friends and wiped the kiss off his cheek. "I couldn't have done it without your help."

As they turned to leave, Chad, Destrey, Donnie, and Stanny jokingly punched Mikey on the arm as they left with the deputies.

"Bye guys." Mikey rubbed his sore arm. "See you tomorrow."

"We get to ride in the patrol car!" Mikey heard Destrey say as they meandered down the hall with the deputies. "I'll turn on the sirens, too. You should see the crowd outside. A television news crew is out there with cameras and microphones! It's so cool! We'll be famous."

§

Mikey chuckled. Then, he turned to his dad.

"Wow, how the heck did the bus driver return to town and become the Reverend without anyone knowing?" Mikey asked his dad.

"Well, probably because so many people around here are new, they didn't recognize him," his dad said. "Frankly, I didn't recognize him either. But I guess old man Stuckey and Mrs. Stevenson began to figure it out."

"I guess so," Mikey said. "But why would he come back and

risk getting caught?"

"Well, sometimes a killer comes back to see if he got away with it. They get a thrill knowing the cops haven't found them yet. Something like that," his dad said.

"So, it's true." Mikey looked up at his dad. "The killer does return to the scene of the crime, huh?"

"Sometimes," his dad said. "...But there was something about him that always bothered me."

"Yeah, what?"

"I don't know. Something about how he never really preached a sermon. He just told jokes and feel-good stories. I guess that's why we stopped going to church," his dad explained. "I never really heard him talk about God or the Bible or anything like that. I always thought that was strange."

Mikey thought about it for a moment. "Well, sometimes we see what we want to see. And sometimes, what's hidden is the most important thing we need to see." He referred to the children under the ice.

His dad turned his head to the side then messed up Mikey's hair. "What an astute observation, son."

"Hey Dad." Mikey grabbed his dad's arm. "I need to show you something."

"We need to have the doctor look at your hand, Mike," his dad said. "Come on, let's go to the hospital."

"We will, but first I need to show you something. Come on, it's this way!"

Mikey took his father's hand and led him to the trophy case with its shattered glass still lying all over the floor. Together, they stood in front of the lit case. The flourescent light dangled by one wire, but it still illuminated the entire case and all its contents spread out in the case and on the floor. Mikey pointed to the photographs in frames and the trophy that read State Champions.

"Dad, how come you never told me about all this?" he asked.

His dad put his hands in his pockets as he stared at the photos. He had a pensive look as though he was remembering back to his high school days.

"Oh heck, Mike, that was a long time ago," he said.

Mikey reached in his pocket and pulled out the letter Kevin had left in the keepsake box.

"Dad, I know you won't believe me, but I have to tell you something," he said. "That night I was pulled under the ice, I saw…well, I saw your little brother."

His dad continued to stare into the trophy case without saying a word.

"I saw his ghost and the ghosts of the other children under the ice of the pond. And ever since then, well…he's been helping me solve this case," Mikey said. "Dad, I know it sounds strange, but I did. I did see Kevin's ghost."

His dad looked down and exhaled heavily as though relieved.

"I know, son." He turned his head to look at Mikey. "I saw him too."

Mikey's eyes grew large. He couldn't believe what he'd just heard.

"Wha…what did you say?" Mikey asked.

His dad walked over to a bench near the gymnasium door and sank down onto it with a deliberate sigh as though he knew it was time he told someone his secret. Mikey followed.

"What do you mean?" he asked his dad as he sat next to him.

"In a way, I feel relieved to finally tell someone about this." The Sheriff rubbed his stubbled chin with his hand. "I can't believe what I'm about to say." He chuckled.

Mikey leaned in to listen.

"Mikey, do you remember how I told you I went to the pond that one night alone to drink beer?"

Mikey remembered.

"And I stood out there yelling at no one in particular? Well, something did happen that night and I've never told anyone about it before. But I guess it's safe to finally tell you," he said. "It was right after your mom left us. I was down in the dumps, feeling low. So, I got pretty drunk. I was angry about…well, I was angry about a lot of things. And while you were sleeping, I ran out to the frozen pond. I stood out in the middle, on the ice, and screamed. I guess I was way too drunk.

"I shouted, 'Why?' as loud as I could. 'Why?' I screamed it over and over again. I wanted to know why Kevin died. Why did your mom leave us? Why was everything so bad when it once had been so good? I wanted answers and I wasn't getting any," he said. He leaned back against the wall and looked up at the tiled ceiling.

"And then, right when I turned to leave, a hand burst through the ice. I jumped back and fell to the ground. I thought for sure I was so drunk I was having some sort of vision."

He chuckled again as he remembered. "I was suddenly stone cold sober."

"But then the hand grabbed my ankle and pulled me under the ice." He turned to Mikey. "And that's when I saw my little brother and the other kids staring at me with ghost-like faces."

Mikey couldn't believe what he'd just heard. It had happened before and to his own father. "Well, what did you do?"

"I could tell Kevin was trying to tell me something. He pointed to the dark waters below, but I pulled away from him and swam to the top."

Mikey looked away.

"I thought I was going crazy, so a couple of nights later, I went back and saw the hole in the ice. Then, I heard his voice," he said. "He asked me to help him. He tried to tell me that it wasn't an accident, but a murder."

His father continued to stare. Mikey knew his dad was remembering the scene in detail.

"'Help me.' Kevin kept saying over and over. 'Help me.'"

Mikey nodded. "Yes. He said that to me, too."

His dad turned his head and looked at his son's young face.

"And then what did you do?" Mikey asked his dad.

A look of disgust came across his father's face.

"What I always do, I got plastered drunk on the couch until the sight of my brother's ghost went out of my mind," he said with tears in his eyes. "I failed him, Mikey."

He took his son's hand in his own. "I failed him."

Mikey turned his body toward his dad as though he was about to say something.

"—But *you* didn't fail him. No, not you. You did it, Mikey" he said before Mikey could interrupt. "You actually kept going. You kept going even when no one believed you. Even when…even when *I* didn't believe you."

He swept Mikey up in his strong arms and hugged him.

"I'm so sorry, son. I should have believed you."

"That's okay Dad," Mikey said could smell the Old Spice on his dad's cheek.

"I'm so proud of you son," he said. "You solved a murder case."

Mikey could hear his dad's voice crack with emotion. "You found a killer."

Mikey felt his own eyes fill with tears.

"You saved lives tonight, son."

Mikey felt his face smile through his tears.

When they parted, Mikey handed his dad the letter from Kevin.

"Dad, he wants you to have this," Mikey said.

"What?" His dad sniffled then looked at the letter. "Who wants me to have this?"

"Kevin," Mikey said. "You see, you may think you failed him, Dad, but you didn't. You were his hero. Kevin was brave because of *you*."

His father crinkled his face as though confused and then opened the letter and read it. Tears filled his eyes when he saw the familiar hand writing, and he stood up to pace the hall as he read. He stopped in front of the trophy case when he finished reading the letter. Mikey could see his dad was weeping. He stood and walked over to him.

He looked at the letter.

"That goofy kid." He shook the letter. "I wish he'd come to me about this. I wish he told me about his suspicions. I would've helped him."

"I know." Mikey patted his dad's back.

"I would've believed him." His dad sniffled. "Why didn't he come to talk to me? That goof."

"I know Dad, but I think he wanted to do something on his own. You know, to prove he could do the right thing."

His dad looked at him.

"Like you?"

Mikey shrugged.

"You're so much like him, Mikey." He messed up his son's hair again. "Maybe that's why he pulled you under the ice. Maybe Kevin knew you would be the one to help him. You did the right thing, son."

"I never knew you were the sports star, Dad. You should have told me," he said.

"Nah, I didn't want to put any more pressure on you than I already did." He wiped his eyes. "Besides, after Kevin died, I never felt like much of a hero anyway."

"Dad," Mikey said. "You're my hero. I don't care why mom left us. I don't care anymore about that. I just want us to be happy."

He hugged his dad around the waist.

"I know, son." He rubbed Mikey's back. "And we will be happy."

Mikey smiled a genuine smile. Something he hadn't done in many weeks.

"Let's go to the hospital so they can x-ray that hand." He turned his son around and they started to head down the hall.

"Yeah, we could do that. We could go to the hospital. *Or*...we could stop by the coffee shop and get some pancakes first," Mikey said.

His dad laughed. "Why not?"

"And maybe Miss Jennings will be outside and we could ask her to come too?" Mikey waited for a response.

"I hope so," his dad said. "Now that would make *me* happy."

§

Together, they passed by the television cameras and reporters to his dad's pick-up truck where they spotted Miss Jennings talking to Destrey's dad. Destrey waved from inside the patrol car.

"There you are!" she ran over and hugged Mikey so tight, he thought he'd burst. "I was so worried about you, Mikey!"

She cupped his face in her gloved hands.

"Are you alright?" she asked. She noticed his swollen hand.

"Yeah, nothing some pancakes and a milkshake can't fix," Mikey said. "You wanna join us?"

She looked at Mikey's dad with a surprised look on her face. "Are you sure? I mean, after all this? Don't you want to go to the—"

"Please." His dad gently placed his hand on her shoulder. "We'd love it if you...No, that's not true. What I meant to say is, *I* would love it if you'd join us."

She smiled that familiar warm smile Mikey loved so much and fingered her hair away from her face.

"*Yes*," Mikey muttered under his breath.

"Well, okay, then," she hopped into the cab of the truck between Mikey and his dad. "It's a date!"

"I like your earrings," his dad said to her.

Her face turned red.

Mikey smiled at his dad. He waved at Destrey and the others as they pulled out of the parking lot.

CHAPTER 32

Seven Months Later…

"Well, looks like the Reverend Johns—I mean Mr. Davis, the former bus driver's trial will begin next week," Mikey's dad said as he sat at the large wooden dining table near the kitchen. He casually flipped through the newspaper that Saturday morning.

"It takes that long?" a female voice came from the kitchen. Miss Jennings came around the corner drying her hands with a dish towel. Of course, her official name was now Mrs. Doug Thompson, the Sheriff's wife. She rubbed her pregnant belly.

"Yep, it takes the prosecution a while to put their case together," her husband said.

The room was flooded with light that shone through the windows framed with red floral curtains. Tastefully framed artwork hung on the light yellow walls behind him.

"Dad, Mom!" Mikey shouted from the family room. "I won't have to testify, will I?"

Mikey walked over to his parents. Mikey smiled at his new mom. He thought she looked cute in her maternity outfit even though she was barely showing.

"You probably will, Mikey. So will I. But your mom and I will be there with you all the way so there's nothing to be afraid of, okay?" his dad said.

"How on earth did that man come back into town and become the Reverend without a single person knowing?" she asked.

Mikey's dad turned the page of the newspaper.

"Well, apparently, Detective Williams discovered that Mr. Davis had settled first in another town nearby and made himself out to be a layman pastor. The town was so small, no one suspected a thing. Raymond, I think that's the name of the town. Anyway, once he established his reputation, he set his sights on Sherman Oaks," he said. "His hair was pure white by then and he grew a beard. So many people in Sherman Oaks were new to the town, it was easy for him to blend in."

"I remember when Reverend Ellis left town. Oh please tell me

Mr. Davis didn't kill him off," she asked.

"No, thank goodness," Mikey's dad said. "He really did retire and move out west."

"Oh good," she sighed.

"I guess Mr. Davis heard about Rev. Ellis retiring then made his move about…what? Five, six years ago?" he said.

"One thing I don't get," Mikey said. "Is how he stole Mrs. Stevenson's car."

Mikey's dad looked up from the paper. "What do you mean, son?"

"Well, when I saw the killer in the car, after he hit Destrey, he was in a white car. But Mrs. Stevenson's car was baby blue."

His dad narrowed his eyes. "Huh. I hadn't thought about it."

"And did they ever find her car?" Mikey asked.

"Not that I know of," his dad said.

"What a shame. I sure hope that monster gets what's coming to him." His mom went back

into the kitchen.

Mikey's dad continued to read the newspaper.

"Hey!" his dad said. He was pointing to an article in the paper. "Here's your article in the paper, Mikey!"

Mikey and his mom rushed over to read it over his dad's shoulder.

"Can a Ghost Help Catch a Killer?" he read the title. "Wow, I can't believe they printed it. That's so cool!"

"It's such a terrific article, explaining what happened, Mikey," his new mom said. "We'll cut it out and have it framed."

"Thanks, Mom," Mikey said and he hugged her. "I like calling you that."

"I like hearing it," she said.

"We're so proud of you, Mike," his dad said. "You're a talented writer."

"Thanks, Dad."

His dad turned the page to the movie section of the paper. He pointed to a large add on the page.

"I don't know, Mikey, a lot of people say this is a great movie," he said.

"You two should go see it today." His mom went back into the kitchen.

"I don't know." Mikey walked over to the antique dresser in the family room. "It's a space movie."

"So? It could be pretty fun," his mom said as she came out of the kitchen with a plate full of pancakes. She placed them on the table and turned to see Mikey holding something.

He held a framed photograph in his hands.

"Whatcha doing with that picture?" she asked.

He rubbed dust off the glass with a cloth.

"I really like this wedding picture," he said. "The photographer did a nice job."

"He did," she said and she walked over to him. "We all look wonderful. What a perfect day that was." She walked back to the table and served her new husband some pancakes.

Mikey studied the photograph of his father's wedding day. Mikey couldn't believe how quickly everyone in town was able to put together a wedding after such tragic events had occurred, but like his new mom said, everyone probably needed to celebrate something to help them deal with the sorrow. In the photograph, they are standing outside by the church with snow still on the ground. Mikey crinkled his face. He was sick of snow and was more than happy to feel the warmth of summer again.

His father looked pretty handsome dressed in a black tuxedo and a white cowboy hat. He thought Miss Jennings's long-sleeved lace wedding gown was perfect for her. He still didn't like the tuxedo and bow tie *he* had to wear, but that didn't matter now. He set it right next to the Kevin's keepsake box on top of her piano which sat near the stairs in the newly decorated living room. It was quite a task moving all of Miss Jenning's furniture into the house, but he was so glad to have it there. All the antiques, rugs, artwork, and books made it feel more like a home.

Mikey went around completing his chores that Saturday morning. It was his turn to dust all the antique furniture. He picked up each trinket, dusted it, and then placed it down on the appropriate lace doily. Then, he straightened out the pillows on the antique couch. He stood and inspected the entire room all bright now and cheery with light colors. He folded his arms and nodded in approval.

Now this is what a home looks like, he thought.

"Come on, school's out and summer's half way over. You two

should get out of the house on this wonderful morning!" his mom said. Then she waved him over to the table to sit and eat his breakfast.

"What do you say, son?" His dad got up from the table and took his coffee cup into the kitchen. "It sounds really neat."

"What's it called again?" Mikey asked.

"Star Wars!" His dad shouted from the kitchen. "Or something like that."

"Oooh, sounds interesting!" His mom's eyes grew wide. "A war in outer space sounds exciting."

"I think you're trying to get rid of us." Mikey smirked. "Alright. I'll see if Destrey and the others want to come."

"Sure, why not?" His dad came out of the kitchen. He hugged his bride from behind. "And I'll finish painting the nursery when I get back. Okay?"

He spun her around and kissed her hard on the lips.

"Oh geez," Mikey said as he walked out the door. He cringed at the sight of his parents kissing. But deep down inside, he liked seeing them together.

He headed down the street along the usual sidewalk. But this time the sun seemed brighter. Not a cloud was in the blue sky that day. It was Fourth of July weekend. He pictured his parents outside cooking burgers on the grill with his grandparents sitting at the picnic bench nearby telling stories. His mouth watered as he imagined all the food that would be served. He could almost smell the wonderful aromas of burgers grilling, potato salad with bacon, and homemade apple pie.

Mikey smiled. He was glad his grandparents knew the whole story about Kevin now. He remembered how his grandpa hugged his dad with tears in his eyes and thanked him for being such a good son when they came over to see them and show them the letter Kevin had written. Mikey knew some boys have never seen their dads cry, but he felt no shame in seeing his dad shed a couple of tears that day.

As he ambled on, he glanced over at the woods across the way. He knew behind those tall trees bending in the wind was the pond. Mikey chortled. He used to hate that pond. Oh, how he hated going out there to practice hockey and then he hated it because of the ghosts. Now, he held no regrets about what happened. He kicked a couple of pebbles off the sidewalk as he continued along.

I wonder if anyone is swimming out there in the pond today, He grinned at the thought. “Swimming at the pond,” he said to himself. “Sounds good to be able to say that again.”

Then, he turned the corner and headed toward Destrey’s house, whistling a tune he heard on the radio. And as he walked, he gazed over at some bushes nearby and spotted a little girl staring at him. He smiled and waved to her. She waved back, but he noticed she didn’t have a smile on her face. He furrowed his brow when he noticed her face was pale and her wave methodical. Mikey stopped walking and turned toward the girl. She wore a plaid dress, white socks, and black patten leather shoes. Her long brown hair was braided and she had on a white cardigan sweater over her dress.

She appeared to be his age, yet she wasn’t dressed like the girls his age usually dressed in the summertime. Her clothes weren’t modern clothes, but more like clothes from years ago. Still, she appeared to be friendly, so Mikey politely waved even though he didn’t know who she was. Then, he turned and started to head to Destrey’s house.

And that’s when he heard it.

“Help me,” the voice said. It was a child’s voice and it seemed to be coming from the girl near the bushes. Mikey turned his head to ask her what she said, but when he did, she was gone.

He stood still for a second.

“*Help me*,” the voice said again.

The girl reappeared even closer than before. Mikey jumped back. It was then that he knew she was a ghost.

She methodically raised her arm and pointed. Mikey took out his small notebook from his pocket and flipped it until he found a blank page. He took out his pencil and prepared to take down everything the girl might say. He carefully approached her.

But she continued to point to something behind him. So, he cautiously turned around to see what she was pointing at. When his eyes focused on what she wanted him to see, all the blood drained from his face.

There, behind him, idling no more than fifty feet away was the baby blue Thunderbird convertible—Mrs. Stevenson’s car.

Mikey squinted and tried to see who was driving it, but the inside of the car was nothing but dark shadows. He took one step toward it and heard the driver put it into gear. The engine revved, and then the car took off in a cloud of dust. Soon, it was gone down the road and out of the neighborhood.

Mikey stood with mouth agape, unsure of what to do next and if anyone would believe his story. He turned around to ask the girl ghost about it, but when he did, he saw that she was already gone.

Mikey closed his eyes and shook his head.

"Oh no," he groaned. "Not again."

THE END.

ABOUT THE AUTHOR

As a substitute teacher back in 2006, **R. A. Douthitt** gave a spelling test one Friday afternoon to a 6th grade class. After noticing how the words on the spelling list fit together, she began to use the list to tell a story about the ghosts of children under the ice of a frozen pond. Years later, she put the story down on paper and now you hold the book in your hand. **R. A. Douthitt** resides in Arizona where she works at a university when she isn't working on her next book. *The Children Under the Ice* is the first in a series of books. **R.A. Douthitt** lives with her husband and their little fat dog.

You can find out more about her books at:

www.thedragonforest.com

Made in the USA
Las Vegas, NV
30 May 2023

72733063R00132